Valerie's heartbeat accelerated when Flaming Arrow swept his arms around her and drew her against him and kissed her.

All doubts, all reservations, all shame were cast to the wind, as Valerie and Flaming Arrow broke apart only long enough to disrobe each other.

When he slid his lips down to her throat, she twined her fingers through his sleek black hair and sought his mouth again with a wildness and desperation.

He had denied himself such pleasures for so long, it was like awakening again to a new world!

Being with Valerie like this began to fill a hollow ache. He was on fire with passion. He felt alive again, as though he had, until tonight, been only a thing, not a person, living mechanically. Oh, how fiercely he loved her!

Nothing could be the same as it had been. She was his world.

His head bent low again.

Valerie closed her eyes. The word "forbidden" was forgotten, forever.

FLAMING ARROW

by

Cassie Edwards

A SIGNET BOOK

SIGNET
Published by New American Library, a division of
Penguin Group (USA) Inc., 375 Hudson Street,
New York, New York 10014, USA
Penguin Group (Canada), 90 Eglinton Avenue East, Suite 700, Toronto,
Ontario M4P 2Y3, Canada (a division of Pearson Penguin Canada Inc.)
Penguin Books Ltd., 80 Strand, London WC2R 0RL, England
Penguin Ireland, 25 St. Stephen's Green, Dublin 2,
Ireland (a division of Penguin Books Ltd.)
Penguin Group (Australia), 250 Camberwell Road, Camberwell, Victoria 3124,
Australia (a division of Pearson Australia Group Pty. Ltd.)
Penguin Books India Pvt. Ltd., 11 Community Centre, Panchsheel Park,
New Delhi - 110 017, India
Penguin Group (NZ), 67 Apollo Drive, Rosedale, North Shore 0632,
New Zealand (a division of Pearson New Zealand Ltd.)
Penguin Books (South Africa) (Pty.) Ltd., 24 Sturdee Avenue,
Rosebank, Johannesburg 2196, South Africa

Penguin Books Ltd., Registered Offices:
80 Strand, London WC2R 0RL, England

Published by Signet, an imprint of New American Library, a division of Penguin
Group (USA) Inc. Previously published in a Topaz edition.

First Signet Printing, May 2000
First Printing ($4.99 Edition), January 2008
10 9 8 7 6 5 4 3 2 1

In appreciation of their wonderful support of my new Dreamcatcher series at Signet, I dedicate my book *Flaming Arrow* to my editors, Claire Zion and Kerry Donovan.

Always,
Cassie

My prayer rises into a darkened night,
Please, Great Spirit, hear my plight,
Our world is slipping from our grasp,
Everything is changing, very, very, fast!

My people have always roamed proud and free,
Now the sky we cannot see,
Give us courage and shower us with love,
Have mercy on us, Great Spirit above.

We live on land that is not our own,
We long for the mountain and rivers of home,
Your wisdom, I know, will come with love,
Please answer this prayer I send above.

The Eagle cries out to us with his heart,
He knows not why we had to part,
Help us to accept what seems to be,
Please bless all of my people and me!

—Harri Lucas Garnett,
poet and friend

1

Should disappointment, parent of despair,
Strive for her son to seize my careless heart,
When, like a cloud, he sits upon the air,
Preparing on his spellbound prey to dart;
Chase him away, sweet hope, with visage bright,
And fright him as the morning frightens night!
—JOHN KEATS

Montana Territory, 1875

With irons on his wrists and ankles, and wearing the breechcloth he was arrested in, Chief Flaming Arrow was being escorted by two soldiers toward the open gates of Fort Harrison.

Defiant, his chin held high, he ignored the stares and snickers of the whiskey-smelled soldiers who were watching his release. He knew that he would still be inside the stinking, rat-infested cell, and would perhaps have been there until he died, if the white leader in Washington had not decided to close down this fort.

Because Flaming Arrow was the only man imprisoned there, Colonel Randall Thiel, the officer in charge, had decided to turn him loose rather than bother with him on the cavalry's move from Montana Territory.

The sun was high in the sky. The high walls of the fort kept out any semblance of a breeze, and the body sweat of the soldiers was permeating the air, along with the stink of the piles of horse dung that lay along the ground. It was so hot, breathing was an effort for Flaming Arrow.

Dust swirled around the chief's moccasined feet as a hand reached out and grabbed him by an arm, stopping him.

His face showing animal anger, his eyes blazing, Flaming Arrow turned and glared at the young lieutenant who began removing the chains and irons. He knew he would wear the white man's brand for the rest of eternity from the irons that had rubbed his skin raw each day until he bled.

As the irons fell away, even now, small pools of blood dropped to the ground from Flaming Arrow's sore wrists, the thick dust grabbing at the blood like a sponge.

Dressed in his blue uniform, with brass buttons down the front and gold epaulets across his narrow shoulders, Colonel Thiel stepped up next to Flaming Arrow.

"You are free to go now," the colonel said, his hands clasped tightly behind him. The gleaming saber at his right side scattered the rays of the sun into Flaming Arrow's defiant, angry eyes as he turned and gazed at the colonel.

The colonel cleared his throat nervously. "Flaming Arrow, I hope you appreciate your early release," he said sullenly. "I hope you appreciate *being* released. You know that I could've hung you instead, to get rid of you."

Flaming Arrow's expression did not change. He would not show any gratitude toward the white pony soldier, now or ever.

Nor could he ever have feelings for white pony soldiers except an intense hate for what they had done, not only to himself but to his Blackfoot tribe as a whole. By 1864, with the United States at war, ostensibly to free the black man from slavery, the white pony soldiers had accepted a policy of extermination for the red man.

This policy had been initiated as early as 1854.

To the Blackfoot, the white pony soldiers had been labeled "squaw killers," for they had not hesitated to gun down women during their surprise attacks on the Blackfoot villages, the women most times carrying their infants in their arms!

No, Flaming Arrow could never feel anything but a loathing for the soldiers. They seemed a different breed from other whites with whom Flaming Arrow had made an acquaintance through the years. When a man put on a uniform it seemed to turn his heart to stone.

"Get on with you, Flaming Arrow, before I change my mind," Colonel Thiel said, waving his hand in a fluttering motion toward the Blackfoot chief. "We've things to do here at the fort besides fool with you."

Flaming Arrow gave the colonel one last cold

stare, then turned and walked past the long line of soldiers.

Holding his anger at bay, Flaming Arrow listened to the soldiers laugh and poke fun at him. They told him he had a long walk before he would find his Blackfoot reservation.

His jaw tightened when one of the soldiers said that he hoped a snake would get him, or the ravages of the sun.

Another soldier laughed and shouted that he wouldn't last in this sun with hardly any clothes on.

Another mocked him by saying that without a weapon he could not go on a hunt for food. He would starve!

Knowing that he had the ability to prove all of these predictions wrong, having learned long ago how to survive the challenges of nature, Flaming Arrow's lips tugged into a slow smile as he continued to walk past the soldiers, whose guns cast long shadows across the toes of his black moccasins.

Square-shouldered and dignified, the thirty-one-year-old Blackfoot chief took one step toward the freedom that had been taken away from him six moons ago when he had been arrested while trying to protect his people from exile on a reservation.

His bitterness ran deep over the arbitrary and unjust department rulings of the U.S. government that sent innocent people like his Blackfoot from land that had been theirs since the beginning of time, and into land that was less fertile and less populated with game.

But Flaming Arrow knew that now was not the time to dwell on such bitterness. He had to find his people and lead them away from this land that was no longer theirs. He had heard of a place called Missouri, where as far as he knew there were no reservations, or strict army rules.

Outside of the wide and high walls of Fort Harrison, Chief Flaming Arrow stopped and lifted his eyes toward the heavens. "Napi, our Blackfoot's maker, guide me," he cried.

He lifted his eyes and hands toward the blue heavens. "I do not know where my people have been taken!" he said mournfully. "Guide me now to them so that I might lead them where they will no longer be imprisoned on a reservation. Hear me, Napi, for my heart is heavy with sorrow for my people!"

The soldiers had followed outside the gate and gawked at him. Although he didn't speak loud enough for them to hear him, it was the way he looked heavenward, his hands beckoning, that made them know he was praying.

"Look at the big Injun chief praying like a baby for salvation!" one of the soldiers mocked. He laughed boisterously, then shouted to Flaming Arrow, "What's the matter, Chief? Are you suddenly afraid? Do you need the help of your 'maker'?"

Others said things that dug deep into Flaming

Arrow's heart as well, as though an arrow were piercing it.

But he would not allow them to know that their words affected him. He walked on away from them with dignity as some talked of how they would have had fun watching him swing from a rope, while others answered by saying that letting him go was the worst punishment, for he was an Injun without a horse and weapon.

They laughed as they predicted Flaming Arrow would die before he found the Blackfoot reservation.

They said he would surely die before he had a chance to steal a horse from some innocent settler, for those who had settled in this area were at least a two-day ride on a horse from the fort.

His waist-length hair, the same hue and as lustrous as a raven's wing, fluttered in the wind as Flaming Arrow walked onward. His faith in his Napi made him know he would find his people. His closest relatives had joined his loved ones in death long ago in the Sand Hills, the ghost place of the Blackfoot. His father and his father's father had been powerful Blackfoot chiefs.

Flaming Arrow was now his people's chief and hungered to lead them as they were used to being led. For six moons they had been denied his leadership . . . his devotion . . . his love.

Soon they would not be denied his presence any longer, for he *would* find them. In his absence, Sky Spirit, the Blackfoot's medicine-pipe man, was to keep a vigil and make medicine daily for Flaming Arrow on his black stone sacred pipe. Once released from imprisonment, that would give Flaming Arrow the knowledge and the power to find his people!

Now far enough from the fort that he no longer heard the white soldiers' cruel, taunting voices, Flaming Arrow was able to relax, look around, and absorb the loveliness of this land that had been denied him while locked away with only four walls to look at.

It pained him to know that soon he would lead his people from this land of such grandeur that it took a man's breath away.

As now. He gazed upon a wilderness of steep, wooded slopes and flowery mountain meadows, where streams tumbled over waterfalls and blue lakes lay in peaceful valleys.

Once, when the world was good and free of white men, great herds of buffalo roamed the river valleys.

They were all but gone now.

But the white man had not succeeded yet at ridding the land of other game, such as the elk, deer, and wild sheep that fed in great numbers on the pine-clad slopes of the mountains.

With determination in his steps and an ache for his people inside his heart, Flaming Arrow continued walking through wind-blown buffalo grass, reminiscing more about the buffalo.

Oh, how he had enjoyed hearing the bellowing

of the buffalo those long years ago when it was their mating season and the bulls kept up a continuous, deep monotone as they charged and fought. He would never hear this again.

But now *was* the season of new beginnings, not so much for the land, since the summer sun had come and scorched everything with its heat. The new beginnings that Flaming Arrow thought of were his people's.

Yes, soon he would find them.

Hope would rise again among them!

Smiling, confident, he walked onward.

2

I breathed a song into the air,
It fell to earth, I knew not where;
For who has sight so keen and strong,
That can follow the flight of song?
—HENRY WADSWORTH LONGFELLOW

Valerie Ross stared from her cabin window. She hungered to be outside, horseback riding. It had been days now since she had been able to leave the cabin. Except to get fresh water from the nearby creek, she had promised her father that she wouldn't leave the cabin until he returned.

Although there were not supposed to be Indians anywhere near their small ranch to threaten her family's safety, since those who used to live in this area had been moved onto a reservation, Valerie's father still said it was possible some Indians were hiding in the mountains.

Since Valerie's family arrived in Montana Territory, her father had only allowed Valerie to go horseback riding while he was with her.

Her father had been gone for several days now. He had gone to get Valerie's Aunt Elaine. Valerie's mother wasn't well. She had been calling her sister's name in her sleep. It was a blessing that her mother's sister Elaine and her husband Harold had also settled in Montana Territory, miles upriver.

Left with Valerie was her ten-year-old brother Brian and another aunt, Hillary, her father's sister, who had become widowed on their journey from Kansas when her husband had taken a bad fall from his horse and broke his neck.

None of Valerie's family had gone to Fort Harrison yet to let the authorities know they had chosen this spot for their ranch. They had been living in the area now for only one month, concentrating on getting the cabin built first. They had brought enough supplies from Kansas to last another six months and planned to go to the fort soon to touch base with Colonel Thiel.

Always loving new adventure, Valerie had been excited about the journey to Montana Territory. But her mother hated the move. She had loved her home in Kansas City, Kansas . . . a home now denied her due to her husband's gambling debts, which had led to bankruptcy and losing everything.

Valerie's father had chosen Montana Territory for their new home because of the promise of quick riches in gold. "Fool's gold," Valerie whispered to herself. That's what her mother bitterly called it when it was obvious her husband would probably never find any.

Valerie's brother stepped up to her side. "Sis, look at my arrowhead," he said, drawing Valerie out of her reverie. "See how it shines?"

Valerie reached a hand to Brian's golden hair and tousled it playfully with her fingers. "It ought to shine," she said, laughing softly. "Brian, you've been polishing that arrowhead since breakfast."

She gazed down at her brother and saw so much of herself in his features. Her hair, which hung long and wavy to her waist, was the same color as Brian's. So were her eyes as blue.

And while looking at his face, it was like looking at herself when *she* was his age eight years ago. They both had the same round face, straight, small nose, and chin that could quickly firm up stubbornly when faced with challenges.

The main difference was the size of Brian's hands and feet. His were large, proving that when he grew into a man he might be well over six feet tall, like his father. His shoulders were just beginning to broaden. And he had muscles that were well developed from working hard alongside his father on the ranch.

Valerie was tiny-boned and was only five-foot-six. At age eighteen, her breasts were well rounded.

When she was Brian's age, her budding breasts had embarrassed her. Now she was proud of the way they filled out her dress. They, as well as other changes that had come with maturing, made her feel like a woman.

"Sis, I love this arrowhead," Brian said, holding it closer for her to take an even better look. "It is a true arrowhead that was once actually used by Indians. Isn't it exciting?"

"Yes, I'd say you have yourself something special," Valerie said, swinging away from the window.

She went to the kitchen table and began clearing away the breakfast dishes, taking them over to a counter and stacking them there for washing.

"I'll never forget the day you found the arrowhead," Valerie said. "I was fishing for trout while father was panning for gold." She flipped her hair back from her shoulders and turned to Brian. "Brian, I thought *you* had found gold," she said. "Father had been panning for hours. When he thought you had found gold before him, he got the strangest look in his eyes. In a way I was glad that your exuberance was only over an arrowhead. Father had looked so long for gold without any luck. I think it would have humiliated him if you would have been the first to find it."

"I was excited that I discovered a place where I found several arrowheads," Brian said, his eyes bright with remembrance. "If not for Father, I would have been forced to leave them there. You didn't want me to keep them."

"Brian, you shouldn't have disturbed what might have been an Indian burial ground," Valerie said, pouring warm water into a basin for washing dishes from a teakettle that she had lifted from the cooking stove. "Indians see such burial grounds as sacred."

"I know, but the Indians are no longer around to know what I do," Brian said, rushing away and returning soon to the kitchen with another one of his relics. "Sis, look at *this*. It's part of an arrow. I wish I had the other half. Look at the beautiful designs of flames painted on the shaft."

"Yes, and I'm sure whoever painted the flames on the arrow did it for a purpose," Valerie said, scrubbing one of the dishes with a cloth. "Brian, most of all, you shouldn't have taken the arrow."

"My having it can't hurt anything," Brian said, curving his lower lip into a pout. "It's broken. What use is it to anyone now but me, who enjoys collecting such things?"

"I just don't know," Valerie said, blowing a fallen wisp of hair back from her eyes. "It just doesn't seem right somehow."

"Sis, take me back there," Brian said, laying the arrow fragment on the table. He picked up a dish towel and began drying the dishes. "I'll help you with dishes for a month if you'll take me back there so I can search for the rest of the arrow. Sis, I'm tired of staying indoors like a scaredy-cat. Don't you need some fresh air? Don't our horses need exercising?"

"Brian, I notice you are helping me with the dishes now without my asking, and you've promised to help me for a month . . . you *must* be desperate to leave the cabin," Valerie said, laughing softly.

"I just want to go and find the rest of the arrow," Brian nagged, taking another dish, drying it. "Please, Sis? Just one more time? Then I won't ask you again."

"I think I've heard that sort of promise before," Valerie said, sighing.

"Admit it, Sis," Brian said. He caught her eye and smiled. "You need to get away yourself, don't you? Don't you miss horseback riding?"

"Father *has* been gone several days," Valerie admitted. "And yes, I do feel all cooped up like a bird in a cage. I do hanker to go riding."

"Then what are we waiting for?" Brian said, throwing down the towel. He tugged on Valerie's shirtsleeve. "Come on, Sis. Let's go now. We can finish the dishes when we get back."

Aunt Hillary had been sitting in her rocking chair embroidering as she listened to Brian and Valerie. She understood restlessness. In her youth, before marrying and settling into a more sedate way of life with a husband, she had even ridden for the pony express. Childless, she looked at Brian and Valerie as her own.

She lay her embroidery aside and reached up and touched the tight bun atop her head. She cringed to realize how matronly she looked. She hated her graying hair more than the wrinkles at the corners of her eyes and around her mouth.

As she saw it, Valerie was wasting *her* youth, one day at a time, as she stayed indoors taking care of things that her aunt could see to. She knew that Valerie's restlessness had to match her own. She saw herself in Valerie when she was young and wild and woolly as an untamed wild horse on the prairie.

"Valerie, go on with your brother," Hillary said,

rising from the rocker. In her cotton dress, her waist no longer tiny like Valerie's, she got up and took the dishrag from her niece. "Go and get some fresh air. Take Brian. I'll take care of things here."

Hillary laid the dishrag aside, went to a cabinet, and opened its door. She stood on tiptoe and, reaching into the cabinet, took out a small pearl-handled pistol. She turned to Valerie and fit it into the palm of her hand. "This was mine when I was your age," she murmured. "Take it with you today. Don't hesitate using it should you and Brian become endangered."

Hillary turned to Brian, whose eyes were wide as saucers as he stared at the firearm. "Brian, scat on out of here," she said, giving him a stern look as he lifted his eyes and gazed at her. "I've got something to show Valerie. It should be done without you watching."

"Aunt Hillary, are you saying that Valerie and I can go and find the rest of that arrow?" Brian asked, his cheeks pink with building excitement. "Can we, Aunt Hillary? Can we go that far from home?"

"I'll probably be horsewhipped by your pa for giving you permission to go there, but yes, Brian, get out of this house and have some fun," Hillary said, placing a gentle hand on his shoulder. "When winter comes, we'll all be cooped up here like a bunch of chickens. Best you get your energies used up now than then."

"Thanks, Aunt Hillary," Brian said, then scurried away to his room to get his leather bag to carry home his prized possessions.

Hillary frowned at Valerie. "I'm trusting that you know how to take care of both yourself and Brian," she said thickly.

"I always have," Valerie said, rolling down the sleeves of her blouse, buttoning them at her wrists. She had put on a comfortable skirt this morning that often had worked well as a riding skirt. She always wore boots instead of mere shoes.

Yes, thanks to her aunt, she was ready to ride *and* feel free for at least a short while!

Hillary reached inside the cabinet and took something else out, then turned to Valerie again. "Let me show you where to wear the pistol," she said.

She lifted the tail end of Valerie's skirt. She then fastened a leather sheath around Valerie's right thigh.

"You wear the pistol hidden beneath your skirt in this fashion," Hillary said. "It works as an element of surprise. Throws most men off guard when a woman lifts her skirt to draw a pistol on them."

Valerie laughed softly. "Why, Aunt Hillary, what a wicked thing to know," she said, her eyes twinkling as her aunt smoothed her skirt back down, the pistol hidden beneath it.

"Perhaps," Hillary said, stepping back from Valerie. She placed her hands on her hips and lifted her chin proudly. "And perhaps someday I'll tell you about my exciting past, which I enjoyed *way* before you were born."

Valerie's interest was piqued, but her hunger for

the outdoors took precedence over any question she might want to ask her aunt about her past.

Valerie and Brian went to the small bedroom at the far back of the cabin.

Valerie knelt down beside the bed and reached a hand to her mother's brow. "Mom . . ." she whispered, but her mother did not respond. She was in a strange sort of sleep, now not even waking to be fed. Brian bent low over his mother and gave her a soft kiss on her cheek. "I love you, Mom," he whispered.

Valerie fought back tears as she took Brian's hand and led him from the bedroom.

"Sis, is she going to die?" Brian asked as they went back to the parlor. He lifted his leather bag and slung it over his shoulder as Valerie secured her hair back from her face with wooden combs.

"Only the good Lord knows the answer to that question," she said somberly.

"You kids be careful," Hillary said, taking them each by the hand and walking them to the door. "I'll take good care of your mother. Nancy means the world to me."

Valerie swung around and hugged her aunt.

Brian took his turn hugging Hillary after Valerie opened the door and stepped out onto the small porch.

Hillary then followed them both outside. She stayed on the porch as they went to the barn and saddled their horses. As they rode free of the barn, she waved. "Don't make me regret giving you permission to leave," she shouted.

"We'll be all right," Valerie said, her voice carrying in the wind back to her aunt.

"Are you truly taking me back to the same place where I found the Indian artifacts?" Brian asked, edging his black mare up next to Valerie's roan. "Are you, Sis? Are you truly?"

"I guess," Valerie said, giving him a weak smile. "Anyway, I remember seeing many wildflowers close by the river there. While you search for the other half of that arrow you wish to have so badly, I will busy myself gathering a bouquet so that our outing won't be altogether selfish. Mother will have fresh flowers at her bedside tonight."

"That's nice, Sis," Brian said, swallowing hard. "Mom always liked flowers."

"Yes, Mom loved flowers," Valerie said. "Snapdragons. They were her favorite. One day I hope she can be aware again of things. I shall plant her a full garden of snapdragons."

They nudged their horses with their heels and sent the snorting steeds into a mad gallop across a wide meadow.

In the far distance lay minor ranges, covered with pine forests. But to Valerie and Brian at this distance what they saw were mere gray silhouettes against a sky of blue.

Valerie slid her hand down and touched the outline of the firearm that lay beneath her skirt.

She hoped that she would have no need to use it.

3

How sweet I roam'd from field to field,
And tasted all the summer's pride,
'Til I the prince of love beheld,
Who in the sunny beams did glide!
　　　　　—WILLIAM BLAKE

The wounds on his wrists like twisted red rawhide, Flaming Arrow stopped beside the Yellowstone River and sank his wrists into the water.

He winced as pain shot through him like searing hot flames.

He closed his eyes and held his wrists in the water for a moment longer as he thought of the miles he had already traveled by foot. Although weakened by his incarceration, where food had been scarce and poor, he still had the strength to travel onward.

He gazed heavenward where the sun had left its midpoint place in the sky and was now making its slow descent toward the mountains in the distance. He had a while longer to travel before it got dark.

And if he had calculated right, he should be near his abandoned village, left barren when his people had been forced to leave for the reservation.

To see it again, deserted, and desecrated by the whites, would fill him with such despair. The pain from such despair would be inside his heart, deep and everlasting.

His stomach rumbled, reminding him of just how hungry he was. The morning meal at the fort had been only some sort of strange-looking liquid with no meat and few vegetables floating in it. The taste had been acrid. It had left a bitterness in his mouth that he could even now taste.

His wrists feeling somewhat better, Flaming Arrow lifted them from the water and blew on one and then the other until they were dry.

Then he determinedly fashioned a spear from a branch of a cottonwood tree.

His dark eyes searching the water, he knelt on his haunches beside the river and waited for a fish to swim past.

When he finally saw a fat trout, he thrust the spear into its side and yanked it from the water.

Flaming Arrow then laid the trout on the ground and busied himself making a fire. He gathered dried twigs and piled them on the rocky shore. With a flint rock he started the fire.

He let the fire burn down to glowing ashes, then wrapped the trout in large wet cottonwood leaves and placed it in the hot coals to bake.

Feeling dirty and wanting to wash the filth of the prison from not only himself but his breechcloth, Flaming Arrow dove into the river and swam for a while.

Then, thinking he had totally rid himself of the stink of the white man, he left the water, lay down on the embankment, and rested until the smell of the fish came to him in its deliciousness, telling him that it was cooked and ready to eat.

His long, jet-black hair hanging in wet streamers across his shoulders, Flaming Arrow sat down beside the fire. Before eating, he prayed to his Napi, asking him to bless the food with his goodness. Then Flaming Arrow tore into the fish and ate in fast gulps until only the bones lay discarded on the ground beside him.

Feeling somewhat refreshed, his hunger at least for the moment alleviated, Flaming Arrow laid rocks over his fire, extinguishing it, then started to walk onward in his mission of the heart.

But he stopped when the wind brought the sound of voices to him. He stiffened as he leaned an ear toward the sound.

He had been told that no one lived anywhere near the fort, much less here, near where his people had been forced from their homes.

It was supposed to be a two-day ride from the fort to a settler's home!

"Then who?" he whispered.

His spine stiff, his eyes narrowed, he crept stealthily toward the sound, knowing that where there was man, there were also horses.

No longer would he have to search for his people on foot. He would steal the white people's horse that had brought them to this land of the Blackfoot!

"Sis, *look*!" Brian said, running to Valerie where she knelt beside the river picking flowers. "Look at what I found! See this strange sort of small hoop with fathers on it? Isn't it mystical?"

"Yes, Brian, it's mystical," Valerie said, laying her bouquet aside to take the hoop and study it. She envisioned an Indian making it. "But I still can't be comfortable about you taking these things."

She shoved it back toward him. "Take this and put it back where you found it," she said, a sudden involuntary shiver riding her spine. "Brian, this belonged to someone. It had special meaning. I . . . feel like we are desecrating graves. You know that we would never approve of anyone taking things from the graves of our loved ones."

"Sis, you've read too many books about Indians," Brian scoffed. "And if there *were* graves, surely we would *see* them. I found this laying beneath some fallen limbs and leaves. Not in a grave. Sis, please let me have it. Let me even go and dig for some more arrowheads. I've only just gotten started."

Valerie sighed. She playfully tousled Brian's golden hair with her fingers. "Oh, all right," she murmured. "But only for a little while longer. I'll pick a few more flowers. Then, Brian, I want to go back home. I don't want to be out here when it starts growing dark."

"Thanks, Sis!" Brian said, his eyes bright with excitement. "Thanks a lot. I'll hurry."

Valerie resumed picking the flowers along the riverbank, which was shaded from the hot summer sun. They were of such vibrant colors! The yellow bells so yellow, the lavender crocus so lavender.

Yes, her mother would have flowers tonight on her bedstead even if she wouldn't be aware of them being there. They would at least brighten her mother's bedroom so that when someone sat at her bedside it would not be as sad.

Flaming Arrow moved stealthily through the thick stand of cottonwoods along the riverbank.

At last he arrived where he had last seen his people, recognizing it from some of his people's personal possessions that had been left strewn along the ground because of the soldiers' haste to make his people leave their beloved home. When he also saw the remains of some lodge poles still sticking like ghosts up from the ground, he soon forgot the voices that he had heard a short while ago from around the bend in the river, which was now only a short distance away. He was caught up in a grief as never before.

He went from item to item and picked them up, then lay them back down again, to pick something else up and study it.

Suddenly he fell to his knees, lifting his eyes and hands heavenward. "My people!" he moaned. "Here are your awls! Here are your bone needles! Here are your moccasins! Where are *you* now?"

A shriek of joy brought Flaming Arrow out of his reverie.

He took no more time with the remains of his people, but instead thought ahead to when he would find his beloved Blackfoot and be a part of their *lives* again.

But to find his people he *must* have a horse!

His jaw tight, his eyes two points of fire, he left his desecrated land behind him and ran stealthily toward a snakelike bend in the river.

When he reached it, he stopped and moved more cautiously, making sure he stayed hidden in the shadows of the trees so that his presence would not be known until he had a horse and was already making his escape on it.

Through a break in the trees he now saw movement. He crept closer and parted the thick brush, peering intensely toward those who were there.

His eyes widened when he saw a young man of perhaps ten winters pulling out the remains of an Indian shield from a hole that he had dug in the ground.

A short distance from the boy was a lovely, golden-haired woman who was sitting by the river peering into it, a bouquet of flowers on the ground beside her. She seemed in deep thought, her mind elsewhere.

Flaming Arrow looked at the boy again. *His* mind was active on what he was doing. He was taking from Flaming Arrow's people that which had been left behind.

Flaming Arrow's insides grew cold at the sight of the many arrowheads the boy had uncovered.

His fingers circled into tight fists at his sides.

*Any*thing of his people must be reclaimed by Flaming Arrow. No whites should ever own anything that once was Blackfoot!

It made Flaming Arrow's heart grow cold when he thought of what his people had been denied. He would most certainly deny this young white man of anything that was Blackfoot!

What was fair, was fair!

While the woman's back was still turned to the young boy, Flaming Arrow circled around behind her. Still hidden in the shadows of the trees, he then rushed out and clasped a hand over the young boy's mouth.

Flaming Arrow had a great knowledge of English from his earlier association with whites with whom he had traded before the evil soldiers came to the land. He leaned low next to Brian's ear.

"Have you taken more than these things of my people that I see here today?" he whispered harshly to Brian. "Nod if you have. Shake your head back and forth if you have not."

Frightened so much that he felt frozen, Brian at first didn't respond. Before the Indian clasped his hand over his mouth, Brian had only briefly seen him as he leaped from the bushes. That had not given Brian enough time to scream a warning to his sister.

An Indian!

An Indian was actually there! Brian could not help but think he might at any moment be scalped!

"Did you take more than these things from the land of my people?" Flaming Arrow whispered again, yet his eyes were on the lovely woman.

His gaze could not help but take in the wonders of the woman's golden hair and the straight, perfect line of her back. He had already seen enough of her face to know that she was a delicate, beautiful thing, like no one he had ever seen before.

But now was not the time to wonder about a woman, he reminded himself. This boy and what he was doing on Blackfoot soil was Flaming Arrow's only concern!

Brian stared at Valerie. She still did not know what was happening behind her. She was in such deep thought, she had not noticed.

Brian had observed his sister's quiet, studious behavior of late since their mother's health had worsened. Otherwise she was attentive to all sounds, smells, her senses alert to everything around her.

He wished that he could cry out and warn her about the Indian. She could at least flee his wrath. Their horses were tethered only a short distance away; she could run fast enough to get to the horse before the Indian could get a chance to stop her.

And she had a gun! She might even take the time to stop and shoot the redskin!

Yet he knew that his sister had never even fired a gun. What if her aim was off? Then the Indian would go after her and kill her. Brian had heard tales of how quickly an Indian was angered to the point of scalping innocent white women!

Flaming Arrow whispered harshly in Brian's ear. "White boy, nod your head if you have earlier than today taken my people's things from this land," he said, his patience running thin. "Have you taken them to your home?"

So hoping that he could keep the Indian distracted from Valerie, Brian nodded.

"You will take me there," Flaming Arrow whispered. He gazed at Valerie again. "Is the woman your mother?"

Brian shook his head no, dying a slow death inside to know now that the Indian was not going to ignore her sitting there.

"Is she your sister?" Flaming Arrow then whispered.

Tears coming to his eyes, fearing for his sister's safety even more than his own, Brian nodded.

"Your sister need not be disturbed," Flaming Arrow whispered. "This is just between you and Flaming Arrow. Walk slowly away. Take me to your horses. Then take me to your home so that I can reclaim what is my people's. Your sister and your family will not be harmed if you do as you are told."

Feeling some hope that Valerie might be safe after all, Brian nodded and edged along in front of the Indian as Flaming Arrow held his arm and shoved him onward.

Then Brian was filled with a sudden panic.

If he took this Indian who called himself Flaming Arrow to his *home,* he would then be placing his mother and Aunt Hillary in danger!

No! He couldn't do that!

Yet what else could he do?

He had no choice!

His eyes lit up as a thought came to him. He would lead the Indian away from his home. The Indian wouldn't know for some time that he had been tricked.

That would give Valerie time to get away. She would know that there had been foul play and she could go to the fort to seek their help. The army could come and rescue him!

"Brian, oh, Brian!" Valerie suddenly screamed. She had turned and seen what was happening.

Just as she started to reach beneath her skirt to get the firearm, the Indian turned quickly with Brian and glared at her.

Her hand froze in midair as the Indian's midnight-dark eyes locked with hers.

4

Mine eyes and heart are at a mortal war,
How to divide the conquest of thy sight;
Mine eye my heart thy pictures sight would bar,
My heart mine eye the freedom of that night.
—WILLIAM SHAKESPEARE

Seeing that Brian was held hostage, Valerie felt that she had to appear strong in the eyes of the Indian. And what gave her even more courage to speak her mind was that the Indian had no visible weapon.

But what if he had companions hiding, watching, their arrows drawn on their bows? She still found the courage to stand her ground. For her brother's welfare, she had to!

She defied Flaming Arrow with a heated stare. "Release my brother," she said stiffly, trying desperately not to show the fear that was building inside her heart.

She had never been this close to an Indian before. This one held her brother threateningly, as though he might break Brian's neck at any moment to show his strength . . . to show that he need not have a weapon to prove his point.

Now, seeing the white woman face-to-face and up this close, Flaming Arrow could not help but be stunned by her earthly loveliness. And he admired her spirit in how she was so bravely defending her brother.

When the Indian didn't respond, Valerie felt at a loss for words, for what else could she do to get her brother freed of his captor?

She could insist, but surely that would also be ignored. It was obvious the Indian could have his way, regardless.

She continued to stare at him. His black hair falling in folds over his broad shoulders, and him being dressed in only a breechcloth and moccasins, made him look like some creature born of the wild.

And oh, how handsome he was! So tall. So spare-built. So sinewy of limb.

His eyes were of the deepest jet and stirred something deeply within Valerie that was unfamiliar to her. It had no connection with fear. It was a strange warmth at the pit of her stomach that seemed to spread throughout her body.

She scarcely breathed as she waited for the Indian to say something. Her eyes slowly moved to his wrists. She shuddered when she saw how raw they looked.

An instant fear leaped into her heart to think of what might have caused such scars. It looked as though they might have been made by prison irons.

Had he escaped from he stockade at Fort Harrison? Was he desperate enough to kill all whites that he might come across?

Seeing the fear deepen in the white woman's blue eyes, and not wanting her or her brother to be afraid, when he, at this moment, needed friends in is life who might be able to tell him where his people's reservation had been established, Flaming Arrow slowly lowered his hand from Brian's mouth.

His spine stiffened as he watched Brian run to his sister. His gaze wavered when the white woman grabbed her brother and hugged him to her bosom. He saw much love between them, which made him think back to how he had loved his own sister so many years ago, before . . . before she had been forcibly taken sexually by a white pony soldier.

His beloved sister had gone into the forest only a few days later and had taken her life with her own knife.

So quickly he had lost his sister!

So quickly he had lost much faith in humanity.

"Flaming Arrow needs two things from you," he finally said, the words helping him put the painful thoughts of his sister from his mind. "You are to take me to your home and return to me all that has been wrongly taken that belongs to my people. Then all that I ask of you is directions to the reservation where my Blackfoot people are imprisoned. You will then be free, as though we never met."

He said this to them, yet Flaming Arrow was not certain he could ever forget this white woman and how she stirred his heart into that which for so long had lain dormant. Although she was white, there was much about her that he could not help but admire.

But he would not dwell on her qualities. His people were foremost on his mind. He had to right many wrongs for them!

Hearing his demands, Valerie panicked. Suddenly not only were she and Brian in danger, but also their entire family.

She had to find a way around leading the Indian to her home. She had to think of how to delay him so that she would have more time to think.

"How can we be sure that what you say is true?" she asked guardedly. "That once we have done as you have asked, you won't harm us?"

"Because I have given you my word," Flaming Arrow said, pride in his eyes.

"You will release us when your artifacts are returned and we have told you where the reservation is located?" Valerie asked softly.

A renewed fear crept into her heart. She had no idea where the Indian's reservation was. She was too new in the area to know such a thing. If she couldn't tell him, would he be so angry he might take it out on her and Brian?

She would play along, as though she *were* able to give him answers he sought. She hoped she and Brian would find a way to flee his clutches before she was forced to tell him the truth.

"Yes, you will both be released," he said

smoothly. "But until you satisfy both of my demands, you and your brother will be my traveling
companions, my captives."

The word *captive* had come so easily to Flaming
Arrow, it had slipped across his lips so quickly,
even he was surprised. He truly wanted no captives.
They were always a burden to the red man.

Yet . . . *this woman*?

No, she could never be a burden. Her mere presence would lighten the load of any man's heart! He
was not sure he could let her go so easily.

"A . . . captive?" Brian stammered, paling. "I
thought you said—"

"Your release will come when it suits this
Blackfoot chief," Flaming Arrow said, his spine
stiffening.

"Blackfoot . . . chief?" Brian said, his eyes widening, suddenly in awe. He was in the presence of
a powerful chief instead of just a mere brave!

Knowing *this* made the venture more exciting for
Brian than frightening. He had heard about a
Blackfoot chief from this area who had been imprisoned for fighting for the rights of his people.
While they were fishing in the Yellowstone River
one day, Brian's father had told him about the
chief. He had just not been able to remember his
name.

But now Brian knew. Flaming Arrow! This was
Chief Flaming Arrow, who had been wronged by
the soldiers.

The chief had a good reason to be angry and defiant—enough to take white captives.

Until now, for the most part, Valerie had found it hard to think logically under the branding of this Indian's midnight-dark eyes. But when he said that she and Brian were captives, her fear again turned into a quick anger.

"You have no right to hold me and my brother captive," she said, placing her hands on her hips. "If you don't leave now, you will be sorry. The soldiers at Fort Harrison will come looking for you. I *know* you escaped from there. Your wrists show the imprint of irons! When the soldiers catch up with you and see you holding white captives, they more than likely will hang you."

Again Flaming Arrow was taken by her fiery spirit, a rare thing in white women. He was even more impressed with her than before.

"There is no more Fort Harrison," he then said, laughing throatily. "Or Flaming Arrow *would* still be a prisoner of the white-eyes. They have disbanded. And to save feeding this Blackfoot chief on their long journey elsewhere, where a new fort awaits them, they have set Flaming Arrow free."

Valerie was somewhat shaken by the truth, that he *had* been a prisoner at Fort Harrison. Yet she still held her stubborn stance, her hands still on her hips. Her eyes were locked in a silent battle with Flaming Arrow, yet she could not help but, deep down, admire this powerful Blackfoot chief.

She knew that such men were always so noble. So strong-willed, so admired!

Yet sometimes they were also greatly feared. She had to wonder if he had killed many whites, taken many scalps.

"Why were you imprisoned at Fort Harrison?" she asked, her spine stiff, her eyes wary.

Seeing how truly spirited the white woman was in the face of what she should consider a real threat to her safety, Flaming Arrow decided to test her. He took a slow step in her direction.

"Why was this Blackfoot chief imprisoned?" he said, his eyes dancing mischievously. "For scalping pretty white women like you."

Valerie gasped and paled. Her hand slid down to where she could feel the outline of the small pistol sheathed to her thigh.

But she was afraid to try to use it. She had never been taught the skills of firearms. She might be endangering herself and her brother even more by brandishing a firearm she knew nothing about. She might even manage to shoot off one of her toes!

And should the Indian get the firearm away from her, it would be too easy for him to rid himself of his "burdens" once he knew that neither she nor Brian could help him find his people.

No. She would wait until later to find a way to take advantage of Aunt Hillary's weapon.

Flaming Arrow was not proud of having told the woman such a lie, when deep inside his heart he would rather say things that impressed her. Again he reminded himself of what was foremost on his mind.

Not a woman. He must always put his people before anything else, especially a white woman!

"Take me to your horses," he said flatly, stooping to pick up Brian's bag of artifacts.

When a knife slid from the bag, Flaming Arrow stared at it for a moment as it lay beneath the sun, the rays reflecting in the blade.

Tumultuous feelings roared through him to know that this very knife was once used by his people.

Perhaps even his father?

He swept it up into one of his powerful hands and slid it beneath the waist of his breechcloth, the blade hot against his flesh.

Brian grabbed Valerie's hand and gazed, questioning, up at her.

She gazed with silent apology down at him. "We have no choice but to do as he asks," she murmured. "Come on, Brian. Things will be all right."

While she was trying to convince Brian that things would work out in the end, she tried to think of what she could do to get away from the Indian. She must figure out a way to keep not only herself and Brian free of harm, but also her entire family.

Her chin proudly lifted, and trying to continue looking strong and courageous in the eyes of the Blackfoot chief, Valerie squeezed Brian's hand reassuringly and walked on ahead of Flaming Arrow.

Brian yanked at Valerie's hand. "Sis!" he whispered, only loud enough for her to hear. "Bend down. While we are walking, listen to what I say. I know how to avoid taking Flaming Arrow to our home. Listen!''

She bent lower and listened to his plan of purposely leading Flaming Arrow in the wrong direction, taking him away from their cabin instead of toward it.

Valerie smiled when she saw that this could work, yet she knew they could delay their return only for a while. Soon the Indian would understand what they were doing.

But she hoped by then their father would have returned home and come searching for them with his shotgun. Any man, red- or white-skinned, would be foolish to go up against the buckshot of a shotgun. Flaming Arrow would be forced to go on his way without them.

She regretted one thing: that she had no idea where the Blackfoot reservation was. If she did, she would tell him. He would hurry onward; it was obvious that his heart was with his people. They were all that was truly important to him—not two white people.

"Quit whispering," Flaming Arrow flatly ordered.

He stepped up to Valerie's other side. "While you are my captives, there will be no secrets kept from Flaming Arrow," he said tightly. "Cooperate and soon you will be free to return to your family."

Valerie was keenly aware of his nearness. In the soft breeze he smelled clean, of fresh river water. She could not help but occasionally glance down at his sore wrists. They looked so raw and painful she could not help but feel some empathy for him.

Yet if what he said was true, that scalping women had gotten him that punishment, it only served him right that he should be suffering! She wondered if he truly would set her and Brian free—or would *their* scalps be taken?

That thought caused her knees to weaken. She stumbled.

When Flaming Arrow grabbed her around her waist and steadied her, his grip so gentle, his eyes filled with a strange, sudden caring as she gazed up at him, Valerie did not flinch and draw away from him.

At this moment, she could not envision him ever being cruel to a woman, much less taking scalps. Yes, surely he had been toying with her, to make her enough afraid of him to do everything he said without rebelling.

His gentleness proved that he could have never removed any woman's scalp, ever!

Flaming Arrow gazed deeply into her eyes and saw something new. Her defiance, her need to prove her courage to him, had melted away into a soft wonder. Could she be feeling some of the same things he was feeling about her?

Or was it only because deep down inside, where his desires were formed, he *wanted* her not to fear him, but instead to have feelings very different that could lead to . . .

Aware of where his thoughts were taking him,

and knowing the foolishness of it since he was so far from his people, and actually helpless until he reached them and was joined by his many warriors, Flaming Arrow yanked himself free of her and walked away, his heart pounding.

He was glad that the horses were now in sight.

He needed a hard ride to clear his thoughts of everything but the pursuit of his people. Of leading them to freedom, of bringing hope into their lives!

No white woman belonged in his world, now or ever!

Valerie's pulse raced. She scarcely breathed once she saw Flaming Arrow's mood change so quickly after that moment when their eyes were locked and strange things happened between them. She now knew that he was battling emotions inside himself that he did not want to feel for her.

She found it hard herself to think it was possible he might feel something besides a loathing, since white people had taken so much from him and his people.

No, she thought, she was only imagining things. This Blackfoot chief had more on his mind than a woman. He wanted his possessions returned to him, and he wanted directions to his people.

She wished again that she could help him.

But she could not ignore the possibility that he might be lying to her and was behaving kind only until after he had gotten what he wanted.

Then what might he truly be planning to do with his captives?

Valerie and Brian mounted her roan, Brian in front, and waited for Flaming Arrow to secure the bag of Indian artifacts to the side of Brian's horse. Once it was secured and Flaming Arrow had swung himself into Brian's saddle, Valerie flicked her reins and nudged her steed with the heels of her boots and rode off, Flaming Arrow close beside her.

She gave him a sly glance as she purposely rode in the direction that was exactly opposite of where her family's cabin sat serene and safe beside a slow trickling stream.

Trustingly, Flaming Arrow followed alongside her, his hair fluttering in the hot breeze, the feel of the horse beneath him something wonderful.

He felt suddenly whole again!

He sank his heels into the flanks of the black mare and rode hard for a moment, savoring the wind on his face and in his hair. Then, not wanting to leave the woman and child alone long enough for them to foolishly get the notion to try an escape, he wheeled his horse around and rode back, settling again beside the boy and beautiful woman.

Strange, he thought, how it seemed natural to be with them.

Strange how he enjoyed their presence.

5

Love, if you knew the light
That your soul casts in my sight,
How I look to you
For the pure and true,
And the beauteous and the right.
—ROBERT BROWNING

Long shadows were cast along the ground. Valerie looked nervously at the horizon where the sun was almost hidden behind the mountains, the topmost pinnacles clothed in scarlet flame. Soon it would be dark.

She now knew that she and Brian would be spending the night with the Blackfoot chief.

She could just imagine Aunt Hillary's desperate fear as she stood on the porch watching for them. She would be envisioning the worst.

And since Aunt Hillary had to stay with her ailing sister, there was no way she could leave on horseback and search for her niece and nephew.

It was apparent to Valerie now that her father had not yet returned home. She knew that if he were home and realized Brian and Valerie were in some sort of trouble, he would have left no stone unturned while searching for them.

"How much farther?" Flaming Arrow asked, edging the black steed closer to Valerie's. "It does not seem that you would have ridden this far from your home."

His lips hardened. His jaw grew tight as he glared at Valerie. "Are you leading me toward—or *away*—from your home?" he said carefully. "Are you tricking this Blackfoot chief?"

Brian reached a hand out and grasped Valerie's arm.

She could feel her brother trembling as he stared at Flaming Arrow, and knew that his fear of the Indian was peaking.

"No one is playing games here," Valerie said, fighting to keep her voice steady, while in truth her insides were quivering with the fear of having been caught.

She had known, though, that Flaming Arrow would eventually discover the truth. Yet now that it was happening, now that he surely knew, Valerie realized the danger she and Brian were in.

"If there is no game, then why have we not arrived at your home?" Flaming Arrow asked, his voice tight.

He looked quickly away from Valerie and searched with his eyes in all directions. Not much was now visible. The shadows had deepened; the sun had slipped behind the mountains in the distance, leaving only faint pinkish hues.

He sent a quick, angry look again at Valerie. "I

see no dwelling anywhere, not close by, nor in the distance," he grumbled.

He thought to reach over and grab her by her golden hair, the deceit he was feeling fueled by his anger, but instead he doubled his free hand into a fist, his other hand tightly gripping the reins.

"That is because . . . I no longer know where my home *is*," Valerie said, unable to hold back the tremor in her voice any longer. She had only a short while ago realized that, although she had *meant* to play the game only on the Blackfoot chief, it was now on herself and Brian.

She truly was disoriented!

Knowing that she was lost gave her an eerie foreboding, a sinking, sick feeling at the pit of her stomach.

She only hoped that Flaming Arrow would believe her and not believe that her being lost was also part of the game of keeping him from her family. He was already so enraged, who was to say what he might do to help release that rage?

She watched his eyes as he seemed to be trying to accept what she had said and believe her.

Flaming Arrow was taken aback. He had never met a woman who could so boldly face him, a proud chief, with such lies, with such games! His gaze moved to Brian. The young man didn't seem so much a part of the game now. Instead of triumph over having duped a Blackfoot chief, there was a deep fear in the boy's eyes, much more than before.

Flaming Arrow gave Valerie a stern look, his lips pursed tightly together. He studied her expression. Strange how in just a matter of moments something about her had changed.

The defiance, the firmness, her stubborn determination—it all seemed to have waned into a soft sort of fear that played in the depths of her blue eyes.

He was confused as to why both the child and his sister had changed in their attitude so quickly. Why did they look so afraid now? He had not threatened them. He did not intend to. He had no plans to harm either one of them.

Actually, the child could benefit the chief at his village. Often white boys were adopted into the Blackfoot tribe. They learned ways of Blackfoot warriors and became as one with them.

They even then fought for the rights of the Blackfoot.

Not the whites!

The woman could fill spaces in his heart that he had refused to allow since the death of his beloved sister. His sister's death had robbed him of feelings of trust that he now felt resurfacing.

The golden-haired woman had awakened much in him that he had for so long denied himself! He tried even now to fight his needs but found himself losing the battle of the heart. He wanted the woman and he would have her, but only after things were made right for his people!

"Tell me . . . are you truly lost?" Flaming Arrow

asked guardedly. "You do not know how to find your way back to your home?"

When Valerie did not answer him, Flaming Arrow sidled his horse closer to hers. "*Awah-heh,* take courage," he said softly. "Do not be afraid to tell me the truth. Could it be that you are truly disoriented? That you are truly lost?"

"Yes, I am," Valerie finally whipped out, fighting back the urge to cry, not only over feeling so helpless, but also over feeling so dumb that she could put herself and Brian in such a position as this.

"How can that be?" Flaming Arrow asked, raising his eyebrows. "You look as though you are an intelligent woman. How could you stray so far from your home that you could not find your way back there?"

Now Valerie was feeling downright foolish. She was looking stupid in the eyes of this powerful Indian chief and that was the last thing that she would have wanted.

But she *was* lost. She *was* disoriented. She had no idea where they were.

She gazed down at Brian, a ray of hope leaping into her heart. "Brian, do you see anything familiar about the land?" she murmured as he turned and gazed at her over his shoulder. "Do you know where we are?"

"Sis, I knew some time ago that . . . that . . . we were lost," he said, his voice breaking. "We might be many miles from home now. Should Father search for us, even he . . . won't find us."

Valerie's throat tightened.

She ran her fingers through her brother's hair as she looked guardedly over at Flaming Arrow. "Neither my brother nor I are familiar with this lay of the land," she murmured. "We both have never been this far from home. We don't know our way back."

Flaming Arrow knew now without a doubt that the white woman and child were lost for a reason. It was obvious to him that they had purposely led him astray, and while doing so, led themselves too far from their home. They had played a dangerous game and it had backfired on them.

He wanted to be angry, yet there was too much panic in both the boy's and woman's eyes to make things worse for them. They had to be feeling helpless. Not only were they sudden captives of a powerful Blackfoot chief, they were lost from their home and those who loved them.

Flaming Arrow again looked up at the sky. The dusky wing of night was flooding the heavens. The moon had replaced the sun. Stars were just beginning to twinkle like small campfires overhead.

Wolves mournfully howled in the distance.

Flaming Arrow lowered his eyes and gazed at Valerie. "Tonight we will travel no farther," he said softly.

He looked over at a small creek that ran through a thick cover of trees. There was a peacefulness in how the water rippled and splashed over the rocks.

It was his first night for many moons that would not be spent behind the four walls of the prison.

He could not help but look forward to sleeping beneath the stars, becoming one with nature again.

He gestured toward the creek. "We will make camp there," he said, seeing a different sort of panic leap into the woman's eyes. "You will be safe here with your brother, not only from four-legged animals, but also two. I will watch over you while you sleep."

Valerie was stunned by his gentleness and his offer of help; in truth, she had been suddenly afraid of being with him through the long night. So many stories had been published in books and newspaper articles about how redskins ravaged white-skinned women. Would this man be guilty of such an act as that at the break of tomorrow's dawn? Or could she truly feel as safe as he was trying to convince her to be?

Were his intentions toward her and Brian truly pure? Oh, she so badly wanted to believe so, for she could not help the feelings she had for him, although knowing they were not only forbidden, but also foolish.

Brian turned slow eyes to Flaming Arrow. "You are no longer mad at me and my sister for anything?" he asked, swallowing hard.

Brian gasped and grabbed at Valerie's arm again when the wolves seemed to be drawing closer, their howls breaking the serene silence of the night. "Flaming Arrow, you . . . know . . . how to protect us from . . . dangerous animals?" Brian asked anxiously.

"I will build a fire," Flaming Arrow said, sliding out of the saddle.

He yanked on the horse's reins, led the steed over to a cottonwood tree, and tied the reins to a low limb. Then he turned toward Valerie and Brian. "Come," he said. "Tie your horse next to mine. We will then work together to get a fire built. Not only will we be safe from intruders in the night, but also our horses will be safe."

"That horse is *mine, not* yours," Brian dared to say as he dismounted. "Father gave me that horse last Christmas."

"The horse is now mine," Flaming Arrow said— not in a forceful, threatening way, but in a matter-of-fact tone.

Brian stopped and stared at Flaming Arrow, his eyes wide, his mouth agape.

When Valerie stepped to Brian's side and slid an arm around his waist, he felt reassured that things would be all right. But he also knew that he no longer owned a horse and there was nothing he could do about it.

"Brian doesn't mind giving his horse up to you," Valerie said, her voice calm, her eyes holding steady with Flaming Arrow's. "I hope you will accept the horse as payment for those things my brother took that belonged to your people. Also, I hope you will accept the horse as payment for keeping me and my brother from harm while we are so far from the safety and love of our family."

Flaming Arrow gazed at her in silence for a moment longer, wondering about her quickness to accept that he now claimed the boy's horse as his.

Was it a ploy?

Or did she truly understand that what he said was law?

He then motioned toward the blankets that were spread out beneath the saddles. "Young brave, you can help prepare our campsite by removing the saddles and getting the blankets," Flaming Arrow said softly as he glanced over at Brian. "Place them beside the water as your sister and I gather firewood. Also, get whatever might be in the saddlebags on both horses that might serve our comforts during the night."

Brian nodded and proceeded to do what he had been told. He was no longer afraid. Now realizing that the Indian meant him and Valerie no harm, Brian actually looked forward to a full night with the Indian beneath the stars and beside a fire.

It was like something someone would only read in books! For certain it was something that he would always remember!

"And he called me a brave," he whispered to himself as he stopped and looked over his shoulder at Valerie and Flaming Arrow picking up dried pieces of wood beneath the trees. Brian smiled, then proceeded to remove the saddles.

While Valerie gathered wood, the thought of

building a fire made her think of her father and how the bright flames might serve as a beacon in the night and lead him to the campsite—*if* her father had returned with Aunt Elaine and realized that Valerie and Brian were missing, she quickly added to her thoughts.

If not tonight, perhaps tomorrow?

As she glanced over at Flaming Arrow and how the moonlight defined his utter handsomeness, Valerie could not help but look forward to being with him tonight instead of dreading it. She no longer felt threatened by him. He seemed to hold much respect for women inside his heart.

And as for Brian, Flaming Arrow seemed to have tender feelings toward children. He had even called Brian a 'brave'!

No, she did not feel threatened. But she was hungry! Now and then her stomach growled.

She had to wonder when Flaming Arrow had eaten his last meal. Surely the food he ate at the fort was hardly fit for dogs. She knew that no soldier had empathy for Indians and would not bother to see that an Indian prisoner was decently fed.

"Are you hungry?" she blurted out, bringing Flaming Arrow's eyes quickly her way.

"Very," Flaming Arrow said, surprising her in how he so quickly allowed her to know his true feelings. "And you?"

"Very," she said, laughing softly.

Then she grew serious. "What can we eat?" she asked. "Not knowing that Brian and I would be

gone so long from home, I didn't bring provisions
for us."

"Do you see the water?" Flaming Arrow said,
nodding toward the creek.

"Yes, I see it," Valerie said, stooping to place
one more piece of wood with the others she carried
in the crook of her left arm.

"Then you are seeing where I will find food for
us," Flaming Arrow said, smiling over at her.

He then winced when the wood he held scraped
against the rawness of his wrist.

Valerie saw him wince and understood why. "I
wish I had some of my mother's medicinal salve
for your sore wrists," she murmured. "I could get
them healed in no time flat."

"I will collect herbs tomorrow as we travel onward and doctor them," Flaming Arrow said, bending to let the wood roll from his arms to the
ground. "Tonight I will build a fire, catch us fish,
and cook them. Then I will bathe my wounds in
the water as you and your brother sleep in the
blankets beside the fire."

"You mentioned traveling onward," Valerie said
guardedly, sliding the wood from her own arms to
the ground beside his. "Are you still determined
to find our home? Is that what we will be doing
tomorrow? Searching for my home? Are you still
determined to have your people's possessions? Isn't
the payment of Brian's horse enough for them?"

"It is payment enough, yes, but only because I
do not wish to waste any more time searching for

your home," Flaming Arrow said. He moved to his haunches as he began to stack the wood for the campfire. "The time will be best served looking for my people. Tomorrow I begin my earnest search."

Valerie absorbed his words, alert to the possible meaning behind them. If he wasn't going to resume his search for her home, then what of her and Brian?

Was he going to leave them alone to find their own way back?

What if they never managed to? Might they die out there in the wilderness? Perhaps her father might never even find them!

"Surely you can't mean that Brian and I are going to—" she started to say, but he interrupted her.

"You and your brother will travel with me," Flaming Arrow said, her gasp drawing his eyes up to lock with hers.

"What do you mean?" Valerie asked, taking a slow step away from him. "Are we now considered your true captives, for*ever*?"

"Only if you consider yourselves that," Flaming Arrow said, slowly rising to his feet.

He wanted to reach out and take one of her hands, but knew that was not a wise move.

Not when she was looking so horrified and confused at him.

"How could we not consider ourselves your captive if we are forced to go with you?" Valerie gulped out, her eyes wide.

"Would you rather I leave you to wander alone and be food for the wolves the next time the moon is high in the sky?" Flaming Arrow asked, gesturing with a hand toward the howling wolves.

"So you are only taking us because you fear for our safety?" Valerie asked guardedly. "You are saying that, should our father search and find us, you will willingly turn us over to his care?"

"Exactly," Flaming Arrow said, a slow smile fluttering on his lips. "But until then, we will continue onward in search of my people. Do you not see? If I stopped to search for yours, you would ask me to give up that which I have already been forced to give up while locked away in the white soldiers' jail: time! Too much time has been taken away from me! My people have been forced to live without my guidance. They will not be forced to give up any more days without their chief."

"I do see your logic, and I know you must be heartbroken, but think of my own pain," Valerie pleaded. "Think of my brother's. We love our family as much as you love your people. Please help us find our home. Please?"

"After knowing what has been taken from me, you would take more yourself by keeping me from my people perhaps for even one more long day?" Flaming Arrow asked, unable to hide the hurt that such words inflicted on his heart.

"I'm sorry," Valerie said, her voice breaking.

Confused by so many things—especially about how Flaming Arrow's tragedy and plight affected her, as though her sorrow were an extension of his—Valerie lowered her eyes.

She noticed that Flaming Arrow was again busy building the fire, and she seemed satisfied that their conversation about this issue was over. Suddenly she realized that no matter how hard she might argue or try to reason with him, his mind was already made up. He would not return her and Brian home.

At this moment, his eagerness to find his people outweighed anything else in his heart.

She felt a stab of guilt for misleading him to keep him from finding her family. She had kept him from perhaps a full day of travel toward his people. She suddenly wanted to help him. He had already suffered so much injustice!

"Flaming Arrow, I don't know where your people were taken," Valerie blurted out, hoping that she was right to make this confession to him. "I have no idea where the reservation was established."

His reaction was very different from what she had expected. He accepted this truth with hardly a trace of emotion.

There was no shock, no anger, not even a twinge of surprise.

"If you say you do not know, I believe you," Flaming Arrow said, giving her a quick glance. "Why *would* you know? My people's plight has never been yours."

Valerie was taken aback by what he said. Her

eyes wavered. She felt a strange sort of guilt knowing that what he said was true, not only about herself, but about *all* whites. Everyone was too busy
being concerned about their own lives to care much
about the Indians.

She now saw the wrong in that.

Silence fell between them as they each stared
blankly at the crisscrossed logs of the fire.

After the flames were burning high and Brian
had the blankets stretched out beside it, Valerie
watched Flaming Arrow catch several small fish on
a spear that he had fashioned from a stick.

Flaming Arrow was deep in thought about having Brian and Valerie with him, and thinking of a
future that might include them. He had admired
Brian's and Valerie's prowess in the face of danger,
with an Indian they knew could kill them at any
moment.

Suddenly aware of something else, Flaming
Arrow turned to Valerie. Their eyes locked. "You
have not shared your name with me," he said
thickly. "I have heard you call your brother by the
name Brian. But yours has yet to be spoken in
my presence."

Valerie smiled, strangely finding this moment
meaningful and mystical. "Valerie," she murmured.
"My name is Valerie."

Flaming Arrow nodded, smiled, then turned back
toward the water and speared another fish.

"Valerie," he whispered to himself. "Just like
her, there is magic in her name."

6

The day is done, and the darkness
Falls from the wings of night,
As a feather is wafted downward
From an eagle in his flight.
—HENRY WADSWORTH LONGFELLOW

Once again the sun was lowering in the sky. Valerie couldn't believe that it was the second day of travel with the Blackfoot chief. She now knew that even if her father searched for her and Brian, he would not find them. He would not think to look this far from their ranch.

Valerie gazed down at Brian as he cuddled against her on the horse, his cheek resting against her chest as he took a short nap.

While they were on their outing, he to search for Indian artifacts, she to pick flowers for her mother's room, Brian had been her responsibility and she had let him down.

She now knew that she should have listened to her father. She shouldn't have ever left their cabin.

Her gaze shifted slowly over to Flaming Arrow. Although she knew that she had been wrong to allow her restlessness to get the best of her, if she had not left home for some fresh air on her horse, she would have never met the Indian chief.

If she hadn't, she realized now just how much she would have missed.

Like a magnet, she was drawn to the mystique of him! Like soft whispers throughout her consciousness, Valerie's every heartbeat now seemed to be speaking Flaming Arrow's name.

If given the chance again, to seek the adventure that had brought her and Flaming Arrow together or to stay home like a dutiful daughter, Valerie knew that, no matter how wrong or foolish, she would have put herself and Brian in Flaming Arrow's path.

Even Brian seemed caught up in the intrigue of the Blackfoot chief. He had voiced no regret over being forced to travel with Flaming Arrow to search for his people. More than once, Valerie had even seen a bright excitement in her brother's eyes when he had spoken of his intrigue of the Blackfoot chief to her.

Yet she wondered if, no matter how much of this was true, she should try to flee tonight when Flaming Arrow fell asleep. Would it be the right thing to do . . . to try to find her way back home?

She could not stop thinking about how much her family must be worrying about her and Brian. It would be cruel not to try to ease their fears.

Yet now that they were so far from home, she knew the risks would be far too great to try finding their way back there now!

Valerie would have to think hard about this. She had until Flaming Arrow fell asleep tonight to make her final decision.

Flaming Arrow could sense that Valerie was in deep thought. It was the way her breathing had become more shallow and how she kept giving him questioning glances.

He could not help but think she was thinking about her family, wondering if she should try to backtrack along the trail to find them.

Although she no longer voiced her concerns about her family and how distraught they would be over her and her brother's absence, surely she knew that she would place herself and her brother in total danger should she try to find her home.

Tonight he would have to keep a close watch on her, for as spirited as she was, she might just try to leave. He understood her need to be with family, which matched his own need to return to his people, but he could not allow her to put herself and her brother in danger. They were now a part of his life as much as the stars were a part of the night sky!

Not wanting to come across any white people who might question a white woman and child traveling with a Blackfoot chief, Flaming Arrow had kept to the ravines away from the river today.

But now he rode down closer to the river and chose a place for tonight's campsite where the prairie reached out on two sides, a butte behind him, the river in front.

He looked over at Valerie, who had followed on her horse. "This is where we will spend the night," he said thickly. "Awaken your brother. He can help prepare the campsite."

Valerie gazed at the river, where fish were swimming close to the surface, and knew that once again their meal would be fish. Although delicious the way Flaming Arrow cooked them, she hungered for something more substantial. All day today, since their breakfast of fish, they had survived on berries they had found along the trail.

Her hand slid down and rested over the pistol that lay beneath the skirt of her dress. Should she give it to Flaming Arrow so that he could kill something for their meal?

No. It was best not to trust him just yet. Although he seemed honest enough, his kindness toward both her and Brian so surprising, Valerie was not yet ready to place a weapon in the Blackfoot chief's possession.

"Brian," Valerie murmured, placing a hand to her brother's cheek, gently rousing him. "Wake up. We've things to do before it gets dark. We're making camp again."

Brian's eyes fluttered open.

He leaned back, yawned, stretched, then smiled up at Valerie. "The nap felt good," he said.

He then gazed over at Flaming Arrow, who had dismounted and was lifting the saddle from his horse. He slid down from his horse to the ground. "Flaming Arrow," he said. "Let me help you."

Flaming Arrow stepped aside as Brian took the saddle and carried it over to lean it against the trunk of a cottonwood tree.

Then, after Valerie dismounted, he took her saddle and placed it beside the other one.

"I'm getting to be an expert at gathering wood," Valerie said, laughing softly as she walked away from Brian beside Flaming Arrow, picking up pieces of dry limbs for their fire.

"If you stay with me, I will teach you many things," Flaming Arrow said, stopping to gaze at Valerie.

Although her clothes were getting dirty and wrinkled from their traveling, it did not detract from her loveliness. Her face was flushed from the exposure to the sun, her hair windblown and thick as it lay down to her waist, and her beautiful sky eyes were drawing Flaming Arrow more each day into caring for her.

But he fought his feelings for her, since he had so many duties to his people to see to. To him women were always a distraction to a man's duties.

Yet the longer he was with Valerie, the more he knew that he enjoyed her distraction, for just to be with her made him feel whole and good. That was something he had not felt for far too long now.

"You said *if* I stayed with you," Valerie said, searching Flaming Arrow's midnight eyes. "Does that mean you are considering turning back and helping me find my home if that is what I want?"

"You are free to do as you wish when you wish,

but no, I cannot change my mind about traveling onward, whether it is with you or not," Flaming Arrow said thickly. "My people beckon to me. I must find them."

"Then if I decide that Brian and I should turn back, you won't stop us?" Valerie said guardedly.

"I did not say that," Flaming Arrow said.

"Then what *are* you saying?" Valerie asked, finding it hard to follow his logic. Sometimes he seemed to speak in circles, perhaps purposely to confuse her.

"Knowing the risks, I do not believe you will take it upon yourself to turn back with your brother," Flaming Arrow said.

He walked on away from her and placed wood where he would soon build a fire. He knelt down on a knee and carefully stacked the wood, nodding a silent thank-you to Valerie as she brought hers to add to the pile.

"But if I do decide to turn back, you won't stop me?" Valerie prodded, moving to her knees beside Flaming Arrow.

Their eyes locked. "Flaming Arrow, answer me," she said, his steady gaze unnerving her. "Tell me whether or not you will stop me and Brian should we decide to leave."

"Yes, I would stop you," he said, his jaw tightening. "But only because it would be to keep you from such a foolish act. *Not* because I wish to hold you hostage."

Valerie sighed deeply. "Although you now say

we are not your hostages, every time we speak of such things, in the end you prove that we *are*," she said.

She sank down onto the ground and stared into the river. "I wonder how my mother is," she murmured. "She was so very, very ill."

"You never before said that your mother was ill," Flaming Arrow said, sitting down beside her as he again prepared a spear from a tree limb to catch their evening meal. "If so, why were you and your brother not with her, but instead where you should not have been—on land that once housed my people's lodges?"

Brian knew now how to place rocks in a circle for their campfire. He was doing this now behind Valerie and Flaming Arrow as he silently listened to their conversation.

Valerie looked quickly over at Flaming Arrow. "I had not meant to be gone for very long," she told Flaming Arrow, suddenly feeling guilty for having left her mother at all. "And . . . and . . . I was picking my mother a bouquet. Had you not come when you did, my brother and I would have returned soon to our home."

"And so now you are blaming me if you are not there if your mother dies?" Flaming Arrow asked, a hurtful expression entering his eyes.

"Well, no, I had not thought to blame anyone," Valerie murmured. She swallowed hard. "And . . . I do not want to even think about the possibilities of her . . . of . . . her dying. Mother will get well. I know she will."

"Do you pray nightly to your God in the heavens for your mother's health?" Flaming Arrow asked, now watching the water for a fish to spear.

Valerie looked quickly over at him again, stunned that he would ask this. She had heard of Indian shamans and medicine men. But she had no idea of the true Indian beliefs, whether they included God or just superstitious hocus-pocus.

"Do you pray?" she asked softly, watching his expression as he turned his eyes slowly heavenward before speaking.

Then he turned smiling eyes to her. "Every night, every day, every needful thing brings prayers into my heart to my Napi, the Blackfoot's Great Spirit, that which might be the same as your God in your eyes," he said thickly. "Prayers are asked, but this Blackfoot chief has learned that sometimes it takes more time for some answers than for others. As for now, while I am searching for my people? Napi has chosen to make me wait for the answer to that prayer. He sees a purpose in making me wait. I accept it."

"I have been praying since my mother first taught me the children's prayer that I always spoke while on my knees beside my bed at night," Valerie said, recalling the very first time her mother had asked her to recite the prayer.

"Children's prayer?" Flaming Arrow said, his eyebrows raising questionably.

"It goes like this," Valerie said, somehow feeling closer not only to God as she recited the prayer, but also to her beloved mother. "Now I lay me down to sleep—"

The prayer was interrupted when Brian let out a loud squeal. "Sis, come here and see this!" he shouted, having left his perfect circle of rocks at the campfire to explore other things. "Hurry, Valerie! Flaming Arrow! I've never seen anything like this!"

Valerie scrambled to her feet and ran to Brian. "What is it?" she asked, searching for whatever had intrigued Brian so much.

"There," Brian said, pointing to what had once been a thriving blackberry bush. All that was left of it was a tangled vine of sharp brown briars.

Valerie gasped when she saw what was trapped on the briars: the remains of small birds, mice, frogs, and even snakes and insects.

"Good Lord, how could those things have gotten pierced onto the briars like that?" she said. "It's so gory, as though something purposely placed them there."

"That is the work of the 'butcher-bird,'" Flaming Arrow said as he stepped up to Valerie's side. He nodded toward her and Brian. "Come. Hide behind bushes. Watch."

"Butcher-bird?" Valerie whispered as she followed Flaming Arrow behind a thick stand of bushes, Brian scurrying alongside her. "What on earth is a butcher-bird?"

"Just watch for now," Flaming Arrow whispered

back as he hunkered behind the bushes with Valerie and Brian. "See what happens. Then I will explain."

Valerie's eyes widened when after only a few moments a gray bird, the size of a mockingbird, appeared. It had a hooked beak, inner white wing bars, and a dark mask covering most of its face, much like a raccoon's. It was carrying a small snake in its beak.

But what it did next caused Valerie to be taken aback with surprise.

The bird impaled the snake on the tangled briars.

Valerie could not believe her eyes when the bird then literally skinned out the snake and hung the carcass several thorns down from the empty skin, where he began to feed on it.

"Loggerhead shrike is the true name of this bird," Flaming Arrow said, no longer worrying whether or not he frightened the bird away by speaking aloud. "Whenever you find such a display of victims as this hanging on briars, you know a loggerhead shrike is near. Because of the way it kills and feeds on the prey, it had been given the nickname butcher-bird."

"But why does the bird display his kill in such a way?" Brian asked softly. "It seems to be so . . . so . . . inhumane."

"Just as a Blackfoot warrior shows off his skills as a hunter, so does the butcher-bird show off his skills as a hunter—to win a mate," Flaming Arrow said.

Brian watched the bird fly away, then he gazed at the various skins on the briars blowing in the gentle breeze. "I'm glad the bird is so small and I am so much larger," he said, laughing. "I wouldn't want to be one of its victims."

"Nor would I," Flaming Arrow said, chuckling. He placed a gentle hand on Brian's shoulder. "Young brave, it is time for us to return to our chores so that we can also have food to fill our stomachs."

More wood was added to the fire. Finally several fish were caught. And again they consumed a meal of baked fish.

Then they prepared themselves for another night in the moon-touched prairie.

Valerie lay beside her brother on a blanket while Flaming Arrow lay on a blanket on the opposite side of the fire.

"Sis, I can't sleep," Brian whispered as he rolled over and gazed at her. "Do you think Flaming Arrow is asleep?"

"I don't know," Valerie whispered back. She pulled the blanket more snugly beneath her chin. "Why?"

"He's been so nice to us I'd like to give him something," Brian whispered back. "What do you think? Should I?"

Valerie propped herself up on an elbow. "What are you talking about?" she asked, watching Brian as he sat up and reached over for his saddlebag.

"Wait a minute," Brian whispered as he opened

the bag and rummaged through it with a hand. "I'll show you."

Valerie sat up beside Brian and her eyes widened when he brought out the half of the arrow shaft that he had brought with him from home.

"You want to give him that?" Valerie asked, reaching over to smooth her fingers over the half arrow shaft.

"I brought it with me, hoping to find the other matching half," he said.

He looked across the fire to see if Flaming Arrow was awake.

He smiled when he saw Flaming Arrow turn on his side and begin staring into the flames of the fire.

"It belongs to Flaming Arrow's people," Brian said. "I want him to have it. Sis, I can't believe how kind Flaming Arrow has been to us. He has never raised his voice or threatened us. I think of him as a friend. Don't you?"

Valerie's insides warmed when she looked over at Flaming Arrow and found that he was now looking back at her through the flames of the fire.

She wanted to tell her brother that, yes, she thought of Flaming Arrow as a friend, and perhaps something more. Each day they were together she could feel a bond forming between herself and the handsome Blackfoot chief.

And he had awakened the feelings of a woman in her, for never before in her life had she felt such a delicious stirring at the juncture of her thighs.

She felt so much that she would not dare speak aloud. Especially to her brother!

"Yes, Brian, he's our friend," she murmured. "Take the arrow shaft to him. He will be grateful for having it."

She stayed behind as Brian scampered up from the blanket and eagerly went over to Flaming Arrow. She watched as Flaming Arrow sat up and took the arrow, his eyes brightening as he studied it.

Something drew her there to hear what he said about it. She sat down next to him, while Brian sat at his other side. Flaming Arrow said nothing, only looked at the arrow, running his fingers over the smoothness of the half shaft that was decorated with paintings of flames.

"This is mine," he suddenly said, looking quickly from Brian to Valerie. "The flames painted on the shaft were painted by my own hands. There were many more arrows such as this, but they were all lost to me on the day my people were uprooted and taken by the soldiers away from their homes."

"It . . . is . . . actually yours?" Brian asked, his eyes wide.

"Truly yours?" Valerie said, amazed that Brian had actually found something that personally belonged to Flaming Arrow.

Flaming Arrow nodded. He smiled at Brian. "Thank you, young brave, for your generous gift," he said thickly. "This arrow is my medicine."

He then looked over at Valerie. "Your brother

has a kind, generous heart," he said, their eyes locking. "I am certain that is because it was taught him by a sister whose heart is as generous and good."

Valerie so badly wished to move into his arms and hug him.

She wished for his lips to cover hers.

She wished for so much more that perhaps she would never get from him.

But the way he looked at her and treated her gave her some promise of what might be in their future. She would hold on to that hope, for she now knew that she loved him.

She would never love another.

"I must take my medicine with me and pray," Flaming Arrow said, rising quickly to his feet.

He was leaving not only to pray, but to put behind him the temptation of this woman whose eyes told him more that her words had ever said.

The longer she was with him, the more he wanted her. For now he had to fight such want.

He must wait until the time was right to tell her his feelings for her.

"I will not be gone for long," he said.

He stopped and gave Valerie a lingering gaze, which seemed to reach inside her very soul with a longing she had never felt before.

He then looked at Brian. "Thank you again, young brave," he said, then turned and hurried away.

Valerie watched Flaming Arrow until he arrived

atop a knoll that overlooked their camp. In the moonlight his silhouette was defined as he fell to his knees and prayed.

She listened to him and wished that she could help him find his people, for that need seemed to be eating away at him.

Flaming Arrow held his half arrow shaft above his head and prayed to Napi, the Blackfoot maker. He called out to Old Man Sun, the Supreme Chief of the Blackfoot.

"Oh, powerful ones, please hear my prayers," he pleaded. "Hear me now. Please bring peace into my life again! Please show the faces of my people soon! They have been too long denied me!"

Then he lowered his voice and said a softer prayer that he did not wish to reach the white woman's ears. "Napi, hear me now," he softly cried. "Please hear my prayer about the white woman! Give me a sign soon about her. Do I allow her to claim my heart? Or do I just look to her as a friend? Lead me into the right decision about the woman, for I am so troubled, oh, so troubled over how I should feel. She is white! I am Blackfoot!"

He had not noticed how his words had gotten louder as he spoke and did not know that Valerie had heard the last of the prayer, which made her now know for certain how he felt about her.

Brian had also heard. He stared with wide eyes and parted lips at his sister as he saw her face light up in a soft radiance that he had never seen before.

7

A thousand suns will stream on thee,
A thousand moons will quiver;
But not by thee my steps shall be,
Forever and ever.
    —ALFRED, LORD TENNYSON

An occasional wolf's howl was the only sound that broke the still of the night as Valerie snuggled next to her brother, both seeking warmth from each other. Although it was hot through the day, after night fell, the dampness crept across the land like seeking, cold fingers.

Valerie was aware of Flaming Arrow's restlessness. Her back was turned to him, yet she could hear him stirring, sometimes putting fresh wood on the campfire. Or she might hear the crunching of his moccasined feet as he paced along the rocky shore of the creek.

She knew that he was troubled by many things, but most of all by the fact that it was taking him so long to reach his people's reservation.

Since none of them knew where the reservation was, she had to wonder if they were even going in the right direction.

How would *he* know which way to go? Did his prayers lead him there? Was his Napi there every inch of the way, guiding him?

Restless herself, Valerie found it hard to sleep tonight. She had many of her own concerns.

How was her precious mother? And had her father arrived home yet with Aunt Elaine? If so, had he searched for his missing children?

There was something else that made it hard for Valerie to sleep tonight. The longer she was with Flaming Arrow, the more her feelings for him were heightened.

She couldn't actually resent him. It was more *her* fault than his that she and Brian weren't with their family.

She was the one who so foolishly led them so far away from her home that she could no longer find it. Flaming Arrow now offered her and Brian safety even if he had not taken the time to help her and Brian find their home.

She understood his need to find his people. She prayed that he would soon. Then she and Brian could concentrate on finding their way back home, she hoped with the safety of many Blackfoot warrior escorts or an Indian agent who might live on the reservation or near it.

She heard Flaming Arrow moving toward her. Her back was turned to him so that she could not actually see him; the uncertainty caused Valerie's heart to do a strange sort of sensual flip-flop. She scarcely breathed when she felt the heat of his hand as he smoothed the blanket that covered her more closely beneath her chin.

Then she sucked in a wild breath when his hand gently touched her cheek and lingered there for a long moment. She did not feel surprised that he might do something like this, for his feelings for her were more and more obvious, yet Valerie's pulse raced to feel the heat of his flesh against hers.

He was ever so gentle.

Her eyes opened wide when Flaming Arrow's hand went to her hair and his fingers wove through her thick, golden tresses.

Slowly she could feel how he let the hair sift through his fingers as though he might be studying it beneath the light of the campfire.

More than once she had seen him gazing in wonder at her hair, as though he might be intrigued by its color. She had also seen him looking at Brian's hair, and in the next moment look at hers again, as though comparing the color.

She was not offended by him coming in the middle of the night to study her, to touch her, for in truth, she wished she could turn to him and reach her arms out for him and lead him into her embrace.

Her heart pounded at the thought of how it might feel to be held by him. She closed her eyes and tried to force the desire for him to leave her, for she knew that this was not the time to be in love, especially not with an Indian!

Brian suddenly flipped away from her to sleep on his other side.

Valerie felt Flaming Arrow's hand leave her hair in a quick jerk as though he had been shot, Brian's sudden movements having surely startled him. She lay quiet as she heard him walk away.

She listened for him to make more sounds, but soon knew that finally he had stretched out on his own blanket and was ready for sleep.

She wished she could crawl over to him and ease the corners of the lone blanket up around him so that at least a portion of his body would be covered from the ravages of night.

He needed a top blanket worse than she and Brian. He was scarcely clothed.

But she knew that it was best to stay where she was. If she went to him and he reached a hand out for her to join him on his blanket, she knew almost for certain that she would do as he bade her. There was no need in chancing such a temptation, not when their feelings for one another were best left unspoken between them.

Sighing, Valerie moved to her side and gazed through the flames of the fire at Flaming Arrow. He was on his side, his legs drawn up. His arms were crossed over his broad chest, a portion of the blanket covering him. His eyes were closed. He seemed to be asleep.

She wondered what he would dream about. She wondered what her own dreams might hold for her tonight. If she went to sleep thinking hard about Flaming Arrow, would she dream of him?

Smiling, the warmth of the campfire on her face, Valerie closed her eyes and was finally able to fall asleep.

Slowly a dream came to her.

It *was* about Flaming Arrow.

He was standing knee-deep in a river, his breechcloth dripping wet, hugging his manhood, defining its long length, its hugeness. Such a sight made a warm stillness envelop Valerie in her dream, yet she did not reach out and touch him to explore his body, though she could, if she dared to. In the dream she was there . . . in the water with him.

She was unashamedly nude!

She could see herself in her dream and how the pearl drops of water glistened on her bare breasts. Her nipples were pink and erect as the cool wind brushed against them. Her golden hair hung in long wet streamers down her back. Her bare, tiny shoulders swayed as passion grew within her.

Flaming Arrow's large, masterful hands reached out and cupped her breasts within their palms. She wanted to scream out to him to do anything to her. She was his! She wanted to tell him to make her shiver with delight, make her experience things a woman experiences.

She wanted to tell him that while she was with him, she was all woman, that all childish desires were like wisps of feathers blowing away in the wind compared to how she felt while truly with him!

In her dream she sensually melted when he reached his arms out and drew her up against him.

His chest was smooth and tautly muscled, his lips warm, his tongue probing. . . .

And then suddenly the dream turned to something else, something ugly, something that made Valerie flinch and recoil in her sleep.

In her dream she was no longer in the water with Flaming Arrow. She was no longer nude. She was no longer being embraced by him.

She was standing aside while a faceless man stepped out of the shadows, his firearm aimed at Flaming Arrow's back.

It was like her feet were stone, for she could not move them. Her voice seemed frozen so that she could not scream and warn Flaming Arrow. She just stood there, motionless, dying a slow death inside when the bullet fired from the pistol and entered Flaming Arrow's back. . . .

Valerie finally found voice enough to scream.

Her screams awakened her.

Sweating, trembling, she sat up in jerks. Her eyes were wild as she gazed over at Flaming Arrow, who had jumped to his feet and was running toward her.

Brian cried out and sat up beside her. "Sis!" he said, grabbing her by an arm. "Why did you scream? What's wrong?"

By then Flaming Arrow was kneeling beside her.

He was gently framing her face between his hands, his eyes searching hers for answers.

"I had a dream," she said, her voice breaking.

She eased her arm from Brian's hand and found herself flinging herself in more powerful arms.

She clutched to Flaming Arrow as she wept.

"First I was dreaming something wonderful," she cried, "And then . . . it changed to . . . to something horrible."

She leaned away from Flaming Arrow and gazed into his eyes. "You were shot," she said, reveling in how he again gently touched her cheeks with his hands. "In the back, Flaming Arrow. Someone shot you in the back!"

"You care enough for Flaming Arrow that you react this way to the dream?" he asked thickly, his heart pounding.

Suddenly Valerie felt awkward. Although she so badly wished to confess her true feelings to him, Brian was there, his ears perked up, his eyes wide as he observed his sister possibly making a fool of herself over the Blackfoot chief.

The good, sensual part of the dream came to her in splashes, filling her very soul with wonder. She gazed into Flaming Arrow's eyes as he still waited for an answer.

His eyes dangerously mesmerized her.

She was afraid of this danger . . . of this passion she felt for this man.

"I . . . I . . . wouldn't want to see you shot in the back," she blurted out. "That's why I reacted in such a way. Only cowards shoot people in the back."

The dream and the horrors of it just would not lessen in her mind.

Again she wished to be held by Flaming Arrow to prove that he *was* all right, that the dream was so far-fetched, it was foolish to think any more about it.

But she couldn't cast it aside as something useless, as something too incredible to truly happen. She knew that Indians lived in danger every minute of their lives because the white pony soldiers had tried everything within their power to totally annihilate the red man from the face of the earth.

One by one they might still try to achieve this.

Thinking this, and truly afraid for Flaming Arrow, Valerie shoved her blanket completely away from her, slid her hand up the inside of her skirt, and unsnapped the sheath that held the pearl-handled pistol safely hidden.

Brian rose up to rest on his knees as, wide-eyed, he watched Valerie pull the pistol out from beneath her skirt and hand it to Flaming Arrow.

"Please take this," she said softly. "Please keep it with you for protection . . . at least until we reach your village and you can have your own weapon."

Flaming Arrow was stunned, not only that she had a weapon all this time, but that she actually trusted him enough to allow him to carry it.

And he was still very much aware how only moments ago she had clung to him as though she were a woman whose heart belonged to him!

For a moment he was at a loss of words, his feelings so tumultuous within him, but when she edged the weapon closer to him and nodded toward it, smiling warmly at him, he reached his hand out and allowed her to slide it into the palm of his hand.

"The dream was very terrifying," Valerie said, glad that he understood now how much she did trust him.

She was even somewhat relieved that he knew how much she cared for him. In the sensual part of the dream, it had felt so wonderful to be with him in such a way.

It would not take much on his part to make it a reality.

"More than once you and your brother have proved that you are generous to this Blackfoot chief," Flaming Arrow said, thinking back on how Brian had given him the broken arrow shaft. And now this. He felt so much at this moment for the woman and the child, he knew that destiny had brought them all together.

"Thank you both," Flaming Arrow said, his eyes locked with Valerie's.

Then, unsure of how to read the desire in the depth of Valerie's eyes, and wanting so badly to take her to a private place away from the eyes of the young boy to show her how a Blackfoot chief made love to a woman he loved, Flaming Arrow wrenched his eyes from Valerie, went back to his own blanket, and spread it on his back.

His heart thumped wildly within his chest as he gazed up at the stars, suddenly not seeing them at all, but instead the face of a woman: Valerie's.

Valerie gave Brian a warm hug, urged him to lay back down on the blanket, then stretched out beside him as he cuddled to again fuse her body warmth with his.

Valerie felt many emotions at this moment. But most of all she tingled with remembrances of the dream, and then later, of how Flaming Arrow had gazed so deeply into her eyes after she had given him the firearm.

He had not said the words that she knew he felt, but it had been there in his eyes.

Yes! She expected the sensual part of her dream to come true. Soon, she softly prayed.

"Sis, you truly trust him, don't you?" Brian suddenly whispered.

"Completely," she whispered back.

"Sis, you've fallen in love with him, haven't you?" Brian whispered, turning to gaze into her eyes.

Valerie blushed. "Brian, honey, go on to sleep," she whispered, bending over to brush a soft kiss across his brow. "We've many miles to travel tomorrow. You need your rest."

Brian gave her a sweet smile, then again snuggled against her as she wrapped her arms around him. "Sleep, little brother," she whispered. "And remember what father always said?"

"Don't let the bedbugs bite," Brian said, giggling.

"Yes, don't let the bedbugs bite," Valerie said softly.

When she knew that Brian was asleep, she turned slowly away from him and gazed through the slow-burning flames of the fire at Flaming Arrow.

A sensual warmth, like sweet, golden honey spread through her veins when she discovered that he was looking at her.

It took much willpower to stay away from him when her every nerve ending cried out to go to him and ask him to make the dream come true . . . the dream of them together, touching, exploring, kissing, holding. . . .

8

Turn away no more;
Why wilt thou turn away
The starry floor
The wat'ry shore
Is giv'n thee till the break of day.
—WILLIAM BLAKE

After another full day of traveling, Valerie saw a cabin a short distance away. She could tell that it was abandoned.

Tall weeds blocked the front door. The garden area was full of scorched, bent cornstalks. Browned, dead green-bean vines hung limply from poles in the ground. Weeds also grew profusely where other crops had once stood green and fresh. Many broken squash lay across a portion of the garden, rotten, where flies and bees battled for space over them.

Hot and sweaty, dust covering her face like powder, Valerie directed her gaze to a stream that trickled soft and sweet not far from the cabin.

She glanced down at her skirt and blouse, moaning to herself when she saw just how wrinkled and dirty they were from the many days of having to wear them. Embarrassing to her, she could even see perspiration circles beneath the arms of her blouse.

Also, she was sorely tired of sleeping on the ground. Just perhaps this one night, after she took a bath in the creek and washed out her clothes, she might be able to sleep on a bed! Often when settlers moved on for one reason or another they left behind the encumbrance of the heavier furniture; they would make new furniture when they again settled.

"Sis, see the cabin?" Brian said, looking quickly over his shoulder at her. "It's abandoned. Can we stop and explore? You know how I like to go through places that have been abandoned."

"Yes, I know how you love to explore . . . *every-*thing," Valerie said, laughing softly.

While on their journey from Kansas City, Brian had been quite the one for wanting to collect things, as now. If not for his love of collecting Indian artifacts, they would be home, clean, rested, and correctly fed.

Her gaze shifted slowly to Flaming Arrow, thinking that at least this one time she would not resent where her brother's curiosity had gotten them. Certainly she did not like worrying her parents, but she was happy she had met Flaming Arrow.

Oh, how she loved him.

Again she looked down at herself and deeply regretted being so filthy dirty and stinky! For Flaming Arrow she wanted to smell sweet. She wanted him to want her.

"Sis, can we?" Brian persisted, drawing Valerie out of her reverie, which she succumbed to now more often, since it felt so deliciously wonderful to fantasize about Flaming Arrow.

"Can we what?" Valerie said, turning her head back so that her eyes were level with Brian's. She blushed when she saw him staring at her with a question in his blue eyes.

"Oh, the abandoned cabin," she blurted out. "Yes, if Flaming Arrow approves, we will stop. Perhaps we can spend the night there."

Flaming Arrow had heard them discussing the cabin, which he had studied closely enough to know that it was safe to stay in for the night. It would be good to allow the woman and child the warmth of a lodge instead of them having to suffer through another damp, cold night beneath the stars.

It was something he wished now . . . to make the woman comfortable and safe. He was tired of fighting his need of her. It was like a slow ache inside his loins, paining him.

Tonight, perhaps tonight, he might approach her. . . .

"We will go and investigate the cabin. If all is well, yes, we will stay the night," he said, drawing both Valerie's and Brian's eyes quickly to him. "Come. Together we will go inside."

He broke away from them and sent his steed into a hard gallop toward the cabin. He gazed cautiously around him, checking for any movement in the brush that grew along the creek.

He then looked intensely through the trees that grew tall and umbrellalike around the cabin, giving it shade from the lowering evening sun.

He was relieved to see that nothing seemed amiss there. The cabin did appear to be totally abandoned.

And by the look of the tall weeds around the house and in the garden, the house seemed to have been deserted many sunrises ago.

He wheeled his horse to a quick stop before the house. As he dismounted, Valerie rode up next to him and drew a tight rein.

Brian quickly slid from the saddle.

Valerie soon followed.

Taking his knife, Flaming Arrow cut through the clutter of weeds at the front door of the cabin.

Valerie gazed all around her, then her eyes brightened when she saw a pump at the side of the house, which meant that a well had been dug to provide fresh water for whoever had lived there.

Without further thought, and throwing caution to the wind, she ran to the pump and grabbed the handle. Pumping anxiously, she laughed aloud when water began pouring from the spout.

"Brian, come here and help me," she shouted, already feeling the crisp coolness of the water flowing deliciously through the fingers of her left hand.

Brian ran to her.

He didn't hesitate to bend his mouth close to the spout. Thirstily he drank from it. Then, wiping his mouth free of water with the back of a hand, he stood back from Valerie.

"Pump it, Brian, while I put my hair beneath the water," she said, releasing the handle to Brian.

She sighed with pleasure as she stuck her hair beneath the spout and Brian churned the handle up and down, pumping fast and furious to bring the water more quickly from the deep well.

Flaming Arrow watched Valerie run her fingers through her hair as she held it beneath the water. His insides stirred sensually when she then held her face up to the water and allowed it to flood her delicate features. The water flowed down the front of her blouse, causing it to cling to her body and define the breasts that rested beneath the fabric.

He longed to hold the weight of those breasts within his palms. He wished to remove her clothes and taste every inch of her creamy flesh with his lips and tongue.

"Flaming Arrow, come and wash your sore wrists beneath the water," Valerie said, stepping away from the pump, lifting her heavy wet hair back from her shoulders.

When the water cleared from her eyes and she could see Flaming Arrow as he still stood at the door, his eyes glazed with desire, her pulse began to race and that only recently familiar ache between her thighs began anew. She realized that he was looking at her breasts, and it excited her to imagine what he must be thinking.

Her gaze slowly lowered and she saw just how

much of her body was revealed, since the blouse and skirt were now so wet and clinging. She blushed to see just how the nipples of her breasts *were* defined beneath the wet blouse. Even her skirt was so tight against her she could see where the triangle started and left off between her thighs.

She was glad that Brian was too occupied with the water, splashing it all over himself and taking deep gulps as he drank it, to notice what was transpiring between his sister and Flaming Arrow as their eyes now met and held, within them a need as old as time.

"Boy, that tasted and felt good," Brian said. He stood back from the pump and ran his fingers through his hair to slide it back from his face.

His voice brought both Valerie and Flaming Arrow out of their reverie.

She swallowed hard, shook the water from her skirt, then moved self-consciously now toward Flaming Arrow.

Flaming Arrow fought the heat in his loins and the need that was brought with the heat. With a pounding heart, he turned and lifted the latch at the door and slowly opened it.

Valerie stepped up next to Flaming Arrow and peered with him into the gloomy interior of the cabin, streamers of failing sunlight the only thing that gave them a faint look of what lay inside.

Brian squeezed between them and went on inside. "Just look at this," he said, a bright excitement in his voice. "Look at everything they left behind. I doubt they took much of anything with them."

This caused Flaming Arrow and Valerie to exchange quick, worried glances. They both wondered what might have caused such a quick exit.

But Brian's excitement was contagious. As he walked around inside the cabin, brushing aside cobwebs and dust and talking about what was there, Valerie could not help but want to see for herself.

Tonight the cabin was theirs!

There would be no sleeping on the ground or worrying about the wolves baying in the distance. Tonight a door could be locked to the outside.

She hurried in. But the more Valerie explored the cabin—finding so much that surely would not have been left behind unless the owners had vacated in a big rush—the more she became somewhat apprehensive about staying there. Could outlaws have caused the settlers' flight?

She looked quickly over at Flaming Arrow, wondering if Indian renegades might have frightened the people away.

Had the settlers even lived through it?

As Flaming Arrow left to collect wood for the fire, Valerie moved more slowly around the room to see if there might be something there to fix for their evening meal.

In the kitchen side of the cabin she found some supplies on shelves that lined the wall.

She smiled when she found glass jars of food that

had been prepared from the garden: green beans, corn, turnip beets, and . . .

"Peaches?" she whispered, holding up the glass jar, marveling over them. She had seen no peach trees in the area, which had to mean that these had to have been canned before the settlers had moved to Montana Territory.

She smiled as she stood several of the jars of food on the kitchen table. Tonight's supper would be special. Finally, they would be eating something besides fish!

She again moved slowly around the cabin, fighting cobwebs. She winced when a lizard scampered across the dust-infested wood floor.

Valerie sighed with relief when the lizard fled through the open door.

She continued looking around and found one bed at the far side of the room behind a blanket that had been strung across a line. She leaned over and tested its strength and softness, coughing when only touching it sent plumes of dust flying from the blankets.

Still coughing, sometimes with a sneeze also troubling her, Valerie stepped away from the bed and gazed at the loft overhead. She went to the ladder, climbed up to the loft, and found another bed there, pillows stacked on one end.

"Sis, look!" Brian cried, bringing her down from the ladder. "Look what I found beneath this pile of blankets! A trunk of clothes. The dresses look your size! There are even some clothes here that are my size. I can change into something clean."

Valerie glanced down at her attire, again grimacing over how dirty and disheveled she was.

She then looked over at the dress that Brian had pulled from the trunk and was holding up for her to see.

In her anxiousness to be more presentable in the eyes of Flaming Arrow, she tossed aside all worries of why a trunk of clothes would have been left behind, and knelt down beside Brian to search through the trunk.

Burdened with an armful of logs, Flaming Arrow entered the cabin and stopped and watched Valerie's exuberance for a moment, enjoying it when she smiled and laughed—for when she did, it was like the heavens opened up and warm sprays of sunshine were everywhere! She lit up this dingy cabin as if she were the sun herself.

Smiling, at least for the moment finding some contentment in his life, Flaming Arrow turned toward the fireplace.

He glanced out the door and saw how quickly night was falling.

He glanced again at Valerie and Brian. Their comforts were important to him now. A fire must be built to ward off the chill of the night. Also, he had found a chicken coop at the back of the house where one chicken had been wandering around only barely alive, yet fat enough for a meal. He had grabbed the chicken and prepared it for the meal.

It even now lay just outside the door, already plucked and washed, a surprise for Valerie, for he knew just how tired she was of eating fish.

He himself had never grown to like the white man's strange birds with their white feathers and funny-looking legs and beaks. But he knew that they must be tasty, for white men to always keep them for the dinner table.

Valerie chose the dress she would wear after her bath in the creek. She even found some delicious-smelling bars of soap at the bottom of the trunk, as well as soft white towels.

But she could not help but feel as though she were intruding on someone's privacy. She again wondered who could have left so much behind. And why?

She glanced toward the door. Soon it would be dark. If she was to have a bath, she would have to leave now, then worry about preparing the food later.

She suddenly realized that Brian was nowhere in sight. She pushed herself up from the floor and looked around the room for him.

When she saw a trapdoor laying open at the far side of the room, she smiled, for she knew that was where she would find her brother. Cellars were the best places to explore. Many things were usually stored there.

But she didn't like the idea of him down there without lamplight. Sometimes things besides food and personal belongings were in the dark confines of a cellar. Spiders, rats . . .

She searched quickly for a kerosene lamp. When she saw one on a table near the fireplace, she laid the dress aside and got it.

"Let me light it for you," Flaming Arrow said when he saw her lift the lamp. He already had flames caressing the logs in the grate. He took a twig and placed it in the fire and got the tip ablaze.

Valerie lifted the smoke-blackened chimney from the lamp and rolled up the wick, then leaned the lamp closer to Flaming Arrow.

She looked nervously at the cellar door, then at the wick as fire slowly waved across it.

Then, just as she replaced the chimney on the lamp and started toward the cellar, Brian's blood-curdling scream made her jump with a start.

"Sis!" Brian cried, a desperation in his voice. "Flaming Arrow! A spider! I was just bit by a huge spider! It hurts! I . . . feel . . . faint!"

Valerie's face paled as she exchanged a quick look of panic with Flaming Arrow.

They then rushed toward the cellar door.

9

As 'twixt two equal armies, Fate
Suspends uncertain victory,
Our souls (which to advance their state
Were gone out) hung 'twixt her, and me.
—JOHN DONNE

As Valerie watched, her heart pounding with fear, Flaming Arrow went down into the cellar and soon brought up Brian, who lay limply and unconscious in his arms.

"Oh, no, it must be so bad," Valerie cried, as Flaming Arrow carried Brian to the bed and laid him on it.

She fell to her knees beside the bed.

Her fingers trembled as she searched for the spider bite on her brother's body and found it on his right ankle.

She rolled his pants leg up to his knee and closely studied the bite, then gave Flaming Arrow a puzzled look.

"It doesn't seem that bad after all," she said softly. "It's barely red or swollen. Thank God it isn't. But . . . why is Brian unconscious?"

She scooted aside and scarcely breathed as Flaming Arrow took a close look. The flames of the kerosene lamp lapped out enough light for him to see that the bite was not a lethal one. It had not been from a deadly spider.

"He will be all right," he said, gazing over at Valerie. "It was not a poisonous spider that bit him."

Valerie sighed. "But Flaming Arrow, why is he unconscious?" she said.

She placed a gentle hand on Brian's brow and slowly caressed it.

"He fainted from the fright, nothing more," Flaming Arrow said, giving Valerie a slight frown as she quickly looked his way. "When he awakens, I do not believe he will be happy about having fainted. He will feel that he showed a weakness that I know he will not be proud of. I have seen much pride in this young brave. I hate to see it taken away by one brief moment brought on by fear."

"Yes, I, too, believe he won't be happy with the situation," Valerie murmured. "But if he speaks of it I will remind him just how lucky he is that a poisonous spider didn't inflict the wound. He could have died."

"Although the bite is not a serious one, I believe it needs special medicines that I can minister to him," Flaming Arrow said, rising to his feet. "Bathe his brow while I am gone. I assure you he will awaken soon."

Valerie nodded.

After Flaming Arrow was gone, Valerie went outside and pumped water into a bucket, then took it back to the house.

After getting a cloth wet and wrung out, she sat on the edge of the bed and began bathing Brian's brow with the damp cloth. She watched his eyes for signs of him awakening.

And the longer he stayed unconscious, the more she became afraid that perhaps Flaming Arrow was wrong.

What if the spider *was* poisonous?

What if it just didn't create a terrible sore from its bite?

When Brian licked his lips and stirred, and then his eyes began showing movement behind the closed lids, Valerie dropped the cloth on a table beside the bed and drew him up into her arms.

"Brian," she murmured, slowly rocking him back and forth as she had when he was a small child seeking comfort from a big sister. "Sweetie, oh, sweetie, you are going to be all right."

Brian's eyes fluttered open. He stared up at Valerie, then became aware of the stinging heat on his ankle.

He swallowed hard and his eyes widened when he recalled having seen the large black spider as it had crawled away from his leg after biting him. There had been enough light from the upstairs room for him to see the spider. He had never seen one as large or as fuzzy!

Even now a cold fear crept into his heart to know

that it would still be down there somewhere waiting for another victim.

"Close the trapdoor, Sis," Brian said, shoving her away. "The spider! It might come up here! It might bite *you*."

Seeing his fear, shivering from the alarm she saw in her brother's eyes, Valerie jumped from the bed, hurried to the trapdoor, and slammed it shut.

"Cover it with the rug, and then hold it down with something," Brian cried. "The trunk! Scoot the trunk over there! Its weight should hold the door down good enough for the spider not to be able to escape!"

When Flaming Arrow came into the cabin with the herbs he had found for the spider bite, he placed them in a wooden basin he had found outside close to the well, then silently watched Valerie as she scooted the trunk over the trapdoor.

He gazed at Brian and saw that he had awakened. It was apparent that the boy was still frightened. He was on his knees, pale and tense, as he watched his sister covering the trapdoor with the trunk.

Flaming Arrow stepped farther into the room, into the light of the flames wafting from the kerosene lamp.

Brian looked over at him. "The spider," he said, swallowing hard. "We're making sure the spider stays in the cellar."

Flaming Arrow and Valerie exchanged worried glances.

Then they both went to Brian and sat down on the edge of the bed, each on opposite sides. "Flaming Arrow has brought something to medicate the spider bite," she said, rolling her brother's pants leg up past his knee.

She gazed over at what Flaming Arrow had brought, grimacing when she saw something that looked like mud spread out in a wooden basin, and then other things in the basin that she did not recognize.

She questioned Flaming Arrow with her eyes, but did not outwardly question him. She didn't want to look as though she didn't trust his judgment about what he had chosen to use on the spider bite. She knew Indians used herbs and all sorts of things found in the forests and along riverbanks. At this moment in time, she welcomed anything that might make her brother well.

"Brian, my people know many ways of doctoring wounds not known by white people," Flaming Arrow said, taking the time to get the boy to trust him before medicating him. He brushed Brian's hair back from his brow and smoothed it down on each side with both of his hands. "Nature offers many cures."

He showed Brian the scars on his wrists that were left there from the prison irons. "See my wrists?" he said. "Herbs made them almost well already."

He smiled at Brian. "Today I have brought what nature offers for spider bites," he said. "Trust me, young brave. What I place on your bite will soon make it well."

"What is it?" Brian asked, craning his neck to look in the wooden basin. He grimaced when he recognized the huge dollop of mud circled around at one side of the basin. "Mud? You are going to put mud on my bite?"

"What I put on the bite will pull out whatever poison *might* be there," he said. "Although I do not believe the spider was a poisonous one, it doesn't hurt to guard against it."

Flaming Arrow sank his fingers into the cool mud that he had collected from the creek embankment. He sprinkled some dried herbs into the mud and mixed them together.

"The spider was so big," Brian said, shuddering with remembrance. "It was so hairy and black."

"Sometimes it is the smallest spider that is the most deadly," Flaming Arrow murmured. "Lay down. Stretch out your leg close to me. Lay still while I medicate the bite. It will feel cool and good."

Valerie placed her hands at Brian's waist and eased him down on his back on the bed.

She then sat stiff and quiet as she watched Flaming Arrow medicate the wound.

Intrigued, she also listened as Flaming Arrow sang a medicine song.

While singing his song of medicine over Brian and holding the mud mixture in his right hand, Flaming Arrow, with his left hand, first wiped the bite with leaves from silver sage. He then sprinkled it with the dust from a puffball and plastered the bite with the fresh mud mixture, in which he had also mixed sarvice-berry juice.

"It is done," Flaming Arrow said. He sank his hands in the bucket of water that Valerie had placed beside the bed, washed them, then rose from the bed with his basin of medicinal supplies.

"That is all you have to do?" Brian asked, staring down at the mud mixture on his leg. "That is truly going to make me well?"

"After a good night's sleep you will be as good as new," Flaming Arrow said, smiling down at Brian.

He then gazed over at Valerie. "Food would also help him recover more quickly," he said. His eyes twinkled as he recalled Brian's stomach growling while he had medicated the bite.

He went outside and brought back the prepared chicken. "This is not what I normally bring to my lodge after a hunt, for I did not have to go but as far as this yard for the kill," he said, handing the chicken to Valerie. "I found the white man's bird you call by the name 'chicken.' I prepared it for you. Now you will prepare it over the fire for Flaming Arrow and the young brave?" He took a step closer to her. "And for you? I believe you have grown tired of fish. Am I right?"

"Very," Valerie said, laughing softly. She was amazed that he had found a chicken. Just the thought of frying it and eating it made her mouth water.

As Flaming Arrow took his basin of medicine outside, Valerie scurried around until she had found enough lard, a large enough frying pan, and salt and pepper, so that she could fry the chicken over the hot coals at the edge of the fire in the fireplace.

She would also open one of the jars of green beans.

And for dessert they would have peaches!

She felt eyes on her as she cooked. She looked over at Brian and saw in his eyes something that worried her. As the grease popped and crackled around the chicken, she went over to Brian and placed a soft hand to his brow.

"What is it?" she murmured, glancing down at his ankle where the mud had dried and was beginning to crack. "What's bothering you?"

"I fainted, didn't I?" Brian asked, glancing toward the door for Flaming Arrow's return. "Like a sissy, I fainted."

"Anyone who became frightened by such a large spider *would* faint," Valerie tried to reassure him. "Please don't worry about it. Brian, it could've been so much worse. What if you'd been bit by a black widow spider? Count your blessings, Brian, that you are all right."

"But Flaming Arrow knows that I fainted," Brian said, wincing when Flaming Arrow stepped inside and heard him.

The Indian chief paused for a moment, his eyes on Brian. Then he sat down and drew Brian into his arms. "Young brave, do not concern yourself over what happened in the cellar, except that you are going to be well soon," he said thickly.

Flaming Arrow's insides warmed when Brian wrapped his arms around his neck and hugged him, his cheek resting against Flaming Arrow's bare chest.

"I feel a kinship with you, young brave, as I would with a son," Flaming Arrow said. "I would never want to see harm come to you. And I would never want you to think that you are less than a man because you fainted. Forget it as though it never happened. In my eyes, it is already gone as though an eagle came and snared your embarrassment in its powerful talons and carried it away."

Brian giggled. "I like the way you explain things," he said softly. He leaned back and gazed into Flaming Arrow's eyes. "Did you truly mean it when you said you liked me so much?"

"There was a special bond that formed between us the moment we met," Flaming Arrow said, placing a gentle hand on Brian's shoulder. "Yes, I care. Yes, it would please me to treat you no less than my son."

Flaming Arrow gazed over at Valerie, who was absorbing all of this with a softness in her eyes, with a wonder.

Valerie felt so much at this moment she was afraid she might speak up and reveal it all to Flaming Arrow.

Suddenly she felt awkward in his presence.

It was as though while he spoke to Brian he seemed to be trying to reach out to her, as well, drawing *her* into the mystique of him . . . and loving him.

Blushing, flustered over caring for him so much, yet unsure of where she should truly allow this caring to take her, she moved from the bed and hurried back to cooking their supper.

But *then* what? she wondered to herself as she took the pan of chicken from the hot coals. What did the night have in store for her? What did it have in store for the kind, handsome Blackfoot chief?

After placing the pan of chicken on the wooden table, she searched through the supplies on the shelves until she had enough plates and cups and silverware for their meal.

Her pulse racing, welcoming a reason to go outside, away from the eyes of Flaming Arrow, Valerie hurried out into the moonlight and to the pump. One by one she washed off the dinnerware.

When she heard footsteps behind her, her insides tightened. A sudden fear swept through her to think someone might have been lurking in the dark, waiting to pounce on the first person who left the cabin.

Dropping a dish to the ground, shattering it, Valerie stood up quickly and whirled around.

She sighed with relief when she found Flaming Arrow standing there, his copper face sheened in moonlight.

He stood there for a moment, his eyes searching hers, a shade of uncertainty hanging between them.

What he did next caused Valerie's breath to catch and her heart to lurch. She melted into his embrace when he placed his hands at her waist and drew her quickly against his hard body.

When his lips came to hers in a searching, wondering kiss, a sweet, soft pleasure spread through her veins. She was basking in sweetness when Brian's voice came to her, wrenching her free of Flaming Arrow's sensual embrace.

Her eyes locked with Flaming Arrow's, Valerie slowly stepped away from him. Then she bent and gathered up the dinnerware and rushed back inside the cabin.

"Sis, you look so flushed," Brain said, raising his eyebrows. "Did you stub a toe or something while you were outside?"

Valerie smiled. "Yes . . . or something," she murmured.

She turned bashful eyes up at Flaming Arrow as he came into the cabin carrying a fresh bucket of water.

His pulse racing hot and anxious through his veins, Flaming Arrow glanced at Valerie. Without actually speaking with her, he knew what to expect later tonight when Brian was asleep. She seemed as anxious as he for that midnight hour when they could finally be together as a man and woman in love.

10

Ascend beside me,
Veiled in the light,
Of the desire which makes thee . . .
One with me.
   —Percy Bysshe Shelley

Flaming Arrow had placed more wood on the blaze
to ensure a fire for most of the night to ward off
the chill. He had left to take a bath in the nearby
creek, the cold night temperatures and cold water
something he had grown used to through the years.

Since so much had taken precedence over the
bath in the stream that Valerie had planned to take
before it had gotten so dark and ungodly cold, she
was now, in Flaming Arrow's absence, only taking
a sponge bath in front of the fire.

Stripped down to only her panties, she sank the
washcloth in the bucket of water that she had
warmed over the hot coals of the fire.

As she washed her arms she turned and gazed
at Brian. Snuggled beneath a blanket, his spider
bite all but forgotten, he was peacefully asleep on
the bed. As soon as they were through with supper
and she had cleared away the dishes, Valerie had

taken all of Brian's bedding outside, as well as that from the loft bedroom, and had shaken it free of dust.

She had then allowed Brian some privacy for a sponge bath as she busied herself in the overhead loft preparing the bed for a comfortable night of sleep.

While doing so, she then wondered about Flaming Arrow, where *he* might sleep.

Because he had been imprisoned in the bleak fort stockade and surely had not been given anything akin to a bed upon which to sleep, she felt wrong to take the upstairs bed tonight.

But earlier when they had discussed it, he had insisted. He said that he would sleep downstairs on the floor beside the fire while Brian slept on the bed nearby.

Remembering their embrace and heated kiss, Valerie wondered just how safe it was for her and Flaming Arrow to sleep beneath the same roof. Their feelings for one another were now out of control. Although she had never been with a man sexually, she was now certain that the feelings that troubled her at the juncture of her thighs were those a women felt when she hungered to have a man's body next to hers.

There had been only one other brief time in her life when she had thought she was in love, but her feelings for that man were not even similar to those she felt for Flaming Arrow.

Bradley Hart, her father's pick of men from

those he knew in Kansas City, had only been a
convenience for her. He had been an escort to balls
and social functions. Nothing more.

Not until one night when they were alone in her
house while her parents were out for a long evening
ride, and things had quickly changed. While sitting
before a soft, gentle fire in the fireplace, Bradley
had gotten bold in his advances toward her.

When she had shoved him away and told him
that she wished not to be kissed by him, *or* held,
he had grabbed her by the shoulders and forced
her down on the sofa. He would have raped her
had her parents not walked in. Her father had
grabbed Bradley away from her and ordered him
from their house and their lives forever.

She shuddered now to think of how Bradley's
hands had already swept up inside her dress. His
fingers had just found her soft and private place.

Shame engulfed her even now to remember how
his fingers had probed and hurt her.

She was so glad her parents understood that she
had nothing to do with the incident . . . that she
had tried to fight him off.

Her father's shotgun had been threat enough for
Bradley never to approach her again.

It had been one year now since she had last seen
him. He had just up and disappeared. She had even
worried that her father might have met him one
night on a dark street and . . . and . . .

Sighing, her cheeks hot from thinking about the
terrible incident, Valerie hurried into the soft silk

long-sleeved gown that she had found in the trunk. She was glad it was somewhat large for her and covered her body so well. While in the presence of Flaming Arrow, wearing something more daring might be all it would take to fuel the fires in his heart again.

Although she hungered for him as she had never hungered for a man before, she did not think it best for them to pursue their feelings for each other. In truth, to all whites, such feelings for a red man were forbidden.

"And so you are ready for bed, I see," Flaming Arrow said, stepping up behind Valerie.

She had been so lost in thought she had not heard him enter the cabin. She turned on a quick bare heel and blushed as she gazed at him. In the soft light of the fire she could hardly control her heartbeat when she saw his wet sleek chest and muscled shoulders, his long thick hair hanging in wet rivulets down his perfectly straight back.

But it was not so much what she saw along his muscled body, how the water droplets shone on his skin like tiny diamonds, as it was what she saw in his midnight-dark eyes. The fires of his passion were there in his eyes as he spoke without words to her of his desire.

Valerie could hardly control her own, weakened by it so much she was not sure she could make it up the tiny ladder to the loft overhead.

"Yes, I . . . I . . . am ready for bed," she said, self-consciously raking her fingers through the thickness of her golden hair. "And you? You are also ready?"

She felt foolish in how her small talk was so obviously forced. By the slight fluttering of a smile on his lips, she knew that he noticed.

This made her even more awkward in his presence, especially since only a silk gown stood between them and their passions.

This was not the same as when Bradley had wanted her so badly. She had not returned the want. She had not wanted him even to touch her, much less kiss her while his large hands groped and assaulted her.

She wished to have *this* man's hands on her! She wished to open herself up to him and let him explore that part of her that tingled even now with rapture as their eyes lingered and silently spoke of sweet promises to one another.

His heart pounding, the heat in his loins like raging fires had been lit there, Flaming Arrow was the first to break the magic spell that had begun to weave between himself and Valerie.

He took the blanket that he had hung over the back of a chair earlier and spread it out on the floor before the fire.

As he stretched out on the blanket, he could feel Valerie's eyes lingering on him. He had to wonder if she could see how she affected him, his manhood swollen uncomfortably beneath his wet breechcloth. The ache was almost unbearable.

Valerie felt a hot blush rush to her cheeks when,

as he turned over to his side, she could see something defined beneath his breechcloth. His manhood had grown as though it had a separate life of its own!

She panicked and turned and hurried toward the loft ladder. When she reached it, she lifted the hem of her gown, took one step on the ladder, then turned again toward Flaming Arrow.

When she found him watching her, she smiled weakly and took a slow step toward him. "I just can't be selfish enough to take the bed," she murmured. "Please, Flaming Arrow. You go to the loft bedroom. You take the bed."

Barefoot, her hair hanging in golden waves down her back, she went and stood over Brian. The bed was too small for them both and didn't look strong enough to carry their full weight.

She then turned back to face Flaming Arrow. "I'll get a blanket and sleep here on the floor beside Brian's bed in case he needs me in the night," she said.

She realized that she was talking unnaturally fast, and that her voice was rising in pitch the longer he stared at her. He had not yet said anything since she had begun her rambling.

She hadn't given him the chance to.

Rattling on and on, she talked nonstop.

Finally she grew quiet. She had said all she could think to say, especially with her heart and mind betraying, wanting to lead her into Flaming Arrow's arms.

Never had she fought feelings as she fought them now. They were consuming her . . . these desires to make love with a man for the first time in her life.

Her breath caught in her throat when Flaming Arrow suddenly rose from his blanket and walked toward her. Her pulse racing, her eyes wide, her insides tightened when he stopped only a heartbeat away, reached out, and took one of her hands.

She questioned him with her eyes as he led her to the loft ladder.

"You will sleep tonight on the bed," he said thickly. "Now go. You need your rest. Tomorrow is another day of traveling."

As though hypnotized by his deep, dark eyes, her whole body feeling as though it were a mass of quivering jelly, Valerie nodded.

When he dropped his hand down away from her, she lifted the hem of the silk gown and again started up the ladder.

She got farther this time—but *still* only halfway—when she turned and gazed down the ladder at Flaming Arrow, who still stood there watching her, his shoulders broad, his chest wide, his jaws tight.

She could not help but take a quick look at his breechcloth to see if . . .

Blushing anew, she realized, that, yes, his manhood was still larger than she remembered it being before they started this soft bantering tonight. She started to resume going up the ladder, but again turned back to him.

"You just can't sleep on the cold, drafty floor,"

she said, her heart pounding. "And since you insist that I sleep on the bed in the loft, so must I insist that you share it with me. It's a much larger and stronger bed than the one Brian is sleeping on. You . . . you . . . need your rest as badly as I."

There!

Now she had said it!

Now she had opened the door to something perhaps far more than she might be able to handle!

But she seemed in such little control of her heart, now that she was allowing herself to have feelings for Flaming Arrow. To hell with how people said it was forbidden for a white woman to love a redskin! she cried silently to herself. How could any woman resist Flaming Arrow? How could any woman not love him?

He was a genuinely sincere, caring man. And, except for her beloved father, Flaming Arrow had been more gentle to her than any white man she had ever known.

Valerie's eyes were locked with Flaming Arrow's. She breathlessly awaited his response. She was stunned when he turned and went back to his blanket and lay down before the fire.

She was in awe of this man who could turn his back on an open invitation to sleep with a woman. It proved that he was a gentleman, through and through.

Or it proved that she had been wrong about him . . . that he truly had no such feelings for her after all. Had *he* been playing a game with *her?*

Had it all been done so that in the end she would feel foolish and degraded?

Hurt, and feeling ashamed for having opened herself up to a man in such a way for the first time in her life, Valerie rushed up the ladder and flung herself on the bed, sobbing.

Oh, how embarrassed she felt! How could she ever face Flaming Arrow again? How could she travel onward with him, as though this had never happened?

When he looked at her tomorrow, and every day after that, would it be with a triumphant mocking that proved that he had bested the white woman in the worst way?

"How could he?" she softly cried, tears moistening the bed beneath her.

"Valerie?"

His voice, so soft, so caring, made Valerie's breath catch.

"Are you crying?" Flaming Arrow asked, settling down on the bed beside her.

When she did not turn and look at him, he reached down and turned her over. Gently he framed her face between his hands.

He bent low and brushed a series of soft kisses across her lips.

Then he enfolded her within his arms and lay down beside her. "Are you certain that you want me, a man with red skin, a man with scars on his flesh made by whites?" he whispered.

He held her so close that he could feel her heartbeat against his chest through the thin fabric of her gown.

"Or did I misread what your invitation to share the bed with you meant?" he said huskily.

"I'm so confused I'm not sure what I'm doing," Valerie whispered back, her skin tingling when he smoothed away the tears streaming from her face.

"Then I shall just lay here beside you, nothing more," Flaming Arrow said, moving away from her. He stretched out on his back on the far side of the bed.

Valerie stretched out on her side, facing him. It was hard to fight back the desire that ate away at her insides, but just now she was not sure if he truly wanted her.

"Thank you for medicating Brian's spider bite," she murmured, the light of the fire wafting up from the lower floor enough for her to see Flaming Arrow's full, handsome profile. "My brother means the world to me."

"I have no brothers," Flaming Arrow said, turning on his side to face her. Gently he took one of her hands and held it. "I had a sister, but she is now a part of those who walk together in the Sand Hills, the forever ghost place of the Blackfoot."

"I'm sorry," Valerie murmured. "Losing someone as close as a sister has to be devastating."

He talked more of his family and of how many of them he had lost in recent years.

He talked more of his plans for his people, of how he must lead them away from the reservation to seek a life elsewhere, where no white leaders would be there to speak his people's minds for them.

"It is my destiny to right all wrongs for my Blackfoot people," Flaming Arrow said, his voice breaking. "For too long now they have been wronged by the whites."

"If that is so, how could you befriend me and my brother so easily?" Valerie asked softly. "I would think that all white-eyes, as you call them, would be your enemy."

"Only those that openly wrong my people are my true enemies," Flaming Arrow said thickly. He reached a hand up and gently shoved some fallen locks of Valerie's hair back from her brow. "You? I could never have feelings but love for you."

"Love?" Valerie asked, her voice filled with wonder. "You can love me so easily?"

"Loving you would be easy for any man," Flaming Arrow said, giving her a warm, slow smile. "Have there been men before me that you have loved?"

Again Valerie thought of Bradley Hart. A bitterness became evident in her voice as she answered him. "No, there has been no man in my life that meant anything to me," she said, swallowing hard.

"What man has caused bitterness to edge your voice when you speak of men?" Flaming Arrow asked, seeing how asking that made surprise light up her eyes.

"You can read me that well?" she asked softly.

"You truly can read my emotions, that you would know that there was a man who . . . who . . . came close to raping me?"

"Rape?" Flaming Arrow said, his jaw tightening. "A man tried to rape you?"

"Father came just in time," Valerie said, lowering her eyes.

"A white man's rape is why my sister is now dead," Flaming Arrow said in a low, angry whisper.

Valerie's lips opened in a soft gasp. "I'm sorry," she murmured. "Oh, so very sorry."

"My sister's death changed much in my life," Flaming Arrow said sullenly. "How I feel about things in general."

"You never mentioned whether or not you were ever married," Valerie dared to say, only now wondering about the possibilities.

She felt foolish for having not thought of it earlier. What if she had allowed herself to love a man and he was not free for marriage? She would die a slow death inside if she could not have Flaming Arrow!

"No, no time for it," Flaming Arrow said softly.

That statement made Valerie unsure of how to feel. She was glad that he wasn't married, yet if he'd had no time earlier for a wife, how could he now? He had much to do for his people!

"Will you ever make time for a wife?" she asked. "Don't you want someone with whom you can share everything?"

"Yes, *now* I do," he said, sliding a hand down

and gently cupping one of her breasts through the silken fabric of her gown. "I . . . want . . . *you*."

Valerie's heartbeats almost swallowed her whole when Flaming Arrow then swept his arms around her, drew her against him, and kissed her with a kiss all-consuming.

All doubts, all reservations, all shame, all thoughts of Brian just below them were cast to the wind as Valerie and Flaming Arrow broke apart only long enough to disrobe one another.

When they were both nude, their eyes absorbing each other's nakedness, Valerie could not help but gaze with fascination at that part of Flaming Arrow that had until now been hidden behind his breechcloth. His manhood was long and thick with arousal.

And when he reached for one of her hands and led it to him, she sucked in a wild breath of surprise when she felt his heat and slowly encircled his throbbing member with her fingers.

"This part of me is forever yours," Flaming Arrow said thickly, wincing with pleasure when her hand tightened, her fingers cool and sweet against his heat. "Move your fingers on me. Feel me."

Unfamiliar with everything about a man, and about this passion that was now overwhelming her caused *by* a man, Valerie gave him a questioning look.

Then with his fingers over hers, she began to move her hand slowly over him.

When she saw how his eyes became glazed and

heard his slight gasps, she knew that she was giving him pleasure.

Flaming Arrow removed his hand from hers, and with both of his hands he explored Valerie's body and began giving her pleasure in return.

She sucked in a breath as he filled his hands with her breasts, his thumbs circling her nipples. She closed her eyes in ecstasy when he bent low and flicked his tongue over first one nipple and then the other.

She would not allow shame to spoil this moment with Flaming Arrow. She knew that things could change as soon as tomorrow. She wanted to at least have this memory to carry with her forever, for never again could she love as did she now.

Feeling himself too near the point of total release, Flaming Arrow swept her beneath him.

As she gazed up at him, questioning him with her eyes, he probed with his manhood until he found her moist, ready place, then sank himself down against her pulsing cleft.

He began slow thrusts as he moved farther and farther inside her, his manhood fitting into her as if it had always belonged there.

Knowing that this was her first time with a man, and realizing that women suffered pain with the first entry, Flaming Arrow held her close and drew her lips to his. As they kissed, he moved his body slowly back and forth, inching himself farther inside her, stopping then, coaxing her to lead him onward.

Feverish with desire, and basking in this moment

of togetherness with the man she loved, Valerie opened herself up to him like a flower opens to the sun.

As he gave one long, last thrust that finally broke through the tiny membrane that had proved her virginity to him, she responded with a soft cry, and then a shuddering breath as the pain turned to pleasure.

Then, as he still kissed her, his tongue sliding between her lips, exploring her mouth, he stabbed deeply within her and sought her center of need.

When she tremored with ecstasy and clung around his neck, he smiled, for he now realized that he had found that one spot within her that would bring her intense joy.

He rubbed himself against her slippery heat, thrust more deeply again, then withdrew and pressed into her again with his hard, throbbing sex.

A tingling sensation was spreading throughout Valerie. She felt rush after rush of exhilaration. Each of his strokes within her made her aware of him as a source of immeasurable pleasure.

When he slid his lips down to her throat and licked her neck in long, sensual strokes, she twined her fingers through his sleek black hair and sought his mouth again with a wildness and desperation.

Understanding her need, a need that matched his own, Flaming Arrow placed his hands beneath her, pressing his fingers urgently into her flesh, and lifted her closer so that he could thrust more deeply and earnestly inside her as they kissed . . . long, deep, and searchingly.

He had denied himself such pleasures for so long, it was like awakening again to a new world! Being with Valerie like this was removing a hollow ache that he had known for so long. He was on fire with passion. He felt alive again, as though he had, until tonight, been only a thing, not a person, moving through life mechanically.

Oh, how fiercely he loved her!

Her warm breath mingling with his, her body locked with his, made him know just how much he had denied himself these past years.

Nothing could ever be the same again. She was his world!

Languorous, floating, so deliciously swimming toward something that dazzled her senses, Valerie closed her eyes as her mind seemed to explode in bright flashes of color, her body tremoring with his in sexual release, dissolving into a delicious heat, spreading, searing their hearts and their very soul into one entity.

Afterward, they lay together.

Valerie was overwhelmed by what had happened, the intensity of it.

Flaming Arrow felt deep gratitude for this woman, who alone had brought him out of his dark world and feelings of hopelessness.

He held her close, brushing soft kisses across her breasts. He smiled when he heard her quiet sighs of pleasure as his fingers massaged the swollen bud between her legs, that which he had awakened to feelings tonight.

"My love," Valerie whispered, quivering as he brought her to the brink of pleasure again with his fingers.

"Tonight is not yet over," Flaming Arrow whispered huskily.

"Do you mean there is more?" Valerie asked, opening her eyes, her cheeks hot from the love-making. She giggled. "I'm not sure if I have the strength."

"You do not have to do anything but enjoy," Flaming Arrow said softly. "After tonight you will want no man but Flaming Arrow."

She questioned him with her eyes, thinking this way of loving her forbidden, then sucked in a wild breath of rapture when he bent low over her and again flicked his tongue over her woman's center, moving over her in a soft pressure.

Moaning, the pleasure rising again within her, she shook her head fitfully back and forth, her golden hair thrashing.

"Slowly," Flaming Arrow whispered, reaching up to still her. "Lie there quietly. Close your eyes. Enjoy it slowly."

His head bent low again.

His fingers separated her folds.

He touched the flowery edges of her womanhood with flicks of his tongue.

She closed her eyes and enjoyed, the word *forbidden* forgotten, forever.

11

Love seeketh not itself to please,
Nor for itself hath any care;
But for another gives its ease,
And builds a Heaven in Hell's despair.
—WILLIAM BLAKE

Morning came with bright sunshine filtering through the cracks in the roof, settling along Valerie's skin in soft rainbow colors.

When she awakened and found herself in bed with Flaming Arrow, an instant shyness enveloped her as she recalled what she and Flaming Arrow had shared the previous night.

As he lay there now so peacefully, so soundly sleeping, one arm thrown across her bare stomach, Valerie still could not believe how completely she had given herself to this man.

Yet if given the chance, she would do it again . . . and again . . . and again!

Their sexual togetherness had strengthened her feelings about him.

Oh, how she did love him! With every beat of her heart, with every breath she took, she loved him.

Although feeling somewhat shy this morning of her nakedness with Flaming Arrow, who was just as naked as she, she was aware of feeling wondrously at peace with herself and the world.

She only hoped that when he awakened he felt the same, and that the torment he had been feeling over so much might be lightened somewhat.

Today she would ride proudly at his side as she helped him search for his people.

"Brian!" she whispered, her eyes widening as she suddenly recalled that he was recovering from yesterday's bite. Although she regretted having to leave the bed when all she truly wanted was to snuggle up against Flaming Arrow and whisper softly in his ear as he awakened, she wanted to see how Brian was faring today. She hoped Flaming Arrow had been right . . . that the bite had not been a poisonous one—that his medicine, strange as it was, had helped Brian enough that he felt like traveling.

She didn't want herself or her brother to be the cause of any further delay in searching for Flaming Arrow's people. Enough white people had already stood in his way! Easing Flaming Arrow's arm from across her, placing it gently at his side, Valerie watched to see if this awakened him.

When she saw that it didn't, and that he only moved over to sleep on his other side, facing away from her, she softly ran her fingers down his thick hair, then bent low and kissed it.

When she heard Brian speak her name from

downstairs, Valerie hurried into the silk gown, ran her fingers through her hair to straighten it back from her shoulders, then went down the narrow loft stairs.

She found Brian clothed in the fresh clean shirt and breeches that he had found in the trunk. His hair was combed and lay neatly along his collar line. His eyes were bright and clear.

"Good morning, sweet Brian," she said, sweeping him into her arms, hugging him. "I don't have to ask how *you* are feeling. You are up and at it even before Flaming Arrow—"

When she spoke Flaming Arrow's name she felt Brian stiffen.

She eyed him speculatively as he stepped away from her, his eyes now wide with wonder.

"Where *is* he?" he asked. "If he isn't up yet, where *is* he? Where did he *sleep?* When I saw that he was not sleeping in the blanket over there by the fireplace, I thought he was up already, perhaps out hunting or taking a brief morning swim."

Valerie's smile faded.

She felt suddenly trapped by a boy's innocence!

How *would* he react to knowing that she and Flaming Arrow slept together all night? If he knew they had been together in bed, would he understand that they had not just slept together, but shared something even more meaningful? Would he understand?

Flaming Arrow was her momentary reprieve as he came down the loft steps, clothed and all smiles, and looked from Valerie to Brian over his shoulder.

"I rarely sleep past dawn," he said, laughing softly. "Today I feel as though I could sleep until the noon hour. But when I heard your voices . . ." When he saw a tenseness between Valerie and Brian, his words trailed off and his smile waned.

As he took the last step from the ladder, he turned and faced them. "What is wrong?" he asked softly. "Young brave, does your ankle pain you? Is not the spider bite well enough for you to travel on horseback today? Is that what is wrong? You do not know how to tell me? You do not want to delay my search for my people?"

His gaze swept over Brian. "Yet you look well enough," he said thickly. "You have even changed into fresh, clean clothes for the rest of our journey."

"I found them in the trunk among the other clothes," Brian said, glancing from Valerie to Flaming Arrow. "And yes, I am well enough to travel."

Flaming Arrow went to Valerie, swept an arm around her waist, and yanked her against her hard body. His eyes seemed to be looking into her soul as he gazed into hers. "My woman, what causes your tension this morning?" he asked. "What causes your brother's?"

"Not now," she whispered, pleading with her eyes. "Please let us talk about it later."

"Talk about what?" Brian asked, raising his eyebrows when he heard her. "Do you two have a secret you aren't sharing with me?"

Valerie's face flooded with a blush. She smiled weakly over at Brian, then knew that she could not delay any longer telling him how things had developed between herself and Flaming Arrow. It was obvious that Flaming Arrow was not going to refrain from touching and holding her in Brian's presence.

"Brian, there is no secret," she murmured, sliding a possessive arm around Flaming Arrow's waist. "I think you'd best know that . . . that Flaming Arrow and I . . . well, we . . . uh . . . slept together last night."

Brian's eyes brightened. He smiled. "Good," he said, sighing. "I was afraid for him to sleep on the floor. More spiders could be lurking somewhere else besides the cellar. One could have crawled on Flaming Arrow and bit him while he slept."

Realizing now that her brother had no idea what "sleeping together" truly meant—that she and Flaming Arrow had promised themselves to one another for eternity after making maddening love for half of the night—Valerie was relieved.

Brian *was* still so innocent of things of this world.

He would not even think to guess how his sister had behaved last night with a man when she had never been so wantonly free with a man before.

He surely never looked to his sister as someone who might be appealing and sexual in the eyes of men. She was his sister, only his sister!

Valerie and Flaming Arrow exchanged sly, amused glances, then laughed softly as they broke away from each other.

"I'll get the dress that I took from the trunk yesterday and go upstairs to get dressed so that we can get on with our morning," Valerie said, grabbing the dress she had left thrown across the trunk.

It was a demure, plain cotton dress, gathered at the waist. It had enough flare in the skirt that it would be easy to wear for riding on a horse.

"Sit down on the bed, young brave, and let me take a look at that leg before we venture onward," Flaming Arrow said.

"It doesn't hurt any longer," Brian said, plopping onto the edge of the bed. He rolled up his pants leg and held out his leg for Flaming Arrow to see.

"There is a slight scab," Flaming Arrow said, noticing Valerie out of the corner of his eye as she returned to the loft to dress in privacy. He pushed tenderly all around the bite, then patted Brian on the head. "But other than that, it is nearly well."

"I still can't believe that mud was used to medicate the bite," Brian said, shoving his pants leg back down.

He jumped from the bed and followed Flaming Arrow to the fireplace. He bent to a knee and handed Flaming Arrow wood for the fire so that they could prepare a breakfast of some sort before continuing onward.

To surprise Valerie, Brian had already placed

coffee grounds and water in a pot for their morning coffee.

"So you found the use of mud strange, did you?" Flaming Arrow said, chuckling as he glanced over at Brian. "Yes, I guess you would, just as I find many of your white doctors' use of medicine strange."

"Well, guys, I'm as fit as a fiddle now and dressed and ready for all that life offers us today," Valerie said as she came down the ladder.

When she reached the lower floor and turned and gazed at Flaming Arrow, their eyes locked with a silent knowing that caused her woman's center to react in a strange sort of warm, gentle twitching.

Aware that Brian was quiet again and watching them, and thinking that he might be wondering what had brought about this change between his sister and the handsome Blackfoot chief—and not wanting him to question her about it—Valerie rushed to the kitchen side of the cabin and searched through the canned goods for something to prepare for breakfast that could be quick yet nourishing.

She knew how anxious Flaming Arrow was to move onward.

She knew that he had taken the time to prepare a morning cook fire only because of her and Brian. Otherwise, he would have headed straight out on the trail and would have worried about food later in the day.

"I'll place the coffeepot in the hot coals," Brian said, breaking their strained silence.

"I think all we'll worry with this morning is a bowl of peaches with our coffee," Valerie said, turning to question Brian and Flaming Arrow with her eyes. "Would that be nourishing enough for the long stretch of travel ahead of us? Or should I go to the cellar and find something more substantial among the food that is stored down there?"

Brian paled. "More substantial like . . . *spiders?*" he said, paling. He jumped up and ran to Valerie to help her find the can of peaches. "Peaches are enough," he said. "Maybe later on today Flaming Arrow can kill a rabbit or something for dinner."

They ate peaches and drank the coffee until both were gone.

Just as they were ready to leave the table to prepare for their departure, a thundering sound of horses approaching the cabin drew them quickly from their chairs.

"Who can that be?" Valerie said, watching Flaming Arrow pick up her pearl-handled pistol and walk quickly toward the window.

Then she paled as she watched him hold the pistol steady, slowing drawing back the curtain that had been sewn from flour gunnysacks.

"Father!" Valerie cried, running to Flaming Arrow and grabbing his arm. "Don't shoot! It might be Father!"

Flaming Arrow had already seen by now who it was. His eyes brightened and he spoke a rush of words in his Blackfoot tongue as he lay the pistol on the table and made a mad rush for the door.

Brian went to Valerie and clung to her as Flaming Arrow opened the door and ran outside.

Stunned by Flaming Arrow's usage of his Blackfoot tongue, and by his exuberance, Valerie took Brian's hand and walked with him to the open door.

Her lips parted in amazement when she saw Flaming Arrow joyfully greet an Indian who had slid quickly from his saddle. He knew the Indians! They were surely not renegades, but perhaps warriors from his very own Blackfoot tribe!

Not knowing how she should feel at this moment about so many Indians arriving, Brian and herself the only white people for miles and miles, Valerie prayed that all she had shared with Flaming Arrow had not been for nothing.

If so, and he saw no further need of her and Brian, what might he do with—*to*—them?

"Who are they, Sis?" Brian asked, watching and listening as the Indians, one by one, left their steeds and greeted Flaming Arrow.

"By their reaction to seeing Flaming Arrow, I have to believe they are from his own tribe," Valerie murmured, placing a hand on Brian's shoulder, drawing him closer. "We'll know soon, Brian, whether or not it is good that they have found their chief."

"What do you mean?" Brian asked, giving her a wide, questioning look.

"Don't worry," Valerie said, still watching Flaming Arrow and the warriors. "I'm sure things will be just fine. Yes, just fine."

Flaming Arrow talked excitedly with Fox Eye, his longtime friend from his village, calling him *nisah,* brother.

They had been children together. Together they had learned how to hunt, swim, master everything young braves were taught so that they would one day be proud Blackfoot warriors.

They had shared everything, almost the same heartbeats, for their feelings for one another were even more closely felt than had they been blood-kin brothers.

"Flaming Arrow, these warriors fled the reservation with Fox Eye," Fox Eye said, gesturing with a slow wave of the hand around him as he looked at each warrior with pride in his eyes. "We have established a home deep in the mountains where no white pony soldier would dare enter. We were on our way even now to Fort Harrison to get you released, either by peaceful means or by force. It has taken us this long to get established at our stronghold and to feel safe enough, to feel bold and strong enough, to go against the white-eye pony soldiers."

"As you see, it is not necessary to lose lives while releasing your chief," Flaming Arrow said, laughing softly. "He is free! Free!"

He explained to Fox Eye just why he had been

released, and how he even now was searching for his people.

"Your search is over!" Fox Eye said, clasping his hands on Flaming Arrow's bare shoulders. "I will take you to them. We will together lead our people from reservation land!"

Fox Eye turned and stared at the cabin, his eyes slowly roaming over Valerie and then Brian. "Who are these white skins?" he asked, again gazing at length at Valerie. "I am surprised to see white-eyes living here. We chased off settlers only a few days ago. Fox Eye could hardly believe it when Flaming Arrow stepped from the cabin!"

Flaming Arrow went to Valerie. He took her hand and led her outside.

He then gestured with a nod of his head toward Brian. "Come, young brave," he said thickly. "I have many friends I would like for you to become acquainted with."

Valerie scarcely breathed as Flaming Arrow explained to Fox Eye how they had met and why they were in the cabin together.

He placed a hand on Brian's head and gently shoved him toward Fox Eye. "This young brave will one day make a great warrior," he said, ignoring the surprise that leaped into Fox Eye's eyes. "He and his sister are going to be a part of the Blackfoot's lives."

Relieved, and feeling ashamed for having doubted Flaming Arrow, Valerie looked quickly up at him when he ventured further to explain to Fox

Eye that she was his woman . . . that she would soon be his wife.

Brian turned a quick glance up at Valerie. "You are going to marry Flaming Arrow?" he asked, his eyes wide. "We are going to live with him forever? We aren't ever going back home?"

Unsure of how Brian truly felt about this, and knowing herself that yes, she wanted to stay with Flaming Arrow and be his wife, Valerie's head seemed to be spinning.

She had truly only known Flaming Arrow for a few days, yet last night she made love with him as though she'd always known and loved him.

Today he was even declaring his love for her to his warriors!

It *did* all seem so unreal. But everything had, since she had left the real world behind in Kansas.

In the wild country of Montana Territory, where life could be so short, it did seem only right to love so quickly . . . to live so quickly! She did know that she couldn't live without Flaming Arrow.

Seeing the tension again between brother and sister, and sensing Valerie's confusion over so much, Flaming Arrow took her by the hands and turned her to face him. "My woman, I know that you are aware there will be danger in staying with me," he said thickly. "You know I am planning the dangerous task of leading my people from the reservation. I would understand if you and your brother wish not to stay with me and my people.

Both you and Brian are free to go. I won't force anything on you, ever again."

"I wish to stay with you," Valerie blurted out, her heart pounding. "I wish to help you."

He drew her into his arms. "Does that mean you will be my wife?" he asked, his voice breaking. "That you will become a part of my people as though you are as one with them? Will your brother?"

"Yes, yes, yes," Valerie murmured, shivering sensually when he lowered his lips to hers and kissed her as all eyes watched.

"Sis."

Brian's voice broke through Valerie's magical moment. She swung away from Flaming Arrow and turned to him. "Brian, how do you feel about things?" she asked softly.

"I want to stay with you and Flaming Arrow," he said, taking one of Flaming Arrow's hands. He gazed up at the Blackfoot chief with much pride and adoration in his eyes. "I wish to learn from you, Flaming Arrow. I wish to understand everything there is about being Blackfoot."

Filled with many emotions, mostly happiness and relief that he could have both Valerie and Brian as a part of his life, he lifted Brian into his arms and swung him around, laughing.

He then placed him back on the ground and turned him toward the warriors. *"Hai-yah!* He is now a part of us!" he cried.

He reached out and drew Valerie to his side. *"She* is *also!"*

When his warriors did not respond right away, but instead only stood there watching with no noted emotion in their eyes or on their faces, Valerie was not sure she and Brian were accepted by the warriors, or ever would be.

She wasn't even sure if she had made the right decision. Was it wrong of her to put such hardships on her brother by urging him to stay with her and the Blackfoot? Should she, instead, if ever given the chance, return him to the way of life he was familiar with?

For now, she felt that she had a struggle of her own, that of winning over these Blackfoot warriors who might be feeling as though they would as soon kill her and Brian as look at them.

Seeking comfort and reassurance, she edged closer to Flaming Arrow's side.

She felt protected as he slid an arm around her shoulders and held her.

12

O! He gives to us such joy,
That our grief he may destroy,
Till our grief is fled and gone.
—WILLIAM BLAKE

Tired from another long day of riding on horse-back, having not yet arrived at the Blackfoot stronghold, Valerie was glad when Flaming Arrow gave the command for everyone to stop and make camp for the night.

She looked over at Brian who had ridden with Fox Eye most of the afternoon. After she had complained to Flaming Arrow that it was cramping her legs for Brian to be confined in the saddle so close to her for so long, Flaming Arrow had swept Brian from her horse and had taken him to the warrior.

Valerie had guardedly watched Fox Eye's *and* Brian's reactions when Flaming Arrow had placed Brian in the saddle with Fox Eye. Both had seemed wary of the other, yet neither questioned Flaming Arrow's decision to throw them together in such a way.

When Flaming Arrow had come back to Valerie

and explained, she immediately thought that it was clever of him to think of such a plan that would help draw his best friend into a close relationship with Brian, which would then ease the tensions among the travelers. The love and understanding of the white child could open the way to a more clear understanding and acceptance of the white woman Flaming Arrow had chosen as wife.

Valerie had kept a close eye on Brian as the afternoon sun crept toward the horizon. When Brian tried conversation with Fox Eye, and Fox Eye responded, she knew her brother had begun breaking down the wall of prejudice between himself and the Blackfoot warrior.

After that, Brian and Fox Eye talked often as they traveled. She could see Fox Eye pointing out things to Brian, explaining the wonders of the countryside. She could see Brian's intense interest. She could also see that a friendship had formed quickly between the boy and the warrior.

While traveling along many broad, deep trails that led them from most of the open land, instead taking them along the wooded river valley and beneath the shadows of the pine-clad slopes of the mountains on which elk, deer, and wild sheep fed in great numbers, Valerie knew that, at all cost, the Blackfoot were avoiding all white travelers.

Time and again she thought of her father. Surely by now he had given up on ever seeing them again.

She, on the other hand, had thought of something that made her heart relax more with having chosen to travel onward with Flaming Arrow instead of insisting on being taken back to her family.

Flaming Arrow had told her he was going to take his people to Missouri! While on their way there, it could take his people's travel in the close proximity of her family's ranch. She would ask him to stop and allow her to explain everything to her family.

Should Brian have by then changed his mind about staying with her and Flaming Arrow; this would give him the opportunity to stay with his family.

"My woman is in deep thought," Flaming Arrow said, shaking her from her reverie.

She looked down at him as he lifted his hands toward her to help her from her horse.

"Come," he said. "While others make camp, we will go downriver and be alone as we bathe the dust from each other's bodies in the water."

Welcoming his hands at her waist, so glad to leave the saddle, Valerie slid down to the ground and stood for a moment gazing into his eyes. She had noticed the blanket slung across one shoulder and now knew why he had placed it there . . . for them to wrap themselves in after the swim as they made love.

There was just enough light left for her to see the passion in his eyes.

She could even see the quick pulse beat in his throat.

"A swim and a bath in the river would be wonderful," she murmured, feeling her own passion peaking at the thought of being alone with him again.

All day they had exchanged knowing, sensual glances. She had known that he had to have been thinking of their sensual time together and eagerly awaited being alone with her again.

"Sis," Brian said, running up next to her, tugging on the sleeve of her cotton dress. "Fox Eye has invited me to go with him to hunt for a rabbit for the evening meal before it gets dark. Can I? He says he will even show me how to shoot his bow and arrow."

"It will be good for the young brave to share the hunt with my favorite warrior," Flaming Arrow said, smiling over at Valerie and then down at Brian.

Valerie glanced over at Fox Eye, who was patiently waiting with his bow slung across his shoulder, his quiver of arrows at his back.

"Sis, please?" Brian insisted, tugging even more determinedly on her sleeve. "Didn't you hear what Flaming Arrow said? Please say that I can go. I'll be careful. I'll stay with Fox Eye. I'll do exactly as he says."

Valerie fell to her knees and drew Brian into her arms. "Yes, go ahead," she said, hugging him. "But *do* listen to everything he says. Bears are out there aplenty."

"We just might even shoot us a bear!" Brian said, returning her hug, then broke away and ran toward Fox Eye.

"Can we shoot a bear if we see one?" Brian asked Fox Eye excitedly, bringing a smile to the warrior's broad, thick lips.

Valerie moved up beside Flaming Arrow. She welcomed his arm around her waist as they both watched Fox Eye and Brian walk away toward the darker depths of the forest.

She turned and watched the activity around her. Some warriors were taking care of the horses, while others were preparing the campfire.

"All is well here," Flaming Arrow said, taking Valerie by the hand. "They have been instructed of their chief's planned absence. They will give us the privacy we seek."

"Perhaps too much privacy might be dangerous," she teased. "What about the bears I warned Brian about?"

"Bears understand privacy," he teased back.

He turned quickly and lifted Valerie into his arms. He snuggled her close and kissed her.

His mouth was warm and moist, and she leaned into the kiss. As he carried her onward, their kiss lasted, his tongue sliding between her lips, hers responding.

As he carried her through the forest, the river beckoning a short distance away where the waning sun cast its golden color like rippling satin in the water, he slid a hand up inside the skirt of her dress.

Valerie trembled sensually as his fingers slid higher along the satiny flesh of her leg. When he reached the valley of promise between her legs, and his fingers slid beneath her panties and separated the flowery edges of her soft folds, a low moan escaped Valerie's throat.

Her head began a slow, rapturous spinning when his fingers pushed, kneaded, and gently pinched the swollen lips where her woman's center grew tight like an unopened rosebud. The more he caressed, the more Valerie became breathless and wanting for more.

And when they finally reached the river and he slid her from his arms and spread the blanket on the ground, her fingers trembled as she hurriedly undressed herself under his watchful gaze.

"I can't believe I am doing these things," she murmured, her cheeks hot with anticipation. "Please believe me when I tell you that before I met you I . . . I . . . was quite timid in the presence of men. Never would I have thought that I could be this brazen . . . this open with a man, especially before I spoke vows with him."

Her clothes tossed aside, Valerie stepped up close to Flaming Arrow. As she placed her hands to the waistband of his breechcloth and she slowly slid it down along his body, she gazed into his eyes.

"Do you think me a hussy?" she whispered, her heart pounding like a sledgehammer within her chest as he gazed with such heated passion back at her.

"I think you are a woman in love for the first time," Flaming Arrow said, stepping out of his breechcloth as it fell around his ankles. "As I, also, am in love for the first time."

"You have truly never loved any women before me?" Valerie asked, quivering from head to toe when Flaming Arrow slowly began to run his hands down her body.

"No one," Flaming Arrow said, his voice thick with a sexual huskiness. "And do not worry about having not yet spoken vows with this Blackfoot chief. Soon. We will speak them soon. Until then, we are married in the eyes of both our gods because our love is sincere."

He lifted her into his arms and carried her into the river until he stood waist deep in the water. She clung around his neck as he again kissed her, then rolled her free of his arms and laughed softly as she spilled into the water and went beneath the surface.

Valerie bobbed back to the surface. She laughed and splashed Flaming Arrow with the water, then suddenly placed her hands to his head and ducked him.

Still feeling playful himself, while he was under the water Flaming Arrow placed his hands behind Valerie's thighs and gave a hard yank, which brought her beneath the water with him. Then he slid his arms around her and brought her against his hard body.

While they kissed beneath the water, Flaming Arrow gyrated his swollen manhood against Valerie's stomach, the feel of her flesh against his heat fueling the fires that had already been lit between them last night in the bed.

His strong arms around her brought her to the surface.

Her arms twined around his neck as they still kissed.

She sucked in a wild breath of pleasure against his lips when she felt his manhood probing her throbbing center. Wanting to make herself more accessible to him, not wanting to delay their togetherness any longer, she swept her legs around him at his waist and lowered herself on his tight sheath, sighing when he began his eager, rhythmic thrusts within her.

"I love you," she whispered as she slid her lips away from his.

She kissed his eyes closed, kissed the long, thick column of his throat. She leaned low and flicked her tongue over his nipples.

When his hands cupped her breasts, she threw back her head and moaned, gasping with pleasure when his tongue moved from one breast to the other, flicking her nipples until they became taut and hard as seeds.

She tangled her hands in his hair and clung to him, their lips meeting again in frenzied kisses as he shoved himself more deeply into her, their moans mingling, their sighs of pleasure filling the night air.

Realizing the noise they were making, Valerie eased her lips from Flaming Arrow's and gazed at him. "What if Brian sees or hears us?" she asked, realizing that their love cries might reach farther than the river.

"Fox Eye knows not to bring Brian close enough to the river to see or hear his sister while sharing sensual moments with her lover," Flaming Arrow reassured her. "This time alone is ours. Only ours."

He scooped his arms beneath her and carried her from the river.

They flung themselves down on the blanket.

He spread her beneath him, and her skin quivered with the warmth of his lips as he kissed his way down her body. Her gasps became long whimpers when he found her soft and wet place where her desires were centered.

Valerie closed her eyes and bit her lower lip to keep from crying out again as he worshiped her body with his lips, tongue, and soft, sensual nips of his teeth.

The pleasure was spreading in hot leaps within her.

His mouth was sensuous.

His tongue was demanding.

Oh, she was so close . . .

"Please . . ." she whispered, twining her hands through his thick hair, drawing him back up over her. "Fill me. Take me."

She could see fire burning in his eyes as he gazed down at her while sliding his manhood inside her again. As he began his slow rhythmic thrusts, she stroked his cheek with her fingertips. She traced his lips.

He swept his arms around her and crushed her up against him so hard she gasped against his lips as he once again kissed her.

She clung to him, slid her legs around him, and

rode him as he darted his tongue moistly into her mouth.

Flaming Arrow felt fluid with fire as his pleasure mounted and spread within him. He pressed endlessly deeper within her, giving her as much pleasure as he was taking. He felt the rapture growing . . . growing toward the bursting point.

He could hold off no longer.

He lay his cheek against her breast, closed his eyes, then took one last deep plunge inside her, soon lost to everything but the great shuddering in his loins as the flood of pleasure swept rapidly through him.

Realizing that Flaming Arrow had reached the ultimate of pleasure, Valerie gave herself over to her own wild ecstasy and sensual abandonment.

She strained her hips up at him and cried out as fulfillment came in great bursts of light throughout her.

Afterward they rolled apart and, exhausted, lay on their backs, their eyes closed.

Somewhere close by a ground owl gave off a low, quivering series of hoots.

Then Valerie became aware of the wondrous aroma of meat cooking over a fire. She leaned up on an elbow and gazed toward their campsite and saw the soft glow of a fire.

"Fox Eye and Brian's hunt must have been a success," she murmured, giggling when Flaming Arrow took her by the wrists and brought her back down beside him.

"Do you wish for food or more private time with Flaming Arrow?" he asked huskily.

Valerie crawled over and lay against him. "Do you truly have to ask?" she whispered, then shuddered with bliss when his fingers sought out her woman's center and began their slow, sensual caresses.

She closed her eyes and began floating as he stifled her moans of pleasure beneath his lips and he kissed her.

Then he slid his mouth aside. "Touch me," he whispered huskily. "Enwrap my heat within your fingers. Stroke me as I stroke you."

Her pulse racing, wanting nothing more on this earth at this moment than to be with the man she adored, Valerie slid her hand down the front of him, slowly and teasingly, then ran it through the thick tangle of hair at the juncture of his thighs.

Folding her fingers around his heat and hearing his quick intake of breath, she stroked him slowly. "Is this what you want?" she whispered, hardly able to recognize her voice in its huskiness. "Or do you wish something more from me?"

He gazed into her eyes as he twined his fingers through her hair and led her lips to him.

She questioned him with her eyes, unsure of what he truly wanted.

As he gave a slow thrust of his hips toward her lips, beckoning them where his manhood ached with need of her, she knew.

She acquiesced.

13

Can I see another's woe,
And not be in sorrow, too?
Can I see another's grief,
And not seek for kind relief?
　　　　　—WILLIAM BLAKE

Another long day had passed. It was just growing dusk when Fox Eye, with Brian still on his horse with him, edged his steed over closer to Flaming Arrow's and told him that they soon would be at their stronghold.

He wheeled his horse around and rode off, leading the slow procession of Blackfoot down, down between towering red cliffs.

Valerie clung to her reins and kept her knees tight against the sides of her horse as she stayed as closely behind Flaming Arrow as possible. The Blackfoot warriors rode in single file on a trail that wound around a dangerous cliff that looked far down into what she felt was a nothingness. A swirling gray mist kept her from seeing what lay below.

She kept straining her neck to see if Brian was all right. She was relieved when every time she checked on him, the tall, thin Blackfoot warrior had a protective arm around Brian's waist, keeping him from slipping and sliding and, worse yet, falling from the saddle to his death way down below on the floor of the deep canyon.

Finally the trail straightened out, widened, and followed a dry wash between towering sandstone cliffs. At a narrow defile, the walls closed in until it seemed Valerie could touch both sides at once.

Then they were again in a clearing. But this time Valerie saw something that made her heart thrill with relief. The arid red-brown landscape had burst into green—a nearby canopy of cottonwoods and willows nourished by gushing springs.

They rode out into the open land, leaving the steep slopes full of fallen rocks behind, and rode through the tall, spring-fed grass. They rode for a while longer, and when they turned a bend, the stronghold came into view. Spread out, with a steep slab of rock on one side, a river in front, and trees, sprays of wildflowers, and grass on both sides, were many tepees and lean-tos, a large outdoor fire in the center of it all.

Valerie was surprised to see so many more warriors. They had apparently stayed behind and protected the stronghold while the others had left to free their chief from chains.

Too curious to keep silent any longer, Valerie rode over close to Flaming Arrow. "There are so many warriors here at the stronghold, yet there were so many who came to release you from prison," she said, his eyes locking with hers. "Did that leave any at the reservation?"

When Flaming Arrow smiled slowly and squared his shoulders, she knew . . . she knew without him even answering her just how large his band of Blackfoot had to be, for they would not have left their people unprotected.

"We Blackfoot warriors are plenty in number," he said. "Enough are with our people to protect them against evil white agents or settlers who still want even the land that my people have been placed on."

His smile faded. "Yet our warriors are not in number enough to ward off the whole white community," he said solemnly. "We are far less in number than the white men who now live on land once owned solely by the red man. We now are only a few little islands of red men in a great sea of whites."

"That is so sad," Valerie said, feeling guilty herself for being a part of the white race who had claimed land she now knew truly did not belong to any of her family or other whites who were settling in Montana Territory.

Yet she, as well as Flaming Arrow, knew that there was no longer anything that could be done about this. It was apparent that the Blackfoot had fought their last battles for land with the whites. If they tried further aggression, the whole tribe might be annihilated.

Fox Eye rode up and wheeled his horse to a stop

on the other side of Flaming Arrow as the warriors
who had stayed behind came running toward them,
their excitement evident in their eyes and the way
they shouted in Blackfoot.

Flaming Arrow gave Valerie a lingering look,
then gazed over at Brian, whose eyes showed he
was totally immersed in the excitement of the
moment.

He then dismounted and walked toward his warriors and greeted each of them in turn until everyone had been given the chance to show their
exuberance to their chief over his arrival.

"Tonight there will be much celebration!" Fox
Eye cried, lifting Brian from his horse. He dismounted and gave his horse over to a warrior, who
then also took Valerie's and Flaming Arrow's
mounts.

Brian ran over and grabbed Valerie by a hand.
He gave her a wide smile, then walked beside her
as Flaming Arrow took her other hand and led
them toward the great outdoor fire where much
food was cooking, and where a skin drum was already being played while the jubilant warriors
began to sing.

Night soon fell, but Valerie hardly noticed. She
was caught up in the wonders of the Blackfoot warriors and their protective love for one another. As
they sat beneath the soft moonlight, the huge fire
bright against the backdrop of night, much deliciously roasted meat was consumed.

Everyone around the fire seemed to be chatting

at once as they made their plans for a return trip to their people. Some were resting on soft buffalo-robe couches, with sloping willow rests at each end, while others sat on blankets or pallets of furs.

Valerie had hardly been able to take her eyes off Flaming Arrow. He had excused himself long enough to take a quick swim in the nearby river. She understood why he hadn't included her in the swim. There weren't any private places.

When he returned to the campfire she had been quickly taken by his change in attire. He was now dressed in a clean buckskin outfit with beautiful leggings embroidered with porcupine quills and bright feathers. His hair was drawn back and held in place by an embroidered headband.

Valerie felt dusty and dirty, and hungered for a bath herself. Brian also needed to have a bath before they retired for the night. She planned to sneak off soon and at least take a sponge bath, if only to get the dust off her face and out of her hair.

She certainly wasn't going to disturb Flaming Arrow's reunion with his warriors by telling him she wished to have a bath before retiring for the night. She had the feeling that the night had just begun. It appeared as though when the Blackfoot got together to celebrate something, it might last into the wee hours of the night.

And she did not want to feel neglected by Flaming Arrow. She understood his need to be with his warriors. He had been denied them for too long as it was.

Brian leaned over closer to Valerie. "Sis, I'm so tired," he said, stretching his arms over his head, yawning.

"Yes, I know," Valerie said, running her fingers through his thick, golden hair. "Come on. Let's go down to the river. We'll get washed off. Then you can go to bed. Before Flaming Arrow went to sit with the men, he pointed out the tepee that we'll be sleeping in."

"I'd like to sit up the rest of the night with Flaming Arrow and Fox Eye and listen to their plans, but I just can't," Brian said, as he rose and walked with Valerie toward the river. "Do you think he's going to think I'm a big baby if I go to bed before everyone else? I already showed him how much of a sissy I was when I fainted after the spider bit me."

"You worry too much about everything," Valerie scolded. "You know that neither Flaming Arrow nor Fox Eye thinks you are a big baby. You have proven time and again how strong you are. Brian, you didn't complain once these past several days while traveling so long and doing without so much that you are used to having. Just please try to accept things, still, as they come to you. As you know, there isn't much we can do about any of it. This is our life now. We must make of it as best we can."

"I love being with the Blackfoot," Brian said, eyes wide as he gazed up at her. He swallowed hard. "But I can't help but miss Mother and Father and Aunt Hillary. Won't we ever see them again, Sis? Won't we?"

"Yes, I hope, and soon," Valerie said, taking his hand as she led him down across the rocky embankment of the river.

"How?" Brian asked, grabbing at Valerie's arm as he stubbed his toe on a huge rock and almost fell down.

"When we are traveling with the Blackfoot on their journey to Missouri, I hope we'll pass close by our home," Valerie murmured. "If we do, we'll stop and see our family."

"Truly?" Brian asked, kneeling down beside the river, reaching a hand into the cold, crisp water.

"Perhaps," Valerie said, kneeling down beside him. "We'll just have to wait and see."

He laughed softly as she sank her hand into the water and splashed some onto his face.

She squealed when he did the same to her.

Then they busied themselves washing off their dust.

Valerie turned with a start when Fox Eye came up from behind them. She questioned him with her eyes as he stopped and stared down at her, then looked slowly over at Brian.

She wanted to question him, ask him what he was doing there. But she was afraid that might show distrust. She didn't want to be the cause of any strain between Fox Eye and Flaming Arrow.

"I have something for Brian," Fox Eye said, reaching a hand out for the boy. "Come, young brave. Come with me. I shall give you my special gift."

Guilt splashed through Valerie for thinking even for a moment that Fox Eye was not to be trusted. He hadn't given her any cause to feel that way. He had been nothing but kind and generous to both her and Brian. He had even gone further with Brian and had become special friends with him.

"A gift?" Brian asked, scrambling to his feet. "For me?"

"Come. I will show you," Fox Eye said, taking Brian by a hand, leading him away from the river.

As they walked away, Fox Eye turned a slow look over his shoulder at Valerie. In his eyes she could see that he knew she had mistrusted him. She glanced away and waited a moment, then followed them to a large tepee that sat next to Flaming Arrow's.

When Fox Eye stopped outside the tepee and then walked behind it, Brian trustingly followed. But Valerie could not help but feel uneasy.

She quietly followed.

When she discovered the reason Fox Eye had brought Brian there, she sighed and smiled. Standing tethered to a low tree limb was perhaps the most beautiful horse she had ever seen. She stifled a sob of wonder behind her hand when she heard Fox Eye tell Brian that this was now his horse, a gift from Fox Eye.

She could hardly hold back her tears when Brian

showed his gratitude by lunging into Fox Eye's arms and hugging him.

"It is a special horse for a special young brave," Flaming Arrow said. He slid an arm around Valerie's waist and drew her attention quickly his way. "The horse is named Bullet. He is one of Fox Eye's favorite warhorses."

"I am stunned that he would give such a horse to Brian," Valerie said. She gazed at the horse again and saw its utter loveliness. It was a mighty black mustang with a lone white spot on its right side.

"Do not be stunned by my best friend's generous nature," Flaming Arrow said, smiling. "Through the years he has given me many gifts of the heart. That is just his nature. It pleasures him more to give gifts than to receive. And to give such a gift to a young brave like Brian shows just how much he has grown to admire your brother."

He placed his hands on Valerie's shoulders and turned her to face him. "Do you not see?" he said thickly. "We, Fox Eye and I, have come face-to-face with many young white boys, and do you not know that most of them laugh at and ridicule us?"

"No," Valerie said, paling. "I had no idea."

"It has happened many times," Flaming Arrow said somberly. "And when your brother shows such friendship and exuberance to be with us Blackfoot? Do you not see how that would touch the heart of even the fiercest warrior?"

"I'm so glad that Brian is Brian," Valerie said,

wiping tears from her eyes. "I'm very proud of him."

"Tomorrow there will be a special gift for you from my best friend Fox Eye," Flaming Arrow said, drawing Valerie into his arms. "For you see, my woman, tomorrow is our wedding day!"

Valerie's eyes widened.

Her heart skipped a beat.

Then she laughed and cried at the same time. "My love," she whispered, so glad when he kissed her.

14

So when she speaks,
The voice of heaven I hear;
So when we walk,
Nothing impure comes near.
Each field seems Eden.
—William Blake

The marriage ceremony had been simple and quick.

Vows had been spoken in the presence of Flaming Arrow's warriors.

The warriors were now celebrating their chief's marriage without the presence of their chief and his new bride.

This celebration would be short. Before midnight arrived, plans would be finalized for the journey to the Blackfoot reservation.

"I wish we could have more time together on our wedding night," Valerie murmured as she lay snuggled against Flaming Arrow in his tepee.

She wasn't worried about Brian and what he was doing while she and Flaming Arrow spent this short time together on their wedding night. He was with Fox Eye.

"But I know it's selfish of me to want that," she murmured. "My love, I will enjoy these spare, precious moments with you. I know what lies ahead for you must be laying heavily on your heart."

"You have lifted my burden more than you will ever know," Flaming Arrow said, slowly running a hand down her silken, nude body. "When I begin feeling somber and angry at the white government over how they have treated my people, I think of you and your goodness and realize that not all whites have greedy hearts. In you, I have learned lessons I would have perhaps never known. It makes those times that lay ahead of me and my people less dreaded."

"I'm glad that I have been able to help alleviate some of your burden," Valerie whispered.

She sighed pleasurably when Flaming Arrow slid her beneath him and blanketed her with his hard, muscled body.

She twined her fingers through his long, thick hair and brushed a kiss across his lips.

"My husband, can I help you now, tonight, even more?" she whispered. "Tell me what you wish of me. I am yours."

"You speaking the word *husband* to me makes my heart sing, knowing that the word binds us together for eternity," Flaming Arrow said.

He leaned up on an elbow and gazed into her eyes. "Let me teach you how to say husband in the Blackfoot tongue," he said softly.

"Oh, yes, please do," Valerie said, her eyes beaming.

"No-ma," Flaming Arrow said. "Say *no-ma,* then you will be calling me husband in my own tongue."

"No-ma," Valerie said softly.

"Nito-ile-man," Flaming Arrow then said in Blackfoot.

Valerie arched an eyebrow. "What does that mean?" she murmured.

"My *wife,"* he said. *"Nito-ile-man* . . . my wife."

He slid a hand beneath her and drew her more tightly against him, his other hand gently cupping and kneading one of her breasts.

"Does my speaking the word *nito-ile-man* make your heart sing, as well?" he asked huskily.

"It thrills me through and through to hear you call me your wife and know that it is so," Valerie said, her cheeks flushing as she felt the heat of his manhood probing where she unmercifully ached to be filled by him.

"Forever, my husband," she whispered. "Forever we are wed. To have fallen in love so quickly surely means that our love will be stronger than anyone else's ever could be."

"Yes, so quickly and endearingly," Flaming Arrow said, his voice low-pitched, husky. *"Nito-ile-man, nito-ile-man."*

He covered her mouth with his lips and gave her a deep, long kiss while he gently shoved his manhood into her warm, flowery folds.

Flaming Arrow's mouth forced Valerie's lips open as his kiss grew more and more passionate while he rhythmically thrust into her.

Valerie's body trembled as she became further alive beneath his hardness. She wrapped her arms around his neck and clung to his rock hardness. As the raging hunger spread within her, she drew a ragged breath.

Flaming Arrow lowered his lips to one of her breasts.

Slowly his teeth nipped at the taut bud of her nipple. He licked first one nipple and then the other until Valerie moaned with pleasure.

His hands swept down Valerie's sides, then he moved them beneath her. His fingers gently digging into her hips, he lifted her closer so that he could go more deeply within her with his eager strokes.

When she lifted her legs around his waist, opening herself more fully to him, as a flower opens to the wishes of the sun, he groaned in whispers against her cheek how much he loved her.

Lost in the whirlwind of rapture, Valerie whispered back to him as his hands now swept up again and cupped her breasts within them. She sucked in a wild breath when he lowered his mouth and again flicked her nipples with his tongue, then enfolded her within his steel-strong arms and held her tight as his thrusts became maddeningly faster.

Moaning, his body on fire, Flaming Arrow buried his face between Valerie's breasts.

She twined her fingers through his hair and held him closer as she felt the urgency building within her. Suddenly an incredible sweetness swept through her as her body exploded in spasms of desire. Her fingers bit into Flaming Arrow's muscled shoulders as his thrusts became faster . . . deeper.

Then Valerie smiled and sighed against his lips while his body exploded in its own magical moment of pleasure.

Still trembling, inside and out, her desires fulfilled for the moment, Valerie watched Flaming Arrow roll away from her and lay on his back, panting.

She turned on her side toward him and gently ran a hand up and down his heaving chest. "I'm too much for you, am I?" she teased, laughing softly.

He laughed throatily, then turned on his side toward her. "I doubt you would like to test me," he teased back, one hand already back at her damp valley, caressing her. "My body speaks again of wanting you. Is yours ready to respond again so soon?"

"I could love you all night and it would not be enough," Valerie whispered, her eyes closing as the ecstasy of his fingers sent a warm, fluid fire throughout her. "Ah, the magic of your fingers. If you only knew . . ."

She gasped with an even more intense pleasure when she felt his tongue flicking where his fingers had just been. Her head reeled as he continued to pleasure her in such a way . . . until again the explosion of ecstasy overwhelmed her, yet leaving her still wanting more.

"I feel so wanton," Valerie whispered as she came back to reality after having achieved a second moment of bliss in only a matter of moments. "I would have never thought a woman could enjoy lovemaking as I enjoy it." She blushed. "My parents never showed much open love toward one another. I wasn't even sure they did love each other."

"Everyone will know of our intense love," Flaming Arrow said, sitting up, drawing her onto his lap facing him. "I shall shout it to the world for everyone to hear!"

"Not everyone would be as pleased as you and I about our marriage," Valerie said, reality setting in as she thought of just how such a marriage would be accepted when the white community would get wind of it. "You do know that the white community sees a marriage between a white woman and Indian as forbidden."

"Just as they declare many ways of redskins forbidden," Flaming Arrow said, his eyes suddenly flashing. "You know that if the whites had their way, there would be no redskins left on the earth. We would be extinct, as are . . . what is the animal . . . I . . . have heard spoken of?"

"The dinosaurs?" Valerie said softly. She flung herself into his arms. "Please, oh, please, never compare yourself . . . your people . . . to . . ." She shuddered, then completed her sentence. "To dinosaurs. That's horrible, Flaming Arrow. Horrible!"

"As you live with the Blackfoot you will see just how much we are forced to endure because of the white community," he said thickly. "But let us speak of it no more tonight. This is *our* time, yours and mine, as new husband and wife. It should be spent with smiles and laughter."

He suddenly lifted her from his lap.

Valerie watched him go to the back of the tepee and lift something from beneath a blanket.

Her eyes widened as she watched him bring a necklace toward her. She had never seen such a beautiful necklace. It was made of beads and shells, and also small circles of copper that picked up the light of the fire in them as Flaming Arrow knelt down before her and held it out.

"Fox Eye gave Brian a beautiful steed," Flaming Arrow said softly. "This is his gift for you."

Her eyes wide, her heart pounding, Valerie stared in wonder at the necklace as Flaming Arrow placed it in her hands.

"It is so beautiful," she said, sighing.

She lifted it closer and studied it. Each bead seemed to have been shaped by hand, as did the magnificently small and beautiful shells of all different colors. The copper trinkets shone as though they were miniature mirrors.

"Fox Eye's wife made the necklace," Flaming Arrow said, sitting down beside Valerie. He leaned over and shoved a piece of wood into the flames of the fire, then turned back toward her and saw her look of surprise.

"He's married?" Valerie said, raising an eyebrow. "You have never mentioned his wife." She looked past him and at the closed entrance flap, then looked into his eyes once again. "She isn't here." She laughed softly. "But of course she wouldn't be. The women are back at the reservation."

"She is not there, either," Flaming Arrow said, his voice suddenly solemn.

"Then where *is* she?" Valerie asked, resting the necklace in a hand.

"She is in the Blackfoot Sand Hills, the place for departed Blackfoot," Flaming Arrow said, his jaw tightening.

"She . . . is . . . dead?" Valerie gasped.

"Yes, two winters ago she died," Flaming Arrow said, staring blankly into the flames of the fire. "She went out one day to look for one of Fox Eye's stray horses. He was not there to search himself for it. He was out on the hunt. It was a cold day. Snow came suddenly. She did not make it back home before she was overcome by the deep snow and cold winds. I found her. I brought her home. I mourned with Fox Eye as though his wife were my own."

"I'm so sorry," Valerie murmured. She spread the necklace out between both of her hands and studied it, then looked softly over at Flaming Arrow. "Why would Fox Eye give his wife's necklace to me?"

"Because you are my woman and he will feel as though a part of his wife is still alive and with him when you wear the necklace she made with her own hands," Flaming Arrow said softly.

He moved to his knees and took the necklace from Valerie. "I shall place it around your neck," he said. "Lift your hair. I shall snap it in place."

Valerie was touched deeply by the gift.

And when it hung around her neck, soft and pretty, she reached a hand up and touched it. "I love it," she murmured. "I even feel as though I have known Fox Eye's wife myself because a part of her is here with me."

She raised an eyebrow. "You have never spoken her name," she said. "What was it?"

"Names of the dead are not spoken aloud," Flaming Arrow said, then leaned his lips close to Valerie's ear. "But I shall whisper it to you."

Valerie leaned her ear close and listened. She whispered back to him, "Tender Heart is a lovely name."

"As lovely as the woman who carried it with her to her grave," Flaming Arrow said.

He reached over and drew Valerie into his arms. "It would be good to make love again, but my warriors wait now to speak of things that do not include women," he said hoarsely. "But if you wish you can join me around the fire as we discuss plans for our journey to the reservation."

"I don't want to intrude on men things," Valerie said, lightly stroking his cheeks with the palms of her hands. "Would I intrude if I sat with you among your men?"

"You will never be an intrusion," Flaming Arrow

said, brushing a soft kiss across her brow. "Now or ever."

They kissed, then dressed and left the tepee.

Already the warriors were nestled around the large outdoor fire, talking seriously.

Valerie did not go immediately with Flaming Arrow to the circle. She spied Brian asleep on a blanket on the ground beside his horse.

"Poor sweet Brian," she whispered, feeling guilty now for having kept him outside for so long while she and Flaming Arrow were snuggled warmly beside the lodge fire making love.

"Brian," she whispered, giving him a light shake on the shoulder. "Come on, honey. Let's go inside the tepee. You can sleep by the fire."

"No," Brian said, sitting up. He yawned and rubbed his eyes with his fists. "I want to sleep here with Bullet. Please let me?"

"But it's going to get much colder as the night deepens," Valerie said, reaching a gentle hand to his cheek.

"Fox Eye gave me many blankets,'" Brian said, nodding toward a neat pile of blankets. "As I need them I shall use them. Go on, Valerie. Do whatever you were doing. I want to stay here with Bullet."

Valerie sighed. "You're sure?" she asked, running her fingers through his thick blond hair. "I don't want you catching a cold. It's much colder here in the mountains than back home, *or* on the trail these past few nights."

"I'm as strong as an ox," Brian teased. "Remember how quickly I got well from that spider bite? I most certainly won't let myself take a cold."

"Well, all right, if you insist," Valerie said. "But let me put another blanket on you."

After Brian was stretched out again on the blanket with two more pulled over him up to his chin, Valerie kissed his brow, then turned and gazed at Flaming Arrow. Her insides tightened when she saw how her husband seemed to be so intense over what he and his warriors were discussing. She knew that the next several days, perhaps weeks, were going to be the hardest of her life, for she would be living the life of a redskin since she was married to one.

She hoped she had the courage to endure all that would be put upon her, for she would die if she ever disappointed Flaming Arrow.

She reached up and touched the necklace. It would help give her courage, for it had been made by someone courageous and special.

Smiling, she walked over and sat down beside Flaming Arrow. When Fox Eye turned toward her, she gave him a smile and whispered a thank-you to him as she touched the necklace.

His smile and nod made her glad she had found a friend in him so quickly. She only hoped that when she arrived at the Blackfoot village they would as easily see her as a friend. She prayed they would not resent her for marrying their beloved chief!

15

Dreaming, she knew it was a dream;
She felt he was and was not there.
      —ALFRED, LORD TENNYSON

Valerie went back inside the tepee, got a blanket, and started to go outside again, but stopped when she saw the arrow shaft Brian had found among the Blackfoot artifacts while searching for arrow-heads for his collection. The arrow shaft lay alone, away from Flaming Arrow's quiver of arrows that were not broken.

Recalling how Flaming Arrow had explained why the flames had been painted on the arrow— that the painting showed possession since his name was Flaming Arrow—she went to his quiver and slowly slid one of the arrows free.

She sighed when she saw how this arrow was beau-tifully painted with the same bright flame. She ran her fingers over the sleekness of the arrow, thinking that Fox Eye proved himself a friend in many ways. He had surely taken great pains to protect this quiver for Flaming Arrow while the chief had been imprisoned.

She gazed around the tepee and saw so many things that belonged solely to her husband. Fox Eye was also responsible for bringing them to the stronghold, certain that his chief—his best friend— would be set free to claim them again.

"I wonder if friendship means more to Indians than it does to white people," she whispered. She had never had a friend as close as Fox Eye was to Flaming Arrow.

She had had many friends in Kansas City, yet she knew that none of them would chance losing their lives to right a wrong for her if she had been falsely accused or imprisoned.

"Although so much has gone wrong for Flaming Arrow, so much is right," she whispered, sliding the arrow back into the quiver. She knew that not only was Fox Eye Flaming Arrow's devoted friend, all of the warriors seemed as devoted to him. And she did not think that was solely because Flaming Arrow was their chief. It was because he drew people to him like honey draws bees because of his caring personality.

"Are you all right?"

Flaming Arrow's voice behind her drew Valerie around with a start. When she saw deep concern in his eyes, she realized that by not returning to sit with him, she had given him cause to worry.

She moved toward him and into his arms. "I'm fine," she murmured. "I came back to your lodge for a blanket. When I saw the arrow shaft Brian had found, I stopped and became lost in thought."

"About what?" Flaming Arrow asked, his eyes smiling into hers. "Your husband?"

"Yes, my husband," Valerie said, laughing softly. "I was thinking about just how lucky you are."

"Lucky?" Flaming Arrow asked, cocking an eyebrow. "You see this Blackfoot chief as lucky? Why is that?"

"Because you have such devoted friends," Valerie said. "And these are friends whom you can trust. In the white community sometimes even friends are not trustworthy. It's hard to find a true friend . . . someone you can depend on."

"Yes, in friendships I do feel fortunate," Flaming Arrow said, nodding. "As do I in other things, as well. Did I not find you? Did I not achieve stealing your heart away?"

Valerie flung herself into his arms and gave him a hard hug. "My darling, darling Flaming Arrow, I hope I never give you cause to regret having married me," she said, then lifted her eyes to him. "I want so much for us."

"In time, perhaps," he said thickly. "In time. But for now there are many people awaiting guidance from their chief."

He stepped away from her and swept an arm around her waist. "I must return to council," he said, walking her toward the entranceway. "Come. Join us. Sit at my side. Learn from the council."

Grabbing up the blanket, carrying it across her arm, Valerie went outside with Flaming Arrow and sat down on a cushion of blankets before the raging fire. She gazed up at the landscape and saw how the fire reflected from the hills and rocks. She wondered if someone from afar could see the fire's glow.

If so, would they investigate? What if soldiers passed by?

Not wanting to think of what might happen should the soldiers discover the stronghold, Valerie scooted closer to Flaming Arrow. She slid the blanket around her shoulders and snuggled into it as she listened to the warriors and Flaming Arrow discuss the upcoming travel to the reservation.

A part of her was excited about arriving there.

Another part of her was afraid.

She could not shake the feeling inside her heart that she and Brian might never be accepted by Flaming Arrow's band of Blackfoot as a whole.

If not . . .

"The reservation is four nights' ride away," Fox Eye was saying, focusing his full attention on Flaming Arrow. "There are no forts between here and there. But there is an Indian agent who might try to stop us. I have observed him. He is a government man . . . an evil man who does not look out for the welfare of the Blackfoot. He might have to be killed, for he is not a man to be reasoned with."

Valerie shivered at the thought of Flaming Arrow and his warriors being forced to kill a white man.

Would they do it in her presence?

Could she condone it even if it meant the safety of her husband and his people?

Murder in cold blood was just that, no matter how evil a man might be, no matter the threat he was to so many!

When she heard the name of the man, everything within her grew cold. She grew pale as she listened to them talking about Bradley Hart!

He was the very man her father had saved her from! This was the man who tried to rape her!

When Bradley Hart had fled Kansas City in anger and humiliation, no one had known where he had gone. Valerie had just been glad to get him out of her life. Not only was he a potential rapist, he was nothing less than a cad and a bigot.

He was an extreme racist—the sort of man who thought the best Indian was a dead Indian!

And now she was going to come face-to-face with him again? This man who hated her with a passion?

The fact that he was the one in charge of the Indian affairs at the reservation was frightening. He would most certainly have done nothing to help the Blackfoot! She now feared arriving at the reservation, feared seeing the total neglect.

She tried to act normal, even with this new knowledge, but the longer she sat, the more she dreaded seeing Bradley again. If he saw her with the Blackfoot, especially after discovering that she was married to their chief, who was to say what he would do? He might go against the Blackfoot purposely because of her. Hadn't Fox Eye said that he was a man who could not be reasoned with?

Unable to sit there any longer with these fears racing through her mind, and memories of the sordid night with Bradley swimming through her consciousness, paining her very soul, Valerie rose to her feet. Stumbling over the blanket, she fell to her knees, then scrambled again to her feet and ran from the council.

She understood that her strange, sudden behavior had caused a quick silence behind her. She could almost feel the warriors' eyes on her as she fled into the dark depths of the forest.

She sobbed as she thought of the night of the near rape. She could even now feel the same helplessness as then . . . when Bradley had held her down, his beady gray eyes filled with lust as he stared down at her.

Oh, how could it be that she was going to face him again? And how could she explain to Flaming Arrow that this very man was the one who—

"Valerie!"

Flaming Arrow's voice behind her made Valerie's heart ache. Oh, how could she tell him that the very man his people had depended on as an agent was responsible for many of her nightmares?

In her worst dreams Bradley had been there, pinning her down, his cold, grappling fingers searching beneath the skirt of her dress. When she awakened it had always been a relief to know that she was still untouched and virginal as she had been before Bradley's attempt at raping her.

Yet, it had been only that—an attempt! It was something she had to forget. She had a husband now. No man would ever wrongly touch her again.

Especially . . . not . . . Bradley Hart, she vowed to herself.

She flinched when a hand grabbed her around the waist and stopped her flight into the darkness.

When she turned and gazed up at her husband, tears rushed from her eyes.

"What is causing your tears?" Flaming Arrow asked, his eyes searching hers. The moon crept through the leaves of the trees enough for him to see the despair and fear in his wife's eyes. "Was something said in council that frightened you? That hurt you?"

"A name was mentioned," Valerie said, smoothing the tears away from her cheeks with the backs of her hands. "But I don't want to talk about him. Your people already have enough hard feelings for him. I don't want to add to their hate! I don't want to be the one responsible for causing added tensions between you . . . and . . . the man!"

"What man?" Flaming Arrow asked.

"I truly don't want to say," Valerie said, pleading with her eyes at him. "Please don't make me tell you. Let things work out without my . . . my . . . interference."

"I have told you that you could never be an interference in my life, nor my people's," Flaming

Arrow said thickly. "Now tell me what has caused you to become someone filled with pain."

"Bradley Hart," Valerie blurted out. "The Indian agent at your reservation. Flaming Arrow, I . . . know him."

"You know him?" Flaming Arrow said, dropping his hand from her waist. "And your knowing him causes you such pain in your eyes? In your voice? How did you know him? *Where* do you know him from?"

"He is the man . . . who . . . Father found attempting to . . . to . . . rape me," Valerie said, watching his expression change from wonder to rage. "Now do you see why I didn't want to mention him to you? Fox Eye has already talked about possibly having to kill him. Now, knowing who he is and what he did, won't it take less for you to decide to take his life?"

Bleak-faced, his eyes filled with fire, Flaming Arrow glared down at Valerie. "This man dares touch such innocence as you?" he said, his voice drawn. "Yes, my wife, it will not take much for me to kill him."

"I shouldn't have told you," Valerie said, burying her face in her hands. "Now I will be at fault if you kill him and then you are taken away by the soldiers and imprisoned again. Oh, Lord, I shouldn't have told you."

He placed gentle hands on her shoulders and turned her to face him. "Do you not know that had you not actually said the words to me, I still would have seen the truth when you came in the presence of this man and your eyes met? I would have read in your eyes of things that had gone wrong between you. I would have known he was at fault, for you are everything good on this earth."

"But I don't want anything to happen to you or your people over something that happened in my past," Valerie said, placing a gentle hand on his cheek. "Please, oh, please do not do anything hasty when you come face-to-face with Bradley Hart."

"I shall weigh everything in my mind and heart before reacting," Flaming Arrow promised. "Now let us put him from our minds. To us he should be just a wisp of wind."

"Yes, just a wisp of wind," Valerie said, so badly wishing it were so.

16

Sweet moans, dovelike sighs,
Chase not slumber from my eyes,
Sweet moans, sweeter smiles,
All the dove like moans beguiles.
—WILLIAM BLAKE

It was the third night on their way to the reservation. The evening meal had been eaten and everyone was settling in for the night.

Becoming more and more a part of the warriors' lives, Brian had been invited to sleep among them.

Flaming Arrow had erected a lean-to of poles covered with pine boughs so that he and Valerie could have privacy. This would be their last night together before Flaming Arrow would be immersed in righting the wrongs inflicted on his people.

"Are you warm enough?" Flaming Arrow asked, smoothing a blanket over Valerie as she snuggled against him. "I could place more wood on the fire."

Valerie laughed softly. "No, I don't think so," she said. "As it is, I'm already afraid our temporary lodge will catch on fire." She gazed at the dancing flames a few feet away from their lean-to.

She then gazed on past it, at the other small fires

that burned amid the sleeping Blackfoot warriors. As always before, she worried about the fires drawing the wrong people. In the darkness of night, they were a beacon to anyone who might want to bring harm to the Blackfoot. Now that she knew about Bradley Hart, how could she not be wary?

"As you have been so often while we have been traveling toward my people, you are lost in thought," Flaming Arrow said.

He turned over and faced her then slipped an arm around her nude body, bringing her close to him. "You are still worrying about this man named Bradley Hart?" he asked. "Is that what lays heavy on your mind?"

"My mother taught me never to hate anyone," Valerie murmured, the heat of Flaming Arrow's body blending in with hers, warming her. "But I can't help how I feel about Bradley. I *do* hate him."

She placed a gentle hand on Flaming Arrow's face. "I hate telling you that," she said, her voice drawn. "I still worry about how this fuels your own hate for the man. Flaming Arrow, if he is an agent for the Blackfoot reservation, he—"

Flaming Arrow slid a hand over her mouth, stopping her from speaking her worries aloud. "Shhh," he said. "You should not concern yourself with things that your husband is capable of handling. This white man? He is but one man."

"You're right," Valerie said, sighing. "And next to *you* . . . he is *nothing.*"

Flaming Arrow chuckled. "Next to my many *warriors* he is nothing," he said, his eyes twinkling.

"How soon after you arrive at the reservation do you plan to start out for land that is free of such confinements?" Valerie asked, sucking in a wild breath when Flaming Arrow cupped one of her breasts and softly, slowly kneaded it.

"As soon as my people can be readied for the travel," he said thickly. "The older Blackfoot might not even want to chance such a journey as it will take to get us to Missouri."

"Or Illinois?" Valerie asked, leaning up on an elbow to gaze at him. "There *is* land, also in Illinois that is free for the taking. I have been there before in the most southern part. It is beautiful, with roaming meadows and beautiful hills of flowers and trees."

"Yes, I have been torn between both places, for recently around the fires with my warriors I have heard tales of both," Flaming Arrow said, nodding.

"And then there is Kansas," Valerie said, memories of her homeland flooding her. If she could, she would live there in a minute!

"Kansas?" Flaming Arrow said. "I do not know as much about Kansas as I do about Missouri."

"I was born and raised there," Valerie murmured. "I loved it."

"Then why did you leave?"

"It was not my decision to leave. It was my father's."

Flaming Arrow became quiet. "No, even though

you would choose Kansas for your home, I do not know enough about it to take my people there," Flaming Arrow said sullenly. "I know now about Missouri and Illinois. Whichever is the most convenient for my people will be where we will settle."

"Kansas City, where I lived," said Valerie, "is close to Missouri. If you choose Missouri for your home, we—you and I, along with Brian—might someday go there so that I can show you my childhood home."

"That is too far into the future to think about," Flaming Arrow said, sighing. He turned over on his back and stared through the openings of the poles and pine boughs at the twinkling stars in the heavens. "There is so much to do to lead my people to safety. Some of the travel must be made on water."

Again he turned and faced her, his fingers slowly weaving through her hair. "My people are not boat people," he said. "But my father, long ago, urged our people to at least learn the art of making canoes should an emergency arise where an escape in water is needed. This journey is that sort of an emergency. Once we have traveled as far as we can on horses, we will then travel by water."

"I truly believe that once you have left Montana Territory behind, things will work out for your people," Valerie said softly. "Yes, the journey will be hard. But hope lays at the end for your people."

"Yes, hope will sustain us," Flaming Arrow said, his hands turning her, again sweeping her silken nudity fully against his hard body. "As does our love, yours and mine, sustain *our* hope. Tonight let us take from each other what we can. For many sunrises, there may be obstacles to such private moments as this for us. Tonight is ours." He brushed a kiss across her lips.

"Tonight, *nito-ile-man,*" he then whispered. "Tonight."

A surge of ecstasy welled within Valerie as Flaming Arrow slipped her beneath him. She could feel how ready he was for her in the way his thick manhood lay heavy against her thigh.

Breathless with building sensations, she twined her arms around his neck. She gasped softly against his lips as he kissed her while he swept his fingers around one of her breasts, just grazing the nipple with his fingertips each time so that it strained with added anticipation.

She swept a hand between them and ran her fingers along his pulsing satin hardness. She slowly, gently stroked him, his moans of pleasure firing her own desires deeply within her.

Wanting him, needing him, Valerie opened herself more fully to him and led him inside her moist, flowery folds. Her body quivered with ecstasy when he pressed gently deeper into her yielding heat, then began his slow, rhythmic thrusts within her, each thrust sending a message of love to her heart.

Flaming Arrow felt his worries melting away as his body became fluid with the fires of pleasure.

He slid his lips down and covered one of her nipples, the nub tight and sweet against his tongue.

When he kissed his way upward, Valerie's throat arched backward and he buried his lips along its delicate column.

Then again his eager mouth covered her lips and kissed her, his tongue surging between her teeth as he came to her, thrusting deeply. He anchored her perfectly still as he dove endlessly into her.

Her insides were blazing, searing.

Her senses spinning, Valerie strained her hips upward.

The intense pleasure stole her breath away. Her pulse raced as the wild, exuberant passion overwhelmed her as never before. A blaze of urgency burned higher with each of his thrusts. She strained against him, her body turning to a warm liquid as the passion mounted to something sweet and wonderful.

Suddenly the longed-for delicious languor stole over her as she went over the edge into the final throes of total ecstasy, the spinning sensation flooding her body.

Holding her tightly in his embrace, knowing that she had found ecstasy within his arms once again, Flaming Arrow felt his own pleasure growing, growing to the bursting point. He slid his hands beneath Valerie's hips and lifted her closer as a great shuddering in his loins sent his seed deeply inside her.

His body jolted, quivered, arched, then relaxed as he came down from the cloud of ecstasy.

Breathing hard, he rolled away from her and

stretched out on his back, his eyes watching the stars, his body still fluid with the fires of passion.

Valerie rolled over next to him and gently stroked his chest. "Life for me was so dull before I met you," she whispered. "I had seemed content enough. But that was because I had no idea what loving a man could bring me."

He turned on his side and drew her against him, reveling in the press of her breasts against his chest. "Nor did I know what life could truly be until I met you," he whispered back, reaching to smooth fallen locks of her hair back from her face. "Until you, the excitement for me was in the hunt, and doing anything men could enjoy together. Women? Yes, they fascinated me. What true man could not want to be with a woman? And I was. Many times. But none touched my inner soul as you have."

"I hate to think that there were women in your arms before me," Valerie said, her lower lip curving into a pout.

"There were women, yes, but only to fulfill the needs of a man," Flaming Arrow said huskily. "I would have not been much of a man had I not bedded women after my body spoke to me of needs that nothing but women could fill."

"Women wait until marriage," Valerie murmured. She smiled softly. "Well, most women, that is." She propped herself up on an elbow and gazed directly into his eyes. "Is it different for Indian women?" she asked softly. "Do they not wait for marriage to be with a man? I mean . . . what women *did* you bed?"

"When a warrior is being raised to be a powerful chief, there are women, always, for that warrior," he said, then placed a gentle hand over her lips. "Shhh, let us not talk anymore about this. I do not wish to speak the names of those I slept with to you. I do not want jealousy to be a part of our lives."

Valerie gently shoved his hand aside. "Are you saying that there are women even now in your village who . . . who . . . want you?" she asked, her voice breaking.

"Always," he said, chuckling.

Then he grew solemn and raised a gentle hand to her cheek. "But, *nito-ile-man,* my wife, you are all this chief will ever want, and once those women who hoped for a future with this chief sees that he was chosen a wife, they will, too, seek a companion elsewhere."

"Will they despise me?" she murmured, eyes wide.

"No one will show any harsh feelings toward you because you are the wife of their chief," he said thickly. "They will show you the respect due a chief's wife."

"I hope so," Valerie said, snuggling against him again as he swept his arm around her and drew her close.

He then brought a blanket up to cover them warmly.

"Sleep, *nito-ile-man,* for tomorrows always come quickly," he whispered. He brushed a soft kiss across her brow. "My people, as a whole, will love you. Who could not? You are everything good on this earth. You spread this goodness everywhere you go."

"You are the good one," Valerie whispered, loving the warmth of his breath against her cheek. "How could any white man ever cause trouble for such a man as you?"

"Because my skin is red and his is white," Flaming Arrow whispered back. "Now sleep. Dream. Bring me into your dreams with you."

"Always," Valerie whispered, shivering sensually when he reached up and enfolded one of her breasts within the warmth of his hand.

17

When the green woods laugh, with the voice of joy,
And the dumpling stream runs laughing by,
When the air does laugh with our merry wit,
And the green hill laughs with the noise of it.
—WILLIAM BLAKE

Valerie could understand why Brian broke away
from the Blackfoot warriors and came back to ride
with her, to enter the village at her side when they
arrived there.

Even she felt overwhelmed by the sight of the
village . . . by the hugeness of it and by the number
of Blackfoot who stood at the outer fringes, silently
watching the arrival of their warriors and chief.

Suddenly Valerie did not feel all that comfortable. Her nagging fears of perhaps not being accepted by Flaming Arrow's people came to her now
like a black cloud enveloping her.

She looked guardedly over at Flaming Arrow,
who rode at her left side. She could not help but
feel that, for him, at this moment, she was not
there.

His eyes were on his people. His jaw was tight,
his back straight, his chin lifted.

She could almost feel the pain of regret that now showed in his eyes as he looked from person to person. Valerie realized now just how much resentment he felt toward the white people for having imprisoned his people on a reservation.

She found it hard to understand, for what she saw beyond his people looked grand and immense. She could see clouds of great pony herds grazing on tall, sweet grass in the distance. Although smoke-blackened, the painted lodges in their village, made from buffalo hides, were as handsome as the Montana Territory landscape and wide, blue sky. The tepees were releasing drifting, lazy smoke up into the breeze. A stream, tree-fringed, fresh from the distant mountains, flowed by the village.

The Blackfoot themselves were dressed in fine regalia.

Flaming Arrow sensed that Valerie was troubled by something. It was in the way he had felt her eyes on him for a moment. And as he gazed at her now, he saw how she studied his people, their horses, and their lodges.

He looked around her and saw how Brian was terribly stiff and quiet in his saddle. He seemed even *afraid*. Flaming Arrow then gazed again in the direction of his village and at the crowd of people who stood there awaiting his arrival.

Yes, now he understood the silence and tenseness of his wife and her brother. Suddenly they saw the true number of his people and might be feeling threatened. If he were entering a white world, himself the only Indian, he might himself feel threatened.

He edged his steed closer to Valerie's. "Soon my people will know the wonders of my wife," he said, reaching a hand to take one of hers. *"Nito-ile-man,* wipe the fear from your face. Take it from your eyes. Lift it from inside your heart. There is no need for that emotion. My people are no different than me and the warriors that you and Brian have grown to know. They are kind and caring. They will welcome you among them."

"They . . . they all look so solemn," Valerie said, not able to take her eyes off them. "I would think they would show some exuberance in seeing you . . . in knowing that you are no longer behind bars."

"Yes, they are happy, but they are also sad," Flaming Arrow said. "They will soon leave this land of wide, blue sky behind them forever. They will be leaving this land of tall, blowing grass. At the end of our journey they do not anticipate finding any land that is as grand as this. They fear there will be no deer . . . no animals at all for the hunt."

Valerie looked quickly over at him. "But they are wrong," she said. "The sky is as blue in Kansas, Missouri, and Illinois. The grass is as tall and green. Deer . . . all *sorts* of animals are everywhere! Has not anyone told them this?"

"They have been told, but they fear it cannot be as true as they wish it to be," Flaming Arrow said sullenly. "It will take showing them to make them know that life can be good elsewhere. When they taste freedom again, they will smile, for freedom is what is truly in question here."

Brian leaned around and gazed at Flaming Arrow. "Where are the children?" he asked. "I see no children."

"They are not with the adults," Flaming Arrow said, giving Brian a smile of reassurance. "They wait around the large outdoor fire where we will all soon have council. They play games while the adults do adult things."

"Are there very many young braves my age?" Brian asked, his fear ebbing away.

"Many," Flaming Arrow said, chuckling.

He squeezed Valerie's hand reassuringly. "I must now leave you for a while," he said. "I will ride ahead of everyone now and greet my people. I will send Fox Eye back to ride with you."

"I love you," Valerie murmured. "And please don't worry anymore about me and Brian. We're fine." She gave Brian a quick look. "Aren't we, Brian?"

"I was a little afraid," Brian said. "But now I'm excited."

"Good," Flaming Arrow said, breaking into a wide smile.

He gave Valerie's hand one last squeeze, then rode away. He stopped long enough to talk to Fox Eye, then rode on toward his waiting people.

Fox Eye wheeled his horse around and edged his

horse between Valerie's and Brian's. He gave them each a smile, then they rode on slowly together.

Tears came to Valerie's eyes as she watched Flaming Arrow dismount and move into the arms of his people as they rushed around him, each taking a turn to greet him.

When she finally reached them, it was apparent that Flaming Arrow had told everyone about her and Brian. Although some of the people seemed tense as they gazed at her and then Brian, most seemed to accept them.

Unless they are great actors, Valerie thought, smiling at the people as Flaming Arrow placed his hands at her waist and helped her down from her horse.

She stood on one side of Flaming Arrow, Brian on the other, as Flaming Arrow made his introductions.

Valerie was touched deeply when the people began filing past her, touching her, hugging her, or just smiling. It seemed to take forever for them all to pay their respects to her and Brian, but the impromptu ceremony did not end until each of them had done so.

"Run on now, young brave," Flaming Arrow said, giving Brian a gentle shove. "A warrior has gone ahead and told the children about you. They await you. Soon you will be as one among them. They know many games. They will welcome your competition."

Brian smiled widely, handed his horse's reins to

a warrior who also took charge of Valerie's steed, then ran through the crowd toward the huge outdoor fire.

Flaming Arrow gazed down at Valerie and saw her smile fade as she looked in Brian's direction. "Do not concern yourself over your brother," he said. He placed an arm around her waist and drew her next to him as he led her through the long line of people who parted to make room for them. "His smile will win over all of the children his age. Soon, except for the color of his hair and skin, you will not be able to tell him from the Blackfoot children."

"This is so new to us both," Valerie said, her cheeks beginning to hurt from smiling so much at Flaming Arrow's people.

"Soon it will be as familiar as that beautiful smile on your face," Flaming Arrow said, chuckling as she gave him a quick glance.

Once they were all seated around the huge, roaring outdoor fire, Flaming Arrow and Valerie sat at the place of honor on a thick cushion of plush animal pelts.

The smell of roasting meat lay heavy in the air. Beef paunches filled with the good inner part steamed in kettles on tripods over the central fire. Dripping their juices into the flames, long strips of meat hung over smaller fires throughout the village.

Valerie was very aware that her husband was the center of attention. The people of the tribe were quiet as they gazed at him. Even the children, who now sat by the fire with the adults, looked expectantly at their chief.

Valerie was not all that amazed to see Brian sitting among the children as though he belonged there. He had always been the sort of child who made friends easily. Even now, when the culture differed, as well as the colors of their skins, he had found a quick, special friendship among the Blackfoot.

Valerie looked quickly up at Flaming Arrow as he rose to his feet. She was filled with much pride and love as he began to speak to his people. She had always known he was their chief, but now, as he stood over them, so majestic and noble, she felt it with intensity.

As he spoke to his people, Valerie looked slowly around her at their expressions as they raptly watched and listened to their chief.

Some of the people's faces were masks of sorrow and anger as they thought of the white man uprooting them from land that had been theirs, and their ancestors' before them, since the beginning of time.

Others had looks of resignation, accepting the fate of their race.

But most looked with adoration at her husband.

"Hai-yah!" Flaming Arrow said, holding his chin high, his shoulders proudly squared. "Your chief has returned to lead you to a free and better land! Tomorrow we will begin our journey! We will not look back! Only forward!"

He paused, then said with a solemnity that sent

shivers up and down Valerie's spine, "The old things have passed away. Our children will not know how it used to be in their fathers' and grandfathers' day."

He gestured toward the great Rockies, towering and majestic and bathed in the ruddy glow of sunset. "We, children and old alike, are like the distant mountains!" he shouted. "We are strong and everenduring! We will survive this ordeal! We will stand straight and tall and be proud!"

He walked slowly around the circle of Blackfoot, every once in a while touching the shoulder of one or the head of another as he continued talking. "I am saddened to know of the passing of one who was so dear to me," he said, nodding slowly as he thought of Sky Spirit, the medicine-pipe man who had promised to keep prayers spoken for him while he was imprisoned.

It was hard for Flaming Arrow not to speak Sky Spirit's name, for speaking it could bring him somewhat closer to the medicine-pipe man at this moment. But he honored the custom not to speak openly the name of the dead.

"Our medicine-pipe man, who was also a medicine man to my father and mother, is now walking with his ancestors in the Sand Hills. When we walk tomorrow away from this land, even the sadness I feel over the passing of my friend will be left behind me . . . behind us *all*. There is much now to be happy over. Freedom for everyone is near!"

Choruses of loud chants of "Freedom! Freedom!" filled the night air, like a low drumming that reached into the distance.

It only stopped when a young brave brought a wrapped pipe and a robe of white fur to Flaming Arrow. The chief took both these things and sat back down beside Valerie. He rested the pipe on his lap as he slid into the robe and drew it tightly around him.

Valerie's eyes were wide as Flaming Arrow slowly removed the wrappings of the black stone sacred pipe. She did not have to be told that it had belonged to the friend to whom Flaming Arrow had only moments ago referred. He had spoken the medicine-pipe man's name to her more than once while on their journey to his people.

Sky Spirit.

This must be Sky Spirit's sacred pipe.

She sat in awe of how reverently her husband held it. In his eyes she could see something she had never seen before . . . such a deep, deep sadness. She could even see traces of tears in his eyes as the fire's glow reflected in them.

"We shall all share smokes from the sacred pipe tonight and pray over it that our journey will be safe from all interference from whites," Flaming Arrow said thickly as he held the long-stemmed pipe out for everyone to see. The stem was eagle-plumed, fur-wrapped, with tufts of brilliant feathers hanging from one end, the bright red feathers of a woodpecker the most prominent.

Valerie watched as a young brave brought a

burning twig toward Flaming Arrow. She looked quickly at her husband as he placed the stem of the pipe between his lips, took the burning twig, and brought it to the tobacco in the bowl to light it, then handed the twig back to the young warrior and waited for him to return to his seat with the others.

Flaming Arrow then reverently lifted the pipe and held it up toward the sun, down toward the earth, then pointed it to the north, south, east, and west as he prayed aloud for health, happiness, a safe journey, and a long life for everyone.

The pipe was passed around to the warriors. Each smoked a few puffs from it, then passed it on to the one who sat beside him.

When the pipe returned to Flaming Arrow, he again took a few puffs. Then, rising, holding the stem extended in front of him, he danced slowly, as somewhere in the distance low, slow beats of a drum could be heard.

Valerie scarcely breathed as so many of the warriors joined Flaming Arrow in the slow, meditative dance, their feet beating out the rhythm in time with the drumbeats as they weaved in and around those Blackfoot who remained on their blankets on the ground, while the women began singing songs of the medicine pipe.

Valerie felt immersed in feelings she had never felt before as her shoulders began to sway in time with the music and the throbbing beat of the dancer's feet. She never took her eyes off her husband, thinking him so mystical at this moment, everything around her seeming seeped in magic.

The moon had replaced the sun in the sky. Its beams seemed to be floating down only on the dancers, as though they were spotlighted by it.

Everything was so peaceful, so . . .

The sound of an approaching horse broke the spell.

Valerie turned her head with a start and saw a lone horseman just entering the perimeter of the village, but at this distance in the dark she couldn't tell who it was, whether he was white- or red-skinned.

When the drums ceased to beat, Valerie turned quickly around again. She noticed how the dancers had stopped.

She also noticed something else: the way Fox Eye hurried to the Flaming Arrow's side and whispered something to him. Fox Eye seemed to know who was approaching.

Flaming Arrow frowned and his eyes became lit with an instant fire as he glared at the approaching horseman, then turned his eyes to Valerie. She wondered why he seemed so concerned.

"Come to me," Flaming Arrow said, hurrying to Valerie. He took her hand and urged her to her feet as Fox Eye came and stood at his side.

Flaming Arrow gazed down at Brian and nodded to him.

"Young brave," he said, his voice drawn. "Hurry.

Go with Fox Eye and your sister to Fox Eye's lodge."

"But why?" Brian asked, voicing the question Valerie wanted to ask. She did not want to question in front of his people anything Flaming Arrow instructed them to do. But Brian, in his innocence, did not think to worry about such a thing.

"Just do as Flaming Arrow says," Valerie said when Brian got no answer. She took Brian's hand, yet gazed questioningly into Flaming Arrow's eyes as she and Brian scampered past him, afraid now to know the reason he wanted to get her and Brian hidden.

A thought sprang to her mind that caused her to go cold inside. Her face drained of color as she stopped and made a quick turn to stare at the man, who was now close enough for her to see his face.

Her knees almost buckled beneath her when she recognized Bradley Hart!

And he was close enough now to have also seen *her*.

She sent Flaming Arrow a quick glance, understanding now that he had wanted to shield her from the man of her past. Also, he knew that, for many reasons, it was best that Bradley Hart didn't know that she was there.

Her eyes wavered when Flaming Arrow opened his arms for her. "It is too late," he said thickly. "He has now seen you. Come. Stand tall at my side." He nodded toward Fox Eye. "Still take the young man to your lodge. Keep him there until the confrontation with this agent is behind us."

Fox Eye nodded and whisked Brian away just as Bradley Hart wheeled his horse to a stop before Flaming Arrow and Valerie.

Her heart pounding, Valerie squared her shoulders and lifted her chin as Bradley stared in disbelief. "Val," he said in a low gasp. "Damn. What are *you* doing *here?* Why aren't you in Kansas City with your family?"

Bradley slid a slow, cool gaze to Flaming Arrow, then back to Valerie. "I also saw your brother," he said warily. "Were you both abducted and brought here?"

He slid another gaze over at Flaming Arrow and saw just how possessive he was of Valerie as he placed an arm around her waist and drew her up next to him. "And who is this Indian?" he said through clenched teeth. "I've never seen him here before."

Valerie groped through her storehouse of courage, and her memories of the near rape, and glared at Bradley through haughty eyes. "Who is this?" she said. "Chief Flaming Arrow. And am I a captive? Is Brian?" She gave off a mocking laugh. "I don't believe a wife is ever considered a captive, now, do you?" she said.

"Wife?" Bradley said, raising an eyebrow. "What do you mean? Whose wife *are* you?"

"Flaming Arrow's," Valerie said, her eyes gleaming.

She wanted to laugh out loud when she saw how Bradley's face suddenly drained of color and knew that the truth was just now sinking home.

But she feared his true reaction too much. If once this truth set in and he wanted to make things rough for her for rejecting him when he had wanted her so badly for himself, she knew that he could achieve this by harming the Blackfoot.

"Why . . . you . . . bitch," was his first reaction.

Valerie forced herself not to react, yet his words made her insides grow cold, then hot with anger.

18

The wild winds weep,
And the night is a-cold;
Come hither, sleep,
And my griefs enfold.
—WILLIAM BLAKE

"Val, are you saying that you actually married one of these heathens?" Bradley said, dismounting.

Valerie had to fight back the urge to slap him for his insulting remark about the Blackfoot.

She had trouble even understanding how the government would hire someone like Bradley as an Indian agent. Surely they had been hard-pressed for agents when they had hired him.

"I am proudly married to Flaming Arrow," she said. "Now why don't you leave? You have no further need to be here. The Blackfoot are . . ."

She stopped short of letting it slip out about the Blackfoot's plans to leave the area tomorrow. Had she told him the plan, it would have been stopped dead in its tracks.

Bradley didn't seem to notice that she didn't finish what she was about to say, or he just wasn't interested. He placed his fists on his hips and glared at her. "I don't understand how you could have become involved with the Blackfoot," he said, his eyes narrowing. "Your home in Kansas City is far from Montana Territory and the Blackfoot never travel that far from *their* home. How did you meet the Blackfoot, Valerie?"

Wanting to keep things civil between them, and hoping that once she gave him the answers he sought, he might leave—and hoping Flaming Arrow would not speak and anger Bradley—Valerie hurriedly tried to explain.

"Bradley, you knew my father well and knew his love for gambling," she said, trying to keep her voice steady, though she hated even to speak to this vile man who had came so close to raping her. "Father gambled his money away. He went bankrupt. He lost everything . . . even our home. When he heard about the discovery of gold in Montana Territory, it lured him here."

"Your parents are in the territory?" Bradley said, an evil smile on his lips. "How interesting."

The color drained from Valerie's face. Bradley's reaction made her realize she shouldn't have told him about her parents. Surely he had never forgotten how her father had stopped him from assaulting Valerie.

There was certainly no love between the two men!

If Bradley wanted to avenge the humiliation he had felt over being treated so roughly by Valerie's father, now he had the chance to do so.

"Don't you go near them," Valerie hissed. "Do you hear? Don't . . . go . . . near my parents."

Suddenly Bradley whipped his pistol from his holster and held it on Flaming Arrow as he reached and grabbed Valerie by a wrist and yanked her back against him, holding her tight in his embrace.

"Back away, Chief, or by damn I'll shoot you," he said, his pistol held steady. "This woman has never belonged to anyone but me and, by damn, I plan to have her."

Without turning his eyes from Flaming Arrow, Bradley shouted over his shoulder to everyone, "If anyone so much as makes a move for their firearms, I'll shoot your chief!" he warned. "And after I get on my horse with Val, *she* becomes my target should one of you become foolish enough to try to stop us from leaving your village."

Flaming Arrow felt the blood running hot and furious through his veins as he watched the white man inch his way backward toward his steed. Seeing Valerie held prisoner in the man's tight grip, he gazed with a silent apology into his wife's eyes, for at this moment he was unable to help her. This white man, who was indeed crazy for trying such a trick, *would* rather kill her than give her back to the life of the Blackfoot.

As for Flaming Arrow, he would give his life to save her. But the way Valerie was being held, there was no way to keep her out of danger should someone even *have* a straight aim on the white man.

Suddenly a blast of gunfire rang through the air.

The pistol flipped like a grasshopper out of Bradley Hart's hand, then landed at Flaming Arrow's feet.

Bradley gasped, let his arm drop from around Valerie, and scrambled to get in his saddle.

Valerie stepped aside so that Flaming Arrow could get to Bradley.

She covered a gasp with her hand as Flaming Arrow placed his arm around Bradley's throat, yanked him from his horse, pulled him to the ground, then straddled him and held him in place.

His pistol still smoking, Fox Eye walked up and stood over them, smiling.

Flaming Arrow sent Fox Eye a quick smile. "Thank you, *nisah,* brother," he said, yet inside his heart thinking about what might have been had Fox Eye's aim been off even a fraction.

"Fox Eye, thank you, thank you," Valerie said, going to give him a big hug.

Brian ran up to Valerie, and as she stepped away from Fox Eye, he flung himself into her arms.

Voices shouting in chants rose into the night air. "Hang him!" the Blackfoot people said almost in unison.

Fox Eye slid his pistol back into its holster as Flaming Arrow stepped away from Bradley. Fox Eye then grabbed the white agent and yanked him to his feet. He placed an arm around the man's throat and held him against his hard body as everyone came by and took turns spitting on the agent's face.

"Kill him!" the people still chanted. "Kill him!"

Valerie gazed anxiously from Flaming Arrow to his people and back at Flaming Arrow again, as everyone seemed hell-bent on killing Bradley.

Since Flaming Arrow had not yet spoken his opinion about what the man's punishment should be, she turned quickly and grabbed her husband by the arm.

"You can't kill him," she said urgently. "Everything you have planned for your people would be endangered. Once the government found out that one of their agents had been murdered, they would find you and punish you. Not only you, Flaming Arrow, but all your people."

"Once the white man saw you at this village, he did not have his duties as an agent on his mind," Flaming Arrow grumbled. "His mind was centered on one thing. On *you*. He endangered your life, a white woman, more than he endangered my people. The government would surely punish him should they know what he did today, instead of making my people suffer for having stopped him."

"Yes, I would think so, but one never knows how the government will react to anything if Indians are involved," Valerie murmured. She had heard of atrocities against Indians over much less than what had happened today.

"Let me go and I promise I won't tell anyone anything," Bradley blurted out. "Val, tell them to let me go. Neither you nor they will ever see me again. I . . . I intended to give up my agent position here in this area anyhow. I hate the isolation of Montana Territory. I'll leave. None of you will ever see or hear from me again."

"Your words are hollow and meaningless," Fox Eye said, turning Bradley to face him. "While you have been agent to my people they have been ignored as though they did not exist. Death is the best punishment for men like you whose sole purpose on this earth is to serve 'self.'"

"But *I will* leave the area," Bradley pleaded. "I will."

"Yes, he will leave," Flaming Arrow said, grabbing Bradley by the arm and turning him quickly to face him. He spoke directly to the agent. "But you will leave without a horse, clothes, boots, and weapon."

Bradley choked back a gasp of horror. "What?" he said, his voice sounding as though it were strangled.

"Fox Eye, unclothe him," Flaming Arrow said, a sly smile on his lips when he saw Bradley try to struggle.

"No!" Bradley cried. "Don't do this!"

Flaming Arrow gazed at one of his other warriors. "Go and burn this man's dwelling and bring his livestock and horses back to our village," he said. "Leave nothing for the man to go back to."

The warrior nodded, went to his horse and swung into the saddle, then rode away.

Valerie wanted to turn her face away from what

was happening as Bradley was quickly being rendered nude.

But she was enjoying his humiliation too much.

In her mind's eye she was recalling her own shameful night . . . her own humiliation with Bradley Hart. Finally he was getting his comeuppance!

Flaming Arrow smiled as Bradley fought to keep his boots from being removed, his naked body already stark white beneath the backdrop of night.

"Also . . . my boots?" Bradley cried, with a pleading look at Flaming Arrow as two warriors held him in place. Fox Eye removed first one boot and then the other.

"You showed my woman no mercy on the night you attempted to rape her," Flaming Arrow said icily. "You showed no mercy tonight when you tried to abduct her. Now you are shown the same sort of mercy."

When the warriors released Bradley's arms, he slid his hands quickly over his private parts, his eyes now locked with Valerie's. "For the love of God, stop what's happening here," he choked out. "For what we once meant to one another, help me, Val."

"You never meant anything to me," Valerie said, easing closer to Flaming Arrow, seeking the comfort of his closeness. "You were forced on me by my father. *He* wanted me to marry you . . . until . . . until you were caught—"

"I'm sorry," Bradley said, interrupting her. "I was wrong. Please don't make me pay for my igno-

rance in *this* way. You are the chief's wife. He'll
listen to you. Tell him to have mercy."

"Take him away," Flaming Arrow growled,
frowning darkly at Bradley as the agent turned
pleading eyes his way.

"I'll probably die out there," he said, his voice
breaking. "There are no forts nearby for me to go
to. There are no homes."

A long, drawn-out wolf's howl in the distance
sent a quick look of fear into Bradley's eyes. He
shuddered. "The animals will seek me out in the
night and . . . and . . ."

"Yes, that is my thought, exactly," Flaming
Arrow said with a grim satisfaction. "And if they
don't find you, and I happen to run across you
again, I will *truly* show you no mercy." Flaming
Arrow leaned closer to Bradley. "Next time I will
kill you."

Bradley's eyes wavered. He swallowed hard.

Then Fox Eye came with a rope and tied it
around Bradley's neck.

After mounting his steed, Fox Eye led Bradley
through the village on foot, the rope swaying between Bradley and the warrior on horseback, the
knot where the rope was tied digging into Bradley's throat.

Again the wolf howled in the distance.

Valerie shivered, for she could not help but think
the wolf's howls might be an omen of Bradley
Hart's final fate.

Brian took one of Valerie's hands. She gazed down at him and saw a silent wonder in his eyes.

She saw in his look that Brian was questioning the way Bradley Hart was being treated. It *did* seem inhumane.

Oh, but if only she knew how to explain the depths of this man's evil nature to her brother.

But there was no way to explain the man's attempted rape to Brian. The child was too innocent, too trusting, to know such a thing in this world existed—where a man would behave like an animal and demand . . . and take . . . a woman's virginity away so heartlessly!

"Sis, what does the word *rape* mean?" Brian suddenly blurted out.

Valerie paled, for now she recalled Flaming Arrow openly talking of the rape while condemning Bradley.

She was at a loss for words. How could she bear the pain of describing this to her brother?

Flaming Arrow heard Brian's question. He understood his wife's reluctance to answer. He saw this as just one more thing the young brave must learn as a part of life. There was no way to shelter him from even the most gruesome acts of mankind.

"Come, young brave," Flaming Arrow said, placing a gentle hand on Brian's shoulder. "Man to man, we have things to discuss. It is time for your lessons as a man to begin."

Valerie reached a trembling hand out for Brian as Flaming Arrow led him away from her. Then she slowly dropped it to her side. She was apprehensive over what Brian was going to be told, yet relieved that Flaming Arrow had saved her from the discomfort.

"Thank you, darling husband, for relieving me of such a task as this," she whispered, tears flooding her eyes as she watched Flaming Arrow kneel on his haunches and explain to Brian, who was raptly listening.

When Brian's eyes widened in horror, yet was stoically silent, Valerie knew her brother had been told the worst and was receiving it inside his heart like a man.

She turned on a heel and was glad she could no longer see Bradley Hart. She hoped that *finally* he was out of her life forever!

Her eyes turned heavenward. In the distance a fire's glow reflected off the clouds. She smiled, knowing that Bradley's home was now ablaze, all signs of this evil man soon to be gone and erased from this land forever.

She doubted that he would survive. She prayed that his body wouldn't be found until the Blackfoot were far from this place of heartache!

19

The night comes on that knows not morn,
When I shall cease to be all alone,
To live forgotten, and love forlorn.
—Alfred, Lord Tennyson

Once more the sun had gone to his lodge behind the mountains.

Valerie was standing outside the tepee that was now not only Flaming Arrow's, but hers. She gazed up to a high hill that overlooked the Blackfoot village.

She watched her husband expectantly. The moon was high, illuminating Flaming Arrow as he knelt and prayed again for his people's safe journey, and for their future.

A soft breeze, bringing with it the chill of night, caused Valerie to shiver.

Hugging herself, she turned and looked at a group of children who were going to sleep tonight beneath the stars close to the large outdoor fire.

She searched the children until she found Brian.

She smiled and felt a surge of well-being and happiness as she watched Brian huddle closer into the group of children to join their laughter and storytelling. She wondered if he had told them some of the ghost stories that she had taught him when he was a much smaller child.

"The ghost of chimney mountain," she whispered.

She laughed softly as she turned and lifted the entrance flap to her lodge, where warmth and comfort awaited her.

Yes, she thought, smiling to herself. She *had* made up quite a tale about a ghost of a mountain that looked like a chimney.

Brian had loved that story above all the others that she had invented only for his ears.

She felt proud that tonight he might have found a way to share them with others. Surely his skills at storytelling would bring him even closer to the Indian children.

She yanked her boots off and placed them close to the lodge fire so that they would be warm in the morning.

She smiled as her thoughts lingered on Brian. He was intrigued by the Blackfoot. *And* he seemed to love and respect Flaming Arrow almost the same as he had loved his very own father.

"Father," she then whispered, disrobing. "I wonder what Father is feeling. What about Mother? Did she get well?"

Every day and every night she thought of her family, sorely missing them. She could not help but think that someday she would see them again. She could not let go of that hope easily. She loved them all too much.

Exhausted from a day helping to gather some of the older people's belongings for the journey, Valerie snuggled into one of the warm, long-sleeved, floor-length cotton gowns she had taken from the trunk she had found in the abandoned cabin.

She then gathered up many blankets and pelts and made herself a pallet beside the fire.

Stretching out on them, she pulled one of the blankets over her and lay on her side, watching the flames of the fire as they wove, ribbonlike, over the logs. She wanted to stay awake until Flaming Arrow returned. She wanted to fall asleep in his arms.

Oh, how she loved to snuggle and feel his warm breath on her cheek, feel the wonders of his powerful, yet gentle hands cupping her breasts.

Smiling, she fell into a soft sleep. In her sleep she dreamed of Flaming Arrow and relived their first moments together, and how she was so stubborn, even arrogant, not knowing whether he was a friend or enemy.

She sighed in her sleep when she dreamed of their first kiss and the wonders of it and how her insides had felt so warm and melting.

She tremored sensually when she dreamed of their first lovemaking and how her whole world had opened up to something new and beautiful.

Then her dreams changed.

She frowned and tossed from side to side when she saw Bradley Hart on a horse approaching her at high speed. She could feel panic again when she tried to run away from him so that he could not pull her on the horse with him . . . or stomp her to death beneath the horse's large hooves!

And then the dream changed again.

Bradley was no longer on a horse. She was standing away from him and seeing him through what seemed to be a hazy, gray film of fog as he stumbled onward away from her, oblivious of her presence.

He wore no clothes. His bare feet were swollen. His body was blistered from the long hours of exposure from the sun. Valerie could hear Bradley groan as he attempted to take each new step.

Something else then entered her dream.

She wanted to scream, yet in the dream her throat felt frozen as she watched wolves gathering along the path, snarling, their fangs exposed, their gray eyes watching Bradley as they all began to stalk him.

Suddenly the wolves sprang forward. The whole pack lunged at Bradley, knocking him to the ground.

His screams of terror and pain ripped through Valerie's consciousness, awakening her with a start, yet the screams came with her from the dream and she soon discovered that they were her own.

Flaming Arrow was wrenched from his meditation and prayers by the screams. When he saw Brian and others rushing toward his lodge, he knew that the one who had screamed was his wife. It was Valerie!

The thought of Bradley Hart possibly circling around after having been set free many miles from the reservation came to Flaming Arrow's mind like a rush of flames, setting him afire with fear. He couldn't get to his lodge fast enough as his moccasined feet scrambled, slipped, and slid down the steep slope of the hill.

Breathless, his heart pounding, he finally arrived at his lodge. He pushed through the silent crowd outside of the tepee and hurried inside.

Fox Eye was holding Valerie in his arms as she wept, while Brian sat before them, wide-eyed and afraid.

"Please, it was only a dream," Valerie said, sobbing. "I'm all right, Fox Eye. I am all right."

When Fox Eye saw Flaming Arrow enter the lodge, he eased Valerie from his arms and stepped aside so that Flaming Arrow could comfort his wife.

"Flaming Arrow," Valerie said in a soft, choking sob. She clung to him and gazed wild-eyed up at his face. "I dreamed something terrible."

"Tell me the dream," he said thickly. "The Blackfoot believe in dreams. If a dream is very clear and vivid . . . it is a dream that one can expect to come true. Dreams sometimes portend one's future."

"Then it surely will come true, for it was as real as you are sitting here, holding me," Valerie said, wiping tears from her eyes with the back of a hand.

She let out a soft, cynical laugh, now feeling foolish that she had behaved so irrationally over such a dream. "And I don't know why I am so upset by it," she said. "The dream was about Bradley Hart, not someone I loved."

"Tell me about it," Flaming Arrow said, gently stroking her thick golden hair.

"There were many wolves," Valerie said softly. She blinked nervously as the dream came to her so vividly she was reliving it. She covered her mouth with a hand. "The wolves . . . they . . . attacked Bradley," she said. "It was so gruesome. His screams! They were so real!"

"If you dreamed this about Bradley Hart, he perhaps will not survive his first full night alone," Flaming Arrow said, nodding. "But he will probably not die in the exact way that you dreamed it. There are many ways for an evil man to die, standing alone against the elements and animals that prey on those who put off the stench of evil."

"Then maybe after tonight I won't have cause to dream of this man ever again," Valerie said, shuddering involuntarily. "Nor will my family. He surely can't travel that far."

Fox Eye placed a gentle hand on Flaming Arrow's bare shoulder. "Would it be best if I sent several warriors out to look for the man, to see if he has died or to see if he has wandered back in our direction?" he asked, his voice tight.

"No, it is not necessary," Flaming Arrow said, although he would never forget those few moments on the bluff when he thought that perhaps the evil man had returned and harmed his wife.

He had to remind himself that the man was weaponless . . . and that his men had led the agent far from the reservation.

"Do you truly believe we won't ever see him again?" Valerie asked, drawing a blanket around her shoulders as Flaming Arrow stood.

"Never," Flaming Arrow said, his jaws tight. He nodded a silent farewell to his friend as Fox Eye nodded, then left the lodge.

"Sis, I think I'll spend the rest of the night with you," Brian murmured, his eyes locked with Valerie's. "With me and Flaming Arrow here for protection, nothing is going to happen to you."

"And so you feel that I need watching, do you?" Valerie said, trying to make light of the situation, even though the dream clung to her, still bothering her in its vividness.

She *shouldn't* feel afraid, for if dreams portended truth, it had nothing to do with her. Bradley had died in her dream! What better way to feel protected than to believe he was dead?

But it was the viciousness of how he died that would not go away.

"It doesn't hurt to have both your brother and husband with you for the rest of the night," Brian said, reaching up and hugging Valerie.

She looked at Flaming Arrow over Brian's shoulder, and when he nodded his approval, she smiled and nodded in return.

"Yes, do stay the night," she murmured, stroking her hands down his back. "But I feel guilty for pulling you away from your friends and the stories beneath the moonlight. I've spoiled your fun."

"I've already told all the ghost stories I know," Brian said, laughing softly as he eased from Valerie's arms. "I think I may have even gone too far with them. I think some of the young braves are afraid to go to sleep tonight."

He chuckled. "Especially after your bloodcurdling scream," he said. "Sis, I had just finished telling them the story about the ghost of chimney mountain when you screamed. You wouldn't believe how the boys jumped with fear!"

"Shame on you," Valerie said, tousling Brian's hair with her fingers.

"Shame on you for screaming at the wrong time," Brian teased back.

"Shame on both of you for leaving me out of the fun," Flaming Arrow said, drawing both of their eyes to him. "What is this about a ghost story? About a ghost of chimney mountain?"

"Oh, it's just something I made up when Brian was small," Valerie said, laughing softly. "There is no such thing as a ghost of chimney mountain, *nor* ghosts at *all.*"

Valerie's smile faded when she noticed how quickly and strangely Flaming Arrow became quiet.

"Darling, what is it?" she asked, searching his eyes.

"There *is* such a mountain," he said. He looked slowly from Brian to Valerie and saw how their eyes widened and their lips parted in wonder. "There *are* such ghosts *on* the mountain. It is not far away. Do you want to see it?"

"But . . . I made that up," Valerie said, her pulse racing. "Surely—"

"Do you want to see it?" Flaming Arrow asked, reaching both his hands toward them. "Come. I shall show you. I shall show you how the ghosts dance and sway all around the mountain peak when the moon is big and full . . . and ghostly."

Pale, Brian backed away. "No, I don't want to see it," he said in a rush of words. He looked at Valerie. "Sis, how could you know?"

"I didn't," Valerie said, just as pale as he. "Honest, Brian, I made it up."

When Flaming Arrow began laughing, his eyes dancing as he looked from Valerie to Brian, Valerie knew that she and Brian had just had a big joke played on them.

"You will pay for this," she said, laughing as she gave Flaming Arrow a shove that made him fall onto his back.

For a moment Valerie forgot Brian was there. She stretched out atop Flaming arrow and held his wrists to the floor as she kissed him, both of them laughing throatily.

"Sis?" Brian said, his voice drawing her quickly away from Flaming Arrow.

Blushing, Valerie sat up and drew the blanket around her shoulders.

Flaming Arrow patted Brian on the back, then

wrapped him in a warm blanket. "Enough ghost stories for tonight," he said, chuckling. "Young brave, I think it is time for you to settle in for the night. Tomorrow comes soon enough with its long journey."

Brian nodded. He hugged Valerie and Flaming Arrow, then went to the back of the lodge and stretched out on his makeshift bed of blankets.

Wanting to give his sister and Flaming Arrow some privacy, he turned his back to them and soon fell asleep.

"You were wicked for doing that to us," Valerie murmured as Flaming Arrow drew her down on the blankets and pelts beside him.

She propped herself on an elbow and gazed into his eyes, then giggled. "But I truly loved the way you teased me and Brian," she murmured. "It's good to know that what lies ahead hasn't robbed you of your humor."

"Humor keeps a man sane," Flaming Arrow said, then drew her lips to his. He gave her a deep, long kiss, then held her in his arms as they watched the fire.

"Tomorrow," Valerie murmured. "Tomorrow everyone's lives change."

"And I hope for the better," Flaming Arrow said thickly. "Time will tell whether or not I have made the right decision for my people."

Valerie said nothing more about it.

She knew all that could be said had been said.

It was now up to fate.

20

The moon like a flower,
In heaven's high bower,
With silent delight
Sits and smiles on the night.
—WILLIAM BLAKE

The many travois were piled high with personal possessions.

Mules were loaded for the flight from the reservation.

There was a long, sad drone of drums and songs from those who feared the long journey on their quest for a new home . . . a new life.

Valerie gazed over at Flaming Arrow as he stood amid his waiting people. Today he was fully dressed in his buckskins, his leggings beautifully embroidered with porcupine quills and bright feathers.

Flaming Arrow had told Valerie earlier this morning that they were his hunting leggings . . . that they were great medicine.

He also wore a necklace of bear claws, a belt of bear fur, and around his head a band of fur.

The music and singing ceased as Flaming Arrow raised both of his hands heavenward, palms up.

Tears came to Valerie's eyes and she drew Brian close to her as once again her husband prayed for his people. She had never realized just how religious he was until he had come among his people, their welfare heavy on his heart.

"Pity us, now, O Sun!" Flaming Arrow cried, his eyes gazing toward the mountains where the sun was still a hot flame as it lowered slowly in the sky. He had decided that for a while this first trek away from the reservation must be done under cover of darkness to keep his people from the eyes of whites who might be wandering along the precious land the Blackfoot were leaving.

"Help us!" he continued to pray. "Oh, Great Medicine Person Above! Look down on your children and lead them to a new land of hope! Keep them safe from whites who would stop their escape! Make them invisible to those who might come upon them! Make the journey one that is not filled with grief and sorrow!"

When his prayer was finished and he lowered his hands to his sides, he gazed around him at those who were elderly. He felt that perhaps they were too old to make the complete journey.

Yet he could not leave them behind to be punished by the white government for those who did escape. Some might even be put to death for having kept quiet about those who had made the plans for the departure.

In a buckskin dress and knee-high moccasins that would protect her against snake and spider bites while on the journey through the tall grass, and her hair drawn back and worn in two braids, Valerie smiled at Flaming Arrow when he came back and stood with her and Brian.

"We are now ready to leave." He glanced from Valerie to Brian, and then regarded Valerie with much adoration. "It is good that you have feelings for my people, so much that you not only married their chief, but also now travel with them to their new land. The journey will not be an easy one."

"Both Brian and I are here to make the journey easier for you, my husband," Valerie said. "Please tell us when we can help. This is such an emotional time for your people."

"Seeking new things is a time for apprehension, yet also my people eventually can look forward to what might be," he said thickly. "But as you see by my people's faces today, there is no joy yet to be found in what we do."

"At the end of your journey, and when they realize that they can be as happy in their new lives as now, there will be happy faces, not sad," Valerie said. "You see, I had to make changes when my father lost everything we owned in Kansas City. At first I hated leaving my home . . . leaving life as I had known it. Then the more I thought of it, of the challenge that lay ahead in a new land, the more I got excited about it."

"And you love this new land as much as you loved Kansas?" Flaming Arrow asked.

"Yes, as will your people love the new land

where they will be raising their tepees and hunting for their meals," Valerie said softly.

"It will be fun to run and hunt with my new friends when we arrive at . . . where did you decide to settle, Flaming Arrow? Illinois or Missouri?" Brian asked, eyes wide.

"We shall see, when we arrive closer to the new land, which will best benefit my people," Flaming Arrow said, placing a hand on Brian's shoulder. "But there are many days . . . many weeks . . . between us and that new land. We had best leave now or we shall never arrive there."

He swung away from Valerie and Brian and went to the head of the long line of readied mules, travois, and horses, his people standing ready for the beginning of their journey.

Suddenly a white-tailed deer ran out from the brush, leaped over one of the travois, and bounded away into the shadows of the fast-falling dusk.

Valerie sucked in a breath at the sight of the deer, thinking its presence at this time might be an omen for good things to come for the Blackfoot.

Yet on the other hand it might represent what they were leaving behind and leave nothing but even a deeper sadness inside their hearts at the sight.

She then spied a flock of catbirds. She recalled having seen them back home in Kansas. Always in spring they had arrived sometime during the night with several other migrators that shared the same valley around her parents' ranch.

She could remember thinking how wonderful, in the mornings after their arrival, was their song of musical notes welcoming the new sun.

She could remember where they had nested each spring. Heavy woodland crowded the borders of a meadow before yielding to the blackberry brambles and bushes. This meadow had become a perfect place for the catbirds. Often they would select a particular hawthorn bush directly below an ailing black cherry tree in which to build their nests. It was a well-hidden nest of twigs and stems that blended in well with the tangles of wild grapes that used the hawthorn to climb to the sun.

Although the female catbirds were secretive while building their nests and then laying their eggs, they still attracted the attention of the males. The male birds spent each morning sitting in the black cherry tree singing a short, whimsical song.

Valerie discovered that female catbirds would receive a male as a mate shortly after laying her eggs. By locating a nest, the male was better able to increase his chances in courtship.

It was good to reminisce about things that took her back home to a time when her family was the central part of her life. But now Flaming Arrow was her total reason for living. Her beloved Flaming Arrow!

"Can I ride with Fox Eye, Sis?" Brian asked, grabbing his horse's reins and pulling Valerie out of her deep thoughts. "I enjoyed riding with him before."

Valerie looked quickly at him. Though she had just thought of Flaming Arrow as her true reason for living, she knew that wasn't entirely true. There was also Brian. She would always be there for sweet Brian.

"Yes, you can ride with Fox Eye," she said, laughing softly as she reached over and tousled her brother's golden hair. "But this time you have your own horse."

"Thanks to Fox Eye I have a masterful steed, *much* more powerful than the mare Father gave me for Christmas last year. I *love* Bullet," Brian said, proudly puffing out his chest. "I can, Sis? I can ride again with Fox Eye?"

"If he doesn't mind," Valerie said, swinging herself into her saddle.

She patted her horse and steadied it as Brian rode away and sidled his black mustang up next to Fox Eye's.

She watched Fox Eye reach a welcoming hand to Brian as he patted her brother on the head.

Her eyes widened when several other young braves Brian's age came with their horses and gathered around Brian and Fox Eye. Theirs was a close camaraderie. It made Valerie happy to know that her brother had fit in so quickly.

When the slow procession began, the youngsters all kept close together, their laughter hopefully becoming infectious among the Blackfoot adults.

Valerie had learned that the Blackfoot were talkative, merry, and lighthearted, and delighted in fun.

In the presence of strangers they were grave, silent, and reserved. But as the Blackfoot became acquainted, the reserve wore off. They were at peace again and appeared in their true lighthearted colors.

Sinking her heels gently into the flanks of her horse, Valerie edged next to Flaming Arrow's steed and rode with him, at first without much conversation. She could see the apprehension in his eyes and the tightness of his jaws.

She could see just how tightly coiled the reins were around his hand.

She understood that he felt all of the responsibility of his people at this time, and she knew it must weigh on his broad, muscled shoulders.

They rode onward until the sun went to its home behind the mountains and the sky became speckled with its twinkling stars and a moon that was no longer full, but just waning from its full circle of white. The farther they rode into the darkness, the chillier the air became.

Having prepared herself for such a change in the weather, Valerie reached inside her saddlebag and pulled out a warm fringed shawl made of heavy buckskin.

After securing this around her shoulders, she glanced over at Brian. She smiled when she saw that he, too, protected himself from the chilly night air. He had slid on a coat made of buckskin, as had his friends.

She looked over at Flaming Arrow. He seemed

so immersed in thought he had not yet noticed the cold air.

Valerie edged her horse closer to his. "Darling, please put on your buckskin cape," she murmured. "You don't want to catch a chill."

Nodding, and glad to be reminded, Flaming Arrow pulled his cape from his bag and slid it on.

"Do you intend to travel all night?" Valerie asked, worrying about the elderly, whose heads were hung from the exertion of the journey.

"We will be stopping soon," Flaming Arrow said, his voice flat. "Many days before Fox Eye found us in the cabin, he and his warriors searched along the trail for resting places for our people as they made plans for this escape. It will be a place where everyone can eat, sleep, and contemplate their tomorrows. It will be a place where you and I can go and be alone, for at least a little while."

"I look forward to that," Valerie said softly. "I look forward to holding you, my darling, to help ease the pain you are feeling inside your heart."

"Wife, did you know that long ago the name *Blackfoot* was one of terrible meaning to white travelers?" Flaming Arrow said sullenly. "The white travelers who passed across the desolate buffalo-trodden waste that lay to the north of the Yellowstone River and east of the Rocky Mountains."

"Yes, I had heard it said about the Blackfoot," Valerie admitted. "But I heard it said about all Indians, not only the Blackfoot. The white children are taught to fear all redskins. They are taught atrocities that I know the white soldiers themselves are capable of. It has never been a fair picture painted for the red man."

"Yes, I am aware of that, and that makes your understanding of me and my people twofold in my eyes and heart," Flaming Arrow said thickly. He gestured with a hand. *"All* of this was Blackfoot land when my ancestors lived and died here, not only a small portion assigned the Blackfoot by the white-eye government."

"Yes, I know," Valerie murmured, seeing now that it was going to take much time for her husband to get over his loss . . . his *people's* loss.

Perhaps he would never get over it.

Perhaps even this journey was useless. When the Blackfoot arrived at a new land, they might miss this land so much they may never adapt.

That was what scared her most, now that she thought of it. She did not want to see these fine, caring people lose heart! Lose hope!

Especially before it even was proved to them that life was as good at one place as another!

They rode on and on, until Valerie thought she might drop from the saddle. Yet she doubted that was possible. It felt as though her behind were glued to the saddle! It ached unmercifully.

Just when she thought she couldn't travel another inch, Fox Eye rode up next to Flaming Arrow and told him their hiding place was near.

Valerie looked where Fox Eye pointed and saw that the land led into a high, deep canyon. There was a high bluff overhead so thickly covered in pine and cedar trees that it would be all but impossible for a man to ride out on it to see down below.

She followed onward the half mile or so it took to get to the canyon, then her eyes widened in surprise when she saw how it opened to a straight stretch of land where a river ebbed, snakelike. It was an isolated place, where the walls of the canyon circled like a protective curtain around the area. Where the Blackfoot entered it, sentries would be posted to keep them safe for the time they needed to rest before venturing onward.

When they finally made camp, Valerie helped everyone make preparations around a warm fire to spend the night.

Food was brought out from their bags. Coffee scented the air with its fine aroma. Pipes were smoked. Baths were taken.

And then everyone snuggled into their blankets and settled in for a long-deserved sleep.

After tucking Brian in, Valerie left the camp with Flaming Arrow. He built them a separate fire beside the river, far enough from the others to be private. He erected a lean-to under which he placed red willow brush to lay upon. Over this he placed several blankets, then held his hand out for Valerie.

Smelling fresh and clean from having bathed with Flaming Arrow earlier downstream from the others, and no longer aware of being so bone-weary, Valerie knelt in the lean-to and slowly slid the buckskin dress over her head.

She laughed softly as she sat down and Flaming Arrow pulled one moccasin from her feet, then the other.

"Let me unbraid your hair," Flaming Arrow said, turning her so that her back was to him.

Still resting on her knees, a giddy warmth spreading through her as his fingers sometimes slid from her hair to her shoulders, and then around to her breasts, Valerie closed her eyes and sighed.

Her hair hanging free down her back, Valerie turned to Flaming Arrow and watched him remove his clothes. The fire cast golden rays of light into the lean-to, sheening Flaming Arrow's copper body as he revealed it to Valerie. She was unable to wait until he was finished. She reached out and softly ran her hands down his muscled chest, then lower, and helped him slide his leggings and pants down past his thighs.

As he slid his clothes on down away from himself, Valerie swept her fingers around his manhood and slowly began moving her hand. When he sucked in quick breaths of pleasure, she was glad, for at least while receiving pleasure he was able to forget that which made his heart ache.

While he was alone with her, she would make his heart sing!

His clothes tossed aside, his eyes hazed over with passion, with quick, eager fingers his hands were in Valerie's hair, bringing her lips to his in a frenzied kiss.

Valerie twined her arms around his neck and

clung to him as his mouth forced her lips open and his kiss grew more passionate. She gasped with ecstasy when he swept his hands downward, cupped her breasts, and kneaded them, then leaned his hard, ready body against hers and led her down on their makeshift bed.

His body covered hers, so warm, so aroused. Valerie opened her legs to him and with a hand led him inside her warm, wet, and ready place.

Desire shot through her as he began his heaving thrusts, filling her more deeply with each rhythmic stroke.

She was imprisoned against him, welcoming it.

Her skin quivered as his hands now explored, seeking her more sensitive spots. His mouth was hot, sensuous, and demanding.

The urgency building, her body yearned for more. She sighed from the pleasurable sensations that overwhelmed her.

A frantic passion was overwhelming Flaming Arrow. He moaned as he felt the surges of warmth flooding through his body. Unable to hold the ecstasy back, he strained hungrily against her and gave one last, deep plunge, then groaned as he felt himself going over the edge.

Valerie felt his release. She closed her eyes and went with him to that private place of lovers as her own body quaked and shook with his.

Then everything was quiet, their bodies lulled by pleasure, their hearts beating as though they were one.

Flaming Arrow rolled away from Valerie and lay at her side, drawing her body up against his.

He lay his cheek against one of her breasts and soon fell asleep.

Valerie slowly ran her fingers through his hair. Tonight was magical, she thought to herself.

But what about tomorrow, and the day after that?

She could not help but be afraid for their future.

For many uncertainties lay in their path!

21

Take heed of loving me;
At least remember, I forbade it thee;
Not that I shall repair my unthrifty waste
Of breath and blood, upon thy sighs and tears.
—JOHN DONNE

Several days into the slow journey across the wide stretches of Montana Territory, Valerie's heartbeats quickened when she became more and more aware of familiar surroundings.

She had ridden often enough in the area close to her family's ranch to know that she was near it!

On the day she had become disoriented, she had taken herself, Brian, and Flaming Arrow much farther.

But now, this close, with bluffs and stands of trees that she had known so well, she knew for certain that once she turned a particular bend she would be home!

She glanced over her shoulder at Brian to see if he was also aware of where they were. She understood why he wasn't when she saw how busy he was chatting with his friends as they walked, leading their horses today instead of riding them, to break up the boredom of the journey.

Also to fight boredom, every once in a while the young braves would stop and have a pitching game with rocks to see who could throw them farthest. Sometimes, even, they would take their bows and arrows and shoot at small creatures such as grasshoppers, or at the bleached bones of buffalo that lay everywhere where the great herds had once grazed.

The young braves had taught Brian the skills of their bows and arrows. One of them, who called himself Dreaming Elk, had given Brian his bow and some of his arrows, and now spent his evenings fashioning himself another bow.

With such distractions, Brian was not aware of being close to home.

It even seemed to Valerie that he had forgotten any other way of life had ever existed.

"You seem suddenly so quiet," Flaming Arrow said, sidling his horse closer to Valerie's. "Is it because you are tired?"

"Somewhat," she murmured, smiling over at him.

Flaming Arrow glanced heavenward and saw how the sun was almost to the mountains. He then looked again at Valerie.

"We will stop soon for the night," he said, reaching a hand to smooth a fallen lock of hair back from her brow.

A thought came to Valerie that lit her eyes with excitement. If they were so close to her parents' ranch, why then could they not spend a night near it?

She knew of a perfect place where the Blackfoot could be hidden from passersby.

She and Brian had found a huge cave not far from where Brian had found his first arrowhead. It was even not far from where Flaming Arrow had once made his home.

Surely Flaming Arrow knew about the cave, as well! Perhaps that was where he was headed. "Flaming Arrow, do you realize where we are?" she finally blurted out. "That you are not far from where you once had your home? That I am not far from my parents' ranch? Both were within riding distance from the other, for Brian and I made the journey in less than an hour on the days we left home so he could search for arrowheads."

"I am very aware of where we are and that my people will soon pass by their original home," Flaming Arrow said sullenly. "Fox Eye's plans were for us to stay the night in a cave where lovers from my village went for their trysts, and where my people sometimes stored weapons that were used against whites."

He arched an eyebrow. "You say that your parents' ranch is also near?"

"Yes. I can hardly wait to see my parents," Valerie said, beaming. "And I can hardly wait for them to meet you, my husband. Will you go with me to meet them? Oh, Flaming Arrow, how relieved they will be to see that Brian and I are all right! I can hardly believe, myself, that we have found our way back home! We could have taken many directions that would have led us away from it!"

"Your eagerness for your parents to meet your husband might be premature," Flaming Arrow said, his spine stiffening. "Do you forget that I am a man with red skin instead of white?"

He paused and looked away from her for a moment, then locked eyes with her again. "Do you forget that in the white culture it is forbidden for a white woman to marry a red man?" he said thickly. "Your father might even shoot me dead for having taken you to my blankets."

Valerie's exuberance quickly waned.

She knew that what Flaming Arrow said about her parents might be true. Yes, her parents more than likely would be abhorred that she had not only slept with an Indian, but married one!

She looked quickly away from Flaming Arrow as a sudden shame and guilt for how the red man had been treated suddenly swept through her, for thinking like she did about her parents, fearing their reaction to her beloved, made her a part of the ugly prejudice.

Oh, how she wanted things to be different! How she wished to be able to ride up to her home and shout out to everyone that she had found the most wonderful man in the world!

Oh, how she wished they could look past his skin color and heritage and be happy for her!

But she knew how just how foolish she had been

to think it might be different. She could recall her father speaking harshly about Indians, calling them a filthy word: *savage.*

He had tried to pound into Valerie's heart the same prejudices, but she had looked beyond such feelings and even then felt regret for how the red man was treated.

She could understand why most Indians had learned to hate and resent white people.

"Is what I said so true it has made you become speechless?" Flaming Arrow asked, interrupting Valerie's thoughts.

She looked quickly over at him. "I would hope that I could expect better from my family, but, Flaming Arrow, you are right," she murmured. "My parents will be *quite* upset about my marriage to you." She swallowed hard. "But my father won't take a gun after you. He respects *me* too much to show such disrespect toward the man I chose to marry."

"And Brian?" Flaming Arrow said, his voice hollow with emotion. "Will they approve of how he has changed? How he mingles so freely among the young Blackfoot braves? Will they allow him to stay with my people? Or will they force him to stay with the whites?"

Valerie sighed deeply. She ran her fingers through her flowing golden hair. "I would hope that they will allow Brian to do as he wishes," she said softly. "Although he is still so young, he *does* have a right to his own choices in life."

"Knowing all of this, do you still wish to stop at your home, or do you think it is best to leave things as they are and continue on past the ranch as though it belonged to someone other than your family?" Flaming Arrow asked, his eyes quickly averting when he saw the high bluff that was the roof of the cave in which his people would spend the night.

"It would be cruel of me not to let my family know that Brian and I are all right," Valerie said, herself now seeing the cave and the thick brush that clung to the sides of the cliff and that grew at the entrance, hiding it from view.

"Then after I see that my people are comfortable in the cave we—you and I and Brian—will ride onward to your family's home," Flaming Arrow said, his voice sounding tired. "But we will not stay long." He reached over and ran a slow hand down her arm. "You need your rest. It has been a long ride today."

"Yes, I'm suddenly very tired," Valerie said, unable to stop a yawn as it fluttered across her lips.

"Tomorrow, and the days it will take after that, to construct the boats we will use for our water journey, you will also get your rest," Flaming Arrow said. His eyes suddenly lit up as he smiled at her. "We will also have time to wander off alone. There is never enough time alone with you."

"I wish we could take a vacation from life as it is and be totally alone for *months,*" Valerie said, laughing softly.

"Vacation?" Flaming Arrow said, arching an eyebrow. "What is that word *vacation*?"

"The word means a period of rest from work," Valerie said. "It means a time to have fun . . . a holiday."

"The word *holiday* is new to me also, but the word *fun* means the same to the Blackfoot as it does the white people," Flaming Arrow said, chuckling. "Celebrations and games are fun times for the Blackfoot."

He became somber again. "There is not much of that today among my people." His voice was drawn. "Perhaps in our new home in our new land fun will be resumed. My people will laugh and sing and enjoy!"

"Yes, I hope so," Valerie said, then grew silent, wheeled her horse to a stop, and watched several warriors cut the debris away from the entrance of the cave. Once the passage was cleared, Valerie watched the warriors enter the cave.

She jumped with a start when several bats came screeching from the entrance, flapping wildly and blindly around it, then flew away into the waning light of day.

The warriors were inside the cave for a short while, then came out and began carrying dried wood into it.

Soon the smell of a fire wafted through the air from the entrance.

"Surely the cave will be filled with the smoke and make it unlivable," Valerie said, glancing quickly over at Flaming Arrow as he dismounted and began loosening his travel bags.

"There are many cracks and crevices in the roof of the cave that will soon draw at the smoke and pull it away from my people's fires," he said. "Come. We will join the others making more fires and see that everyone is comfortable enough. After we share the evening meal with them, we will ride to your family's ranch."

"It will be dark by then," Valerie said, sliding from her saddle. "Is it wise to wait until dark?"

"It is wise *not* to," Flaming Arrow said, slinging one of his travel bags over his shoulder. "I cannot forget how close we are to Fort Harrison. Although the pony soldiers have left, I cannot shake my uneasiness about the fort's nearness."

"Thus far we've been lucky not to be confronted by anyone on the journey," Valerie said, lifting a rolled blanket from the back of her horse. "The gold fields are elsewhere, thank goodness."

She laughed softly. "My father thought he was near them when he built our home," she said. "When he discovered that he was many miles from the fields, he just contented himself panning for gold in the nearby river."

"Did he ever find any of the shiny gold rocks?" Flaming Arrow asked, reaching out a hand for Valerie.

She took his hand and walked with him toward the cave entrance, her attention drawn suddenly to

Brian, who was running and laughing with his friends as they chased a frightened jackrabbit.

A sudden shot rang out, silencing the laughter and causing the children to stop almost in midstep.

Fox Eye walked over, picked up the dead rabbit, and strolled casually away with it into the cave.

"His dinner," Flaming Arrow said, smiling over at Valerie as she looked quickly up at him. "But he will share it with others."

They went on inside the cave to join the others who were preparing themselves for their stay there.

Small fires popped and crackled. Blankets and thick animal pelts were spread out beside the fires.

After the evening meal had been eaten, the most elderly, men and women alike, rested against plaited willow rests, puffing their pipes.

Children huddled together, laughing and playing games with rocks and sticks.

Valerie went to Brian and led him away from the children. She stopped and turned him to face her.

"Brian, it's time to go now to let Mother and Father and Aunt Hillary know that we're all right," she said. "But I must warn you, honey, that things might not be all that pleasant when they know that I've married Flaming Arrow. And they will be adamantly against you staying with me instead of with them."

She framed his face between her hands. "Brian, are you certain that's what you wish to do?" she said, her voice drawn. "You truly wish to stay with me and the Blackfoot? You have to know that things will never be as easy for you with the Blackfoot than with the comforts of a white man. You have to know that no white woman will marry you once it is known you have associated so closely with Indians. Are you ready for those things? Can you accept them?"

Brian's sudden silence and a strange look in his heart sent a feeling of dread through Valerie's heart. Was he having second thoughts? Was he thinking that perhaps it was best not to stay with her and Flaming Arrow after all?

Had she painted too clear a picture for him of how it would be in the future if he remained with the Blackfoot? Did he want to cling to life as he had known it before he had met the Blackfoot, after all?

She was not sure if she could stand saying goodbye to her brother, although she was willing to say it to her parents. There had always been such a camaraderie between herself and her younger brother!

Life without him would not be the same.

"Brian?" she said guardedly.

22

Never seek to tell thy love,
Love that never told can be;
For the gentle wind does move—
Silently, invisibly.
        —WILLIAM BLAKE

"How can Mother and Father, and especially Aunt Hillary, who seems to have an open mind about so many things, be so unhappy about your marriage to Flaming Arrow, if they know that's what *you* want?" Brian said in a rush.

Valerie was relieved to know that the strange look in her brother's eyes was a look of puzzlement over *that,* instead of a look caused by suddenly realizing he was wrong to want to be a part of the Blackfoot's lives!

"Honey, I hope I am wrong," she murmured, drawing him into her embrace, hugging him. "And yes, surely I *am.*"

"I want to stay with you, Sis," Brian said, clinging to her. "No matter what Mother and Father say, please let me stay with you and Flaming Arrow."

"There is only one thing I can think of that might

make me think you should stay with our parents," Valerie said softly.

Brian crept from her arms and gazed up at her. "What is that, Sis? What could change my mind? What could change yours? I thought you truly wanted me to stay with you. Don't you?"

"Oh yes, I do," Valerie said, placing a gentle hand on one of his cheeks. "But perhaps I am being selfish. What if Mother is still not well and she wishes you to stay with her? Can you so easily deny her? Remember how ill mother was?"

She swallowed hard. "Oh, Brian, what if she has died?" she said softly.

Brian's eyes widened. "Do you think she might have?" he asked, swallowing hard.

"Oh, Lord, I hope not." She gave Flaming Arrow a worried glance as he came to her side.

"Sis, if she is still ill and she asks me to stay, must I?" Brian blurted out, giving Flaming Arrow a soft, worried look.

He again looked up at Valerie. "Sis, I love Mother, but I . . . but I . . . love *you*," he cried. "I could not bear being parted from you."

"Nor I, you," Valerie said, bending to her knees to take him again in her arms. "Let's just wait, Brian. Let's see how things are at home. Come on. The horses are ready. We'll go now and see. Surely things are just fine with Mother, Father, and Aunt Hillary."

Brian clung to Valerie for a moment longer, then eased from her arms and felt suddenly self-conscious for behaving so childishly when he discovered that his Blackfoot friends had come and had watched him with his sister.

He smiled awkwardly, then walked from the cave with Valerie and Flaming Arrow.

The moon was high and full as they rode away from the cave.

And when the bend in the road was reached where Valerie could see her family's ranch, a keen coldness swept through her when she saw no lamplight in the windows or any smoke spiraling from the fireplace chimney.

She gave Flaming Arrow a quick look of panic. "Something is wrong," she said, then sank her heels into the flanks of her horse and rode off in a hard gallop toward the ranch.

Flaming Arrow and Brian rode after her and did not yet catch up with her when she came to a sudden halt before she reached the fence that circled the ranch.

Flaming Arrow watched her slide quickly from her saddle and stand over something that he could not yet make out in the dark.

When he came closer and he saw a mound of dirt and a rugged grave marker made from a large stone, he knew that the news was not good for his woman.

Someone in her family had died.

Brian gave Flaming Arrow a questioning look after he also saw the grave and marker. Then he rode onward and wheeled his horse to a stop beside the grave. He scrambled from the saddle and fell to his knees beside Valerie.

Feeling almost paralyzed with fear, Brian studied the large mound of dirt, then ran his fingers over some etchings on the stone.

"Oh, Lord, no, the name on the marker is Royal Ross. It's Father's grave," Valerie cried, wiping tears from her cheeks with the backs of her hands. "Father is buried here, Brian. The moon is bright enough for me to read the inscription on the stone. It's Father's name, Brian. Father's!"

"Father . . . is . . . dead?" Brian stammered, tears streaming down his cheeks like falling rain. He crept into Valerie's arms and sobbed. "Father, oh, Father!"

Valerie held her brother close and was catapulted back in time when she had had the terrible nightmare about Bradley Hart and the wolves. When she told Flaming Arrow about the dream, he had told her that dreams portended the future.

Had her dream had nothing at all to do with Bradley? Had it, instead, portended her own father's death?

Knowing that she must be strong now for Brian, Valerie cast the troubled thoughts from her mind. She worked hard to hold her grief inside her.

She gazed over her shoulder at Flaming Arrow as he came and stood over her and Brian, then knelt on his haunches beside her.

"Father is buried here," she said as Flaming Arrow questioned her with his dark eyes. "His name is scratched on the stone, Flaming Arrow. My father is . . . dead."

"I am sorry," Flaming Arrow said, drawing both Valerie and Brian into his muscled arms.

Flaming Arrow looked past them at the silence of the cabin.

Why was there no lamplight in the windows, or smoke rising from the chimney from their lodge fire?

"I will go first to the cabin and see how things are there," he said.

He looked slowly from Valerie to Brian as they rose to their feet. "You both stay here," he said calmly. "Let me go first and discover the way of things. If it is safe enough for you to come on to the cabin, I shall motion for you to come."

"You think the rest of my family might be . . ." Valerie shivered at the thought of the words she could not bring herself to say.

"All I can say is that things are not normal at your family's lodge and I would prefer that you both wait until I see what is causing it," Flaming Arrow said, swinging himself into his saddle. "I shall go and look. If it is safe, then, and *only* then, do I wish for you to follow."

"All right," Valerie murmured, agreeing only because she knew that was how he truly wished it to be.

"Father was so strong," Brian said, bending to a knee to pluck a wildflower, placing it then on his father's grave. "How could anything happen to him? I . . . thought he was invincible."

"You should have realized that wasn't so when he lost everything we all loved in Kansas City," Valerie said, hating herself for having said it the moment the words slipped across her lips. This was no time to show any resentment toward her father for having loved gambling more than his family!

Especially now, when that had sent him to his grave, for it was for certain that had he stayed in Kansas City he would still be alive.

"I don't want to be like father," Brian blurted out. "I never want to gamble! I never want to pan for gold again! I . . . thought it was fun while doing it. Now . . . now . . . I know that had Father not hungered for this gold he might never have come here and died!"

Valerie looked quickly down at Brian, stunned that his logic was identical to hers. He seemed so grown up, of late.

At least that was one of the advantages of having come to the Montana Territory, as well as them both becoming so immersed in the lives of the Blackfoot.

Both seemed better for it!

As Flaming Arrow opened the door of the cabin and peered inside, silence and darkness greeted him. He looked cautiously around. The moonlight through the windows allowed him to see that at least *this* room was empty.

His hand on as knife sheathed at his waist, he

crept on into the cabin and moved stealthily from
room to room.

He soon discovered that there were no signs of
anyone living there.

The rooms had been stripped of their furnishings.
There were no cooking utensils in the kitchen.
There was only a strange odor in one of the bed-
rooms, something akin to medicine that white men
used on their ill. He had smelled it at the fort when
one of the soldiers had fallen sick. He had watched
the stricken man drink from a bottle that he called
his white man's medicine.

He recalled Valerie speaking of her mother's ill-
ness. Surely if she had died she would be in a grave
alongside her husband! The fact that she wasn't
had to mean her health had improved enough to
travel, for it was obvious everyone had left this
cabin.

Certain that there was no danger now, Flaming
Arrow went outside and, in the moonlight, waved
to Valerie and Brian.

He watched them ride toward him, and wondered what his wife's reaction would be when she
learned her family was gone, yet knowing not
where.

He knew by the family's absence that they had
concluded Brian and Valerie were dead, or surely
they never would have left until they knew for certain of their children's welfare.

Knowing that her father was dead was enough
of a burden for Valerie, but not knowing where

the rest of her family was would be like having lost them also to the dark claws of death.

As Valerie slid from the saddle, her eyes never left the cabin. Then she gazed at Flaming Arrow as he stood at the open door. Her heart sank. It was written on Flaming Arrow's face and in his eyes that the news was not good. Brian crept to Valerie's side and took her hand. They exchanged quick glances, then went on to the cabin.

Flaming Arrow stepped aside and watched them enter. He waited a moment, then went inside and watched them go from room to room.

Valerie fought back the tears that stung her eyes to know that her family *was* gone! But, oh, Lord, where? And why had they left?

Because her father had died? Yes, surely they had left because they did not feel safe enough staying there without her father.

"We'll never see them again, will we?" Brian suddenly blurted out.

"I . . . don't know," Valerie murmured, covering her mouth with her hand. "Oh, Lord, I doubt it!"

Brian fought the urge to cry. He had been a baby too often in the presence of Flaming Arrow! And now, with his father dead, he realized he was the man of the house!

Except that there was no house . . . no family for him to be the man for!

Brian could no longer hold back the tears. He brushed past Valerie and Flaming Arrow and ran outside, then held his face in his hands and sobbed.

"He's had so much to accept so quickly," Valerie said, going to the door to gaze out at her brother.

She welcomed Flaming Arrow's arms as he swept them around her. She turned and leaned into his embrace. "So have I," she whispered, choking back a sob. "So have I. I don't even know how Father died, or . . . or . . . why!"

23

Now quick desire hath caught the yielding prey,
And glutton-like she feeds, yet never filleth;
Her lips are conquerors, his lips obey.
     —WILLIAM SHAKESPEARE

Silent with their own thoughts, warm blankets snuggled around their shoulders to ward off the chill of early evening, Valerie walked with Flaming Arrow farther from the cave so that they could spend some time alone before returning to those who were preparing the evening meals over the campfires.

No white people had been seen in the vicinity since the Blackfoot had arrived there, and the warriors had felt it was safe enough to wander farther on their horses today to assure a good hunt so that their women and children could have meat in their bellies.

The wonderful aroma of cooking meat even now wafted through the air from the cave, stirring Valerie's stomach into several low growls.

After three days of hard labor for the Blackfoot—cutting the birch trees taking more time than actually building the canoes and rafts—the journey to the Blackfoot's new homeland could now proceed. But one more night in the cave was required to give those whom had worked endlessly building the canoes and rafts time to rest.

Tomorrow the true test came for the Blackfoot . . . when they would be traveling down the Missouri River.

Not only were their sailing abilities going to be tested, but also they would be setting themselves up as targets in the water as they traveled down the long river. They would be targets for whoever might decide to shoot at them.

It gave Valerie a sense of dread and foreboding to think of what could happen should the wrong whites see the Blackfoot. If they were like Bradley Hart, they would not even grimace while killing the innocent.

Flaming Arrow stopped and placed his hands on Valerie's waist. He turned her to face him. "Is it your family that you are thinking about?" he asked softly. "Is it your father's death, and not knowing where your family has gone, that causes your silence? Is it the fear of the approaching journey in the river? Or is it both?"

"It will take me some time to get over the death of my father, if I ever can, and I sorely miss my family now that I am totally denied them," Valerie said.

She reached her hands to her hair and ran her long, lean fingers through it to draw it back from her face. "Even Aunt Elaine and Uncle Harold," he murmured. "I'm not certain where they are. Yesterday, when you took me to their home and I found it also abandoned, I felt so . . . so . . . empty."

She sighed. "And yes," she said, "I am truly worrying about the river journey. What if—"

Sensing what she was about to say, himself carrying the same worries heavy on his shoulders, Flaming Arrow gently placed a hand over Valerie's mouth to seal her words behind her lips.

"It is only natural that you would be concerned about the river journey," he sad thickly. "But Napi, *and* your God, will guide us and protect us. Place your fears from your mind until you are given true cause to worry. Only when danger stares you in the face should you trouble your mind about things."

He laughed loosely, dropped his hands to his sides, then turned and walked again toward the river as Valerie walked beside him. "I preach to you about worries when I am guilty myself of being burdened so much with them I sometimes feel dizzy from it," he said.

He gave her a soft smile. "*Nito-ile-man,* my wife, we must learn from each other how to fight this worry demon," he said. "We need not have it in our bed with us when we make love. Nor should it be with us any other time. Shoo it away as you would a playful dog. Laugh about it as you would the feisty animal. Both our lives will be better for it."

"I don't want *any*thing to share our bed as we

make love," Valerie said, laughing softly as she tried to respond in the way he wished in his search for lighthearted talk. "Only you and I, Flaming Arrow."

She stopped, grabbed his arm, and spun him around to face her. "Only you, my love, my wonderful *no-ma*, husband," she whispered.

She twined her arm around his neck and brought his lips to her mouth. Their blankets fell away from their shoulders as they shared a frenzied kiss.

Flaming Arrow's hands slid up the inside of the skirt of Valerie's dress. She shimmered with ecstasy when he splayed his hand over the soft patch of hair at the juncture of her thighs.

When he began to move his palm over her there, she arched her hips forward and made it easier for him to touch that sensuous spot that always awakened to pleasure at even the mere *thought* of his hands, lips, and manhood being there.

Waves of liquid heat pulsed through her veins as he sank a finger deeply inside her hot, moist valley.

Her shoulders swayed as the ecstasy spread, his tongue surging through her lips, touching her tongue.

Skilled at keeping the magical spell that was weaving between them, Flaming Arrow held Valerie with one arm and led her downward, his knee spreading the blanket beneath her just before she touched the ground. Amid kisses and caresses they both quickly unclothed each other.

Valerie gasped with pleasure when Flaming

Arrow spread the full length of his body over hers. As he filled his hands with her aching breasts, the smoky pink nipples hard against his palms, with one thrust his manhood was inside her.

He swept his arms around her then and cradled her close as he began his rhythmic thrusts, his hard, taut body leading hers in a rhythm that matched his.

Flaming Arrow slid his lips from her mouth and whispered to her, his warm breath tickling her ear. "Tell me now what is on your mind," he whispered huskily.

"You, only you," she groaned in a whisper back to him.

She arched her neck back and moaned as he swept his tongue along its delicate curve while making his way down to her breast. When he clamped his lips on one of her nipples, she tremored.

She ran her hand slowly down his sleek, copper back and rested her fingers on his hips. She pressed them into his flesh, urging him to fill her more deeply with his heat, his magic.

Silvery flames licked through Flaming Arrow's consciousness. He moved faster inside Valerie, with sure, quick movements. His manhood throbbed. It felt as though it might burst as he held back the pleasure that knifed through his body in hot stabs. He wanted to postpone the final throes of ecstasy so that he could share these moments, which after today, until their journey was over, would be few.

Today was forever! It had to last forever!

He slowed his strokes within her. He leaned slightly away and gazed down at her, taken anew by her sweetness, by her utter loveliness.

"Do you know that you are more precious to me than breathing?" he said, his voice breaking with emotion when she reached a hand to gently trace the outline of his lips, then leaned a soft kiss to them.

"My *no-ma,* you *are* my breath, my heartbeat, my everything," she whispered back, then tremored sensually when he gave a deep shove and resumed his rhythmic strokes within her

"I cannot wait any longer," he whispered against her cheek. "I need you . . . I need fulfillment . . . now. *Now.*"

"Yes, yes," Valerie whispered back, her face flushed with the heat of the moment. "Now, my darling. Now!"

He twined his fingers through her hair and brought her lips to his in a demanding, hot kiss.

She swung her legs around his waist and her arms around his neck and rode him, her mind splintering into great bursts of light as she shared the moment of bliss with her husband while their bodies rocked and quaked.

When it was over, and they lay side by side, staring up at the darkening heavens, Valerie caught herself just short of speaking again of worrying about the journey on the river. The ecstasy of the lovemaking had lasted for only so long and now she was back to reality.

But instead of saying what she was thinking, not wanting to get Flaming Arrow immersed in the same concerns, she rose on an elbow and gave his cheek a soft kiss. "I'm hungry," she murmured.

"How can that be?" he said, his eyes twinkling into hers. "I just fed your hunger. You fed mine."

"I mean *hungry,* silly," she said, giggling as she sat up and grabbed her dress. "For *food.* For *food.*"

Flaming Arrow reached for his own clothes. "The word *silly* is a strange one," he said, drawing on his breeches. "I have never heard it used before."

Valerie was startled by Dreaming Elk's shouting her name, his voice growing louder as he searched for Valerie and Flaming Arrow. The young brave sounded worried.

Valerie could only believe it had to do with Brian. Why else would Dreaming Elk be seeking her out?

"Flaming Arrow, something has happened to Brian," she said, hurrying into her clothes. She ran her fingers through her hair as she waited for Flaming Arrow to finish dressing. Then they both grabbed up the blankets and ran in the direction of Dreaming Elk's continued worried shouts.

When they finally reached him, Valerie stopped and stared questioningly at Dreaming Elk. He peered up at her with a strange sort of foreboding in his eyes.

"Well? What is it?" Valerie asked, her heart

beating wildly within her chest. "Has something happened to Brian?"

"He is gone," Dreaming Elk said, his voice breaking. "I thought he was with other braves but discovered that no one has seen him. He has been gone for some time. We do not know where."

Alarm filled Valerie's eyes and heart. Since they had discovered her father's grave, Brian had been subdued. He hadn't joined the others in their games. He had sat away from the others, alone, forlorn, and strangely quiet.

She knew Brian was not yet mature enough to accept death as well as she.

"He's probably returned to Father's grave," Valerie said, her eyes lighting up with the hope of that possibility. She turned to Flaming Arrow. "Let's go and see if he *is* there," she urged. "And we must go quickly. Soon it will be pitch-black. I hate to think of Brian out there weaponless at night. He could become prey to many things."

"Dreaming Elk, run back to the cave and ready my horse and my wife's," Flaming Arrow said, taking Valerie's hand.

Dreaming Elk nodded. He turned quickly and ran ahead of them to the cave.

When Valerie and Flaming Arrow arrived, the horses were ready, and several warriors awaited on their mounts to ride with them in the search for Brian.

Valerie's pulse raced as she swung herself into the saddle. The cold air brushed against her cheeks and through her hair as she sank her heels into the flanks of her horse and sent him into a hard gallop across the shadowy land.

Impatient to see if Brian was at the grave saying a last good-bye to his father, Valerie could not ride fast enough.

"I wish you could sprout wings!" she shouted at her horse. "Hurry! Faster! I must find Brian before it turns too dark!"

A thought came to her that made her feel sick to her stomach.

Bradley Hart! What if Bradley had survived? What if he was responsible for Brian's absence? Yet there were no signs of the man anywhere.

No one had known how to take that news. No one knew if he was alive or dead.

"Oh, Lord, oh, Lord . . ." she whispered, her heart sinking as she worried that Bradley had found a way to get back at her through her beloved brother!

24

Hot, faint, and weary with her hard embracing,
Like a wild bird being tamed with too much handling.
—WILLIAM SHAKESPEARE

Armed with a bow, quiver of arrows, and a rifle provided by Fox Eye, Flaming Arrow was tense as he watched Valerie's abandoned family home come into sight. He had wanted to voice aloud his concern that it was not best for her to return where she had found such heartache.

He heard her quick intake of breath when the grave was only a few feet away. He saw the pain on her face and in her eyes, yet at this moment he could do nothing to alleviate it. Not only was she reliving the discovery of her father's death, she now also had concern for her brother to burden her heart.

If he could, he would wipe away all of this that lay before her. If he could, he would speak Brian's name and the young brave would be there!

But that wasn't possible. He could only hope that at the end of this search, Valerie would have cause to laugh, not cry.

Valerie wanted to stop at the grave and speak a soft prayer over it again, but her concerns for Brian took precedence. She had been foolish to think she could ride up to the grave and so easily find Brian there! He had been gone for many hours. Had he come to visit the grave, he would be gone by now.

She gave the desolate cabin a long, lingering stare as she rode past the grave. Although she saw no horse reined outside, perhaps Brian had left it elsewhere out of caution. Perhaps he was in the cabin, revisiting memories of his family.

She, too, would like to take the time to sit down inside the cabin, close her eyes, and allow the memories to flood her. Perhaps if she thought hard enough about her mother's arms wrapped around her, she might feel them! If she thought hard about her Aunt Hillary's laughter, she might truly hear it! If she concentrated hard enough she might even smell her father's pipe tobacco as he sat beside the fireplace smoking!

She shook her head. There was no time to get sentimental. She had to find Brian!

And once she did and saw that he was all right, oh, how she would like to take a switch to his bare legs like Father always had when Brian had been too mischievous for his own good. Going away today alone and not telling anyone where he was going was the worst of her brother's careless behavior. She had thought that he had matured at least enough to know better!

Oh, but if only she could find him at the cabin,

no, she wouldn't spank him. She wouldn't even
scold him. She would hug him until her arms ached
and he begged to be released!

Her horse barely stopped when Valerie dismounted and ran to the cabin. It was dark now,
and in the moonlight, the cabin looked mysterious
and very alone in the middle of the stretch of land
her father had claimed as his own upon their first
arrival in Montana Territory.

She became lost in thought again, remembering
how much fun it had been to build the cabin, log by
log, then to fill it with laughter once it was finished.

She would never forget the first fire on the grate
or the first meal eaten on their dinner table. She
would never forget the family's plans for their first
Christmas there, how they would place the tree in
front of the living room window.

Her fingers trembling, and paying no heed to
Flaming Arrow and his warriors as they rode up
outside and stopped, Valerie shoved the door open.
She held her breath when she stepped into the
room and looked slowly around her.

She placed a hand to her mouth and stifled a sob
behind it when she saw no one there, heard no
sounds other than a lone cricket that hid in one of
the corners.

"Brian," she said, still holding out hope that he
might be in one of the other rooms. She looked
overhead at the loft bedroom . . . *Brian's* bedroom.

A keen hopelessness assailed her when she saw

no movement, heard no sound when she spoke Brian's name again . . . and again.

"He is elsewhere," Flaming Arrow said, as he stepped up behind Valerie. "His horse is not tethered anywhere outside the lodge. There are no signs that he has been here."

Valerie spun on a heel and gazed up at her husband. The moon was seeping through the window enough for her to see his face and the pain in his eyes—pain for her, for he knew her so well, and knew how she would be worried over Brian.

Feeling helpless, Valerie moved into her husband's arms. Sobbing, she clung to him. "Why did he do this?" she cried. "Brian knew the risks of going out alone. I've warned him enough times. So did Father and Mother! Why would he not listen to anyone but his own sense of adventure?"

"We shall look until we find him," Flaming Arrow said, holding her close. "Come. Let us leave now and resume our search."

"Yes, let's go," Valerie said, easing from his embrace.

She wiped her cheeks and her eyes free of tears with the backs of her hands, then walked outside with Flaming Arrow. She turned and took one last look at the cabin, then followed him to the horses and mounted her steed as Flaming Arrow swung himself into his own saddle.

They turned away from the cabin and rode again past the lonesome grave.

Feeling empty inside, Valerie stared at the

mound of dirt with the wilting flower Brian had placed on it earlier when they had visited it together and whispered the final farewell to their father.

"I will see you in heaven someday," she whispered. "I love you, Father. I love you."

The moon now high overhead, gilding the land even more with its sheen of white, Valerie rode alongside Flaming Arrow as they searched in the night. Just as they were ready to turn back and return to the cave, a voice filled the night air that caused Valerie's heart to lurch with joy and gladness.

"Brian!" she cried as she saw his black mustang riding toward her, Brian waving at her from his saddle.

She sank her heels into the flanks of her horse and rode in a thunderous gallop toward him. When she reached him and they drew a tight rein beside each other, Valerie reached over and gave him a firm hug.

"Where have you been?" she cried, her voice almost hysterical. "Brian, you gave us all such a scare."

Brian returned her hug, but his eyes were on Flaming Arrow, who had pulled up alongside Valerie. He could hardly wait to tell Flaming Arrow what he had found! Never had Brian been as excited as the moment he discovered it lying beneath a thick brush of briars. The scratches on his hands and arms were worth having rescued such a gift!

It had been good for himself, also, to have something special to do to help erase the heaviest burden of grief from his heart. He now felt as though he could move on with his life. He had been childish long enough, pining away over his losses!

"Brian, answer me," Valerie said, leaning away from him to study his face, so glad to have an opportunity to see it again!

Then she gasped and paled when she saw how bloody and torn his hands were.

She reached for his hands slowly. "How did this happen?" she said, her voice breaking. "Did some wild animal claw you?"

Brian eased his hands away from hers and smiled at her. "No, Sis, there was no animal," he said. "And I'm sorry I frightened you. When I left the cave I had no idea it was going to get dark so soon. You know how I so badly judge time."

"Yes, I know," Valerie said, reaching over to tousle his already wind-whipped golden hair. "Now tell me. Why *did* you leave the cave without telling anyone? Why did you venture out like this alone? Didn't you know how much you would worry me? How much you would worry Flaming Arrow and all of your friends?"

"I'm sorry," Brian said, again gazing over at Flaming Arrow. "But I had good intentions."

"Like what?" Valerie dropped her hand away. "Did you return home? Did you revisit father's grave? Is that where you've been?"

"Yes, I did both those things," Brian said, his

eyes now locked with Flaming Arrow's. "But I did something more than that."

He turned his eyes down to his saddlebag. He winced when he scraped his sore fingers and hands against the leather as he reached inside to get his prize. When he pulled free the other half of the painted arrow that he had found earlier, Valerie gasped.

Flaming Arrow's eyes widened and his heart raced.

"I just could not rest until I searched again for the other half of Flaming Arrow's arrow," Brian said, resting the shaft in his hands, holding it toward Flaming Arrow. "Flaming Arrow, I found this today. Please take it. You now have a complete arrow."

Flaming Arrow was so touched by what Brian had done he was at a loss of words.

His eyes misting, so filled with gratitude toward this child, he took the arrow shaft and held it over his heart.

"Thank you, young brave," he finally managed to say. "What you have done today goes beyond friendship. We, you and I, are sealed now forever in a special bond."

Valerie was so touched by the scene, renewed tears streamed from her eyes. She flicked them away and smiled when Flaming Arrow held the arrow into the air and emitted a series of cries and chants, his warriors soon following, filling the night air with the marvel of it!

"Let us return now to our people," Flaming Arrow said, sliding the arrow shaft into the quiver of arrows at his back. "Napi has kept this brave safe! As did Napi guide him to my medicine! My arrow! I feel assured now that all will be well for us on our journey to our new home! Tomorrow! Let us look forward to tomorrow with glad hearts and wide smiles!"

As they rode off, Brian, flanked between Flaming Arrow and Valerie, gave Valerie a look of apology. "Sis, I am so sorry that I worried you," he said.

He then laughed softly. "I'm sorry I worried my-*self*." he said. "For a while there I felt as though I were lost. You know how we got disoriented that day when Flaming Arrow wanted us to take him to our home? Well, when it got dark and everything seemed as though it were fusing into one place, I got scared. I had just found my bearings when I saw you. I was on my way back to the cave."

"But it *could* have been so different," Valerie said, frowning at him. "You could have been lost for*ever*. You . . . could have died out here and no one would even find your body. Don't you recall the bleached bones of the animals we've seen on the trail? Brian, do you think those animals were ready to die? It could be your bones lying there someday for someone to stare at . . . for someone to . . . to shoot at with their guns or bows and arrows!"

She knew that she was painting a horrid picture for her brother, but she felt it was necessary. She wanted to put such a fear in his heart that he would never be this recklessly foolish and foolhardy again. No arrow was worth what might have been. Nothing was worth it!

"I had to find the other half of the arrow, or at least give it one last try," Brian said, seeming not to have listened to one word Valerie said. "It's his medicine, Valerie. To Indians, their medicine is more important to them than the prayers we say to our God."

"Brian, I don't care *why* you did this." Her voice was sharp. "Just don't you ever do anything like this again or . . . or . . . by God, I'll appoint someone to keep an eye on you."

"You wouldn't," Brian gasped.

"Try me," Valerie said, stubbornly firming her chin.

"You would be treating me like some helpless baby!"

"I would do anything to keep you safe," Valerie said, reaching over to gently touch his cheek.

She was glad when he didn't brush her hand away.

And she could tell by the wavering in his eyes that he understood that, though her warnings were a bit far-fetched, they were spoken only out of her intense love for him.

"I'll not scare you like this ever again, Sis," Brian

said, smiling at her. "I'm sorry I did tonight. Forgiven?"

"Forgiven," Valerie said, then reached for his hand and turned it from side to side. "Now let us get back to that cave and take care of these hands."

"We don't have any medicine," Brian said, flinching when just moving his fingers pained him.

"The Blackfoot medicine has healed their people from the beginning of time," Valerie said, gazing over at Flaming Arrow, admiring him anew as he rode so straight and tall in the saddle, his long hair flowing on his broad shoulders. "I'm sure it will be adequate for us."

"I wonder what sort they will use on my cuts," Brian said, sliding his hand away from Valerie.

"Made from herbs gathered in the forest, I'm sure," Valerie said. "You know . . . similar to the medicine Flaming Arrow made for you when the spider bit you."

"Oh, no, not mud again," Brian said, groaning.

Valerie threw her head back in a long, sweet laugh.

Flaming Arrow looked quickly over at her. Although he did not know the reason for her laughter, it was good to see her laugh again. It made his heart sing!

25

Love me, that I may die the gentle way.
To let me live, O, love and hate me, too.
—JOHN DONNE

Valerie sat with Brian just behind Flaming Arrow in their canoe, her eyes absorbing everything around her as her husband took long, masterful strokes with his paddle through the water.

The windblown grass had been left behind, as well as the Yellowstone River that ran through the Montana Territory.

They were now several days into the river voyage down the Missouri. The many canoes filled with the Blackfoot people rhythmically glided through the river, while the most muscular of the Blackfoot warriors manned the great, large rafts that carried horses, mules, and supplies.

As the sun set each evening, the procession stopped. The people rested, ate, and slept until the break of the next day.

And then the journey began anew, one long day seeming now to blend into another.

Valerie could not help but worry about the most elderly of the travelers. Each day of travel seemed to take more toll on them. Their faces showed their weariness, their eyes seemed to have lost their luster. Many had grown ill on the days when the wind blew incessantly, the high, quivering waves thrashing against the sides of the canoes seemingly endless.

But they had much more to endure before it was over. It was still quite a distance to the state of Missouri.

The sun was sinking in the sky, bringing an end to another day on the water. Valerie frowned when she looked on either side of the river and saw huge clay banks looming gray and somber in the waning light. If they did not find a place where there was easily accessible land, they would have to travel onward into the night.

And there were dangers in that. The moon was now only a tiny sliver in the sky at night and made no light for which to guide travelers. The water as well as the land blended into the blackness of night like an ink blot, making navigation impossible.

"Sis, I'm so tired," Brian said, scooting closer to her, snuggling beneath her blanket with her. "Will we ever stop today? I'm beginning to hate this river. Will *it* ever stop?"

Valerie gently placed a hand on her brother's head and brought it down to rest against her chest. "You'd best get used to the river, Brian. We have many more days to spend on it," she murmured.

"*Then* I imagine you will grow weary of land travel, for I am certain Flaming Arrow won't make his village the minute we reach Missouri's soil. He has a vision for what he wants for his people's home. He will search until he finds it."

"At least while we are on land me and my friends can find ways to fight off the boredom," Brian said, sighing.

As a spray of water hit him in the face, he shivered. "And I'm so cold," he said, taking the corner of the blanket to wipe his face dry. "I can hardly wait to sit by a warm, cozy fire tonight."

Again Valerie looked at the high bluffs on each side of the river. She then gazed at the sun and saw that it was just now slipping behind those bluffs. Soon it would be gone from sight, as would the warmth it gave to the travelers, and its light.

"Damn the bluffs," she whispered, drawing Brian's eyes up to stare at her. "Whoops, sorry about that, Brian. Seems my language fits my mood, for I am also bone-tired and weary of the journey."

"When we traveled to Montana Territory with our family I don't remember it being so grueling and long," Brian said, reaching for a drier corner of the blanket, drawing it up more closely beneath his chin.

"That was because we traveled on a comfortable paddle wheeler," Valerie murmured. "Thank goodness Father had enough money left to pay, at least for the most part, our passage from Kansas to Montana in a boat."

"I wish we could find a paddle wheeler that would take pity on us and sail us the rest of the way to Missouri," Brian said, again sighing. "But that's wishful thinking, isn't it, Sis? It just won't happen."

"Even if a riverboat came by, it would not offer passage," Valerie said, her voice drawn. "No captain of a riverboat would offer passage to Indians, especially so many."

She looked over her shoulder at the large rafts and the animals being held steady on them by warriors. "Although I know that riverboats carry animals, they most certainly wouldn't carry as many as the Blackfoot are trying to transport," she said.

"So far the Blackfoot are lucky to have lost only four horses in the water," Brian said, himself looking across his shoulder at the animals. "And that was because the waves frightened them the other day when the wind was so strong. I bet more will be lost before it is over."

"Yes, I imagine," Valerie said, hoping it would only be animals that would go overboard in the river—not innocent people!

A sudden long whistle slicing through the air jolted her. She jumped with a start at the second blast, the whistle this time long and ear-splitting.

Brian jerked quickly away from her and clasped his hands over his ears, straining his neck to look past Flaming Arrow and see where the whistle was coming from downriver.

Flaming Arrow's insides splashed cold at the

sound of the riverboat's whistle. It was too near! And where there were riverboats, there were many white people.

Thus far they had not encountered a paddle wheeler while in the water. But often, while still on shore making camp, they had seen more than one slide past, lamplight bright on the top deck and in the windows.

Seeing Flaming Arrow's back go stiff and his jaw tighten, Valerie scampered from her seat and crawled closer behind her husband. "It's a paddle wheeler," she said, her voice showing that her fears matched her husband's. Not only was a riverboat filled with white people cause for alarm for the Blackfoot, but also the great paddle itself, which churned the water into something dangerous for smaller river vessels.

Especially canoes!

"I do not see it yet," Flaming Arrow said, looking ahead to a bend in the river. "We might have time to get our canoes closer to land before the boat gets this far."

"But the river is low," Valerie cried. "There are so many sandbars. Your canoes might get grounded on them or, worse yet, capsize."

"We have to take our chances," Flaming Arrow grumbled, making a wide swerve left toward shore with his canoe. He looked over his shoulder at his warriors and shouted at them to follow him.

Valerie's eyes widened when they rounded the bend enough to see the riverboat. It was no threat to them at all! *It* was grounded helplessly on a large sandbar on the right side of the river. That was why it incessantly blew its whistle—the crew were trying to attract attention any way they could to secure help in getting freed from the sandbar.

"Flaming Arrow!" Valerie cried. "Look! The river boat is going nowhere! It's stuck! Please hurry and instruct your warriors to continue traveling mi-driver. We can get past the riverboat without problems! Hurry, Flaming Arrow, or our fate might be the same as the paddle wheeler's."

When Flaming Arrow saw the large white boat, he smiled broadly and guided his canoe back away from the dangerous shore and once again toward the middle of the river, his warriors following his lead.

Valerie went back to her seat behind Flaming Arrow and clung to it. Her knuckles were white with the tight grip as Brian sat down beside her again, his eyes wide. As they reached the large white paddle wheeler, there was still enough light to see the passengers standing along the rail of the deck, and the surprise in their faces as they watched the long procession of canoes and rafts approaching them.

Valerie's pulse raced as Flaming Arrow guided the canoe onward and soon came side by side with the paddle wheeler. She looked guardedly up at the people, so close now. She tightened inside when she saw the ship's captain standing away from the others, his fists on his hips as he glared at the Blackfoot passing by.

She could tell by the slow smile on his lips that he purposely nodded to one of his crew to blow the whistle now, surely in an effort to frighten the animals on the rafts enough that they might spill over the sides. But the man in charge of the whistle seemed transfixed by the sight of so many Indians. He reached up to yank on the rope but did not pull it.

Valerie could see the captain turn and shout at him. She could even make out the word "fool" as he stamped over to the man and took the rope away from him.

Fearing the worst, Valerie sucked in a wild breath and waited for the whistle, but was stunned when she saw a man step up to the captain and force him away from the whistle. It was a man whose skin was the color of the Blackfoot's, though his hair was golden and he wore white man's clothes.

"Sun Dance," Flaming Arrow gasped, recognizing the man as a friend he had made many years ago at a trading post. Sun Dance was a half-breed—part Blackfoot, and part white. The two men had hunted together many times since then.

Flaming Arrow had lost track of his friend when the government interfered with their lives and ordered the Blackfoot onto a reservation.

Sun Dance, being part white, had gone elsewhere.

"You know him?" Valerie asked, amazed at the coincidence.

"Yes, I know him well," Flaming Arrow said, giving a proud wave to his friend. "We are *nisah*, blood brothers."

Valerie gazed at the half-breed and smiled as he looked down at her.

Then her face paled and everything within her went cold as she discovered another face among the crowd . . . a face she had seen in many of her nightmares . . . a face she thought she would never see again!

"Bradley," she whispered, the word like poison on her tongue and lips.

"What did you say?" Brian asked, turning quickly to stare at Valerie.

"Nothing," Valerie was quick to say, for she didn't want anyone but herself to know that the man everyone hated was still alive.

Someone had found him and took pity on him and had surely not offered him lodging and clothing, but booked passage for him on the riverboat.

What was worst of all was the direction of the paddle wheeler. It was headed away from Montana Territory. Its destination was somewhere to the south, which could include Missouri.

Valerie realized that as long as this man was alive, he was a threat to herself and her husband's people. Especially now . . . now that he had seen the Blackfoot's exodus from Montana Territory and knew that they had fled reservation life, which was illegal in the eyes of the white authorities.

"Sis, tell me what's wrong," Brian begged, turning to look up at the boat as the canoe continued to slide past. "You look as though you've seen a ghost."

"I wish I had," Valerie said, swallowing hard.

"What do you mean?" he persisted.

When Valerie turned a stern look toward him, his eyes widened and he became quiet.

"Brian, *please* quit being so inquisitive."

She felt it was best not to tell anyone she had seen Bradley Hart. She would keep her fears hidden inside her heart and pray that they were needless—that Bradley wouldn't be able to ever again stand in the way of the Blackfoot's destiny. He had no idea where they were going, so how could he become involved in their lives again?

Something drew her eyes to stare again at the riverboat as Flaming Arrow's canoe took her on away from it. Her heartbeat quickened when she saw a lone man at the far end of the paddle wheeler watching the Blackfoot procession of canoes and rafts. He had separated himself from the others to take a better, lingering look.

Valerie was still close enough to the boat to see the man's face. Her heart sank. It truly *was* Bradley!

Suddenly their eyes locked in silent battle and she knew for certain that they were not yet finished with one another.

She knew him well enough to be certain he would search until he found her again, especially now that he knew she was a challenge again to fight for. Away from the reservation, and the laws that guarded it, she and the Blackfoot people were vulnerable to anything that that madman might try to do to them!

26

The last I saw in all extremes is fair,
And holds me in the sunbeams of his hair,
Her nymph-like features such agreement have
That I could venture with her to the grave.
                    —JOHN DONNE

The canoes and rafts beached now forever, the horses and travois now once more the Blackfoot's mode of transportation, the city of St. Louis, Missouri, was not far from where they had chosen to leave their water travel behind.

As they traveled onward toward the city, Valerie looked around her at the rolling hills and forests, at the small streams that worked their way across the fertile land. It was a beautiful place, one that she recalled with much fondness when her parents had ventured through on their way to Montana Territory before they booked passage on the riverboat. It was a good land that was good to the people.

She gazed at a field of sunflowers. "Towers of life," her mother had called them, so tall, their golden flowers with their central black seeds so elegant.

She had learned one particular day long ago to call the sunflowers "ambush flowers"! She smiled as she recalled a time when she was a child and she had been visiting Aunt Elaine and Uncle Harold's farm on the outskirts of Kansas City.

Sunflowers dominated her aunt and uncle's flower beds in front of their big red barn. The sunflowers had become "towers of life," all right, expanding the size of the flowerbeds with their height alone.

The cavernous mouth of her uncle's barn served to attract paper wasps. Valerie remembered watching one such wasp one day as it was investigating every crack and crevice of the barn's structure and its curiosity carried it closer to the open door and the wall of mature sunflowers that bordered both its edges.

As the wasp neared the heavy growth of sunflowers, a gray form lashed up from its concealed place and seized the wasp. A sharp, spikelike tube protruding from the mouth of the wasp-killer penetrated the wasp's body.

When Valerie ran to her uncle and told him what she'd witnessed—horrified yet also intrigued by it— her uncle explained how a bug similar to a preying mantis yet smaller, called a mantid, hunted for its prey in the lower stalks of the sunflowers. It was nettled in grays and browns, and judging by its actions, it was always hungry.

Valerie and her uncle went to the flowers and watched the mantid, and every time a fly came close, the mantid's head and predatory eyes would swivel and focus on the fly's movement as the fly explored the plants, then suddenly the fly was caught and consumed.

When one area of the sunflower plants failed to produce enough food, the mantid would move to another where the flies seemed more numerous.

This went on and when it was growing late Valerie and her uncle decided to help the mantid. They stunned several houseflies and a hover fly with a fly swatter.

Each of these they offered to the mantid by placing them on the upside down sunflower head where the mantid waited in ambush.

The mantid eagerly accepted the houseflies but refused the hover fly. Perhaps the brightly contrasting black and yellow bands of the hover fly warned the mantid of a toxin or poison found in the fly's tissues.

Realizing they were now within close proximity of St. Louis, Valerie was brought from her deep thoughts and glanced quickly over at Flaming Arrow. "Where are you going to make our village?" she asked, holding back a queasiness that now troubled her each morning, so much that she dreaded even the smell of food, and much more the taste of it. "I think this, right *here,* would be a wonderful place for your children to grow up into adults."

"You are familiar with the area?" Flaming Arrow asked, sidling his horse closer to Valerie's.

"You do know this place where we are at well enough to advise establishing our village here?"

"Yes, it's a place of peace and beauty," Valerie murmured. "And with St. Louis now so close, you would have a place to trade. Along the waterfront many people come with their pelts and garden products for trading, red and white alike."

"The Blackfoot would be accepted?" Flaming Arrow asked. "There are no nearby forts where there might be conniving colonels and agents?"

He frowned when he saw her gulp hard, as though she were swallowing back something that was distasteful to her. He had seen her do this the past two days, and when he had questioned her about it, she just brushed it off as nothing. He was beginning to think that it was more than that. He was afraid that his wife might be ill.

"Yes, there *is* a fort," Valerie said, feeling dizzy now from the queasiness. This time it just wouldn't leave. It was worse than any of her previous attacks. "Fort Jefferson Barracks is up the Mississippi River from St. Louis. But it is a friendly fort to Indians. If you wished to go there and introduce yourself to them, you would be readily accepted. I'm sure they would offer a pipe to be smoked to prove their peaceful intentions toward you."

"I doubt there is any white man's fort that is without some prejudice against redskins," Flaming Arrow said.

But his heart leaped when he saw Valerie's shoulders begin to sway. He reached out and grabbed her as her eyes closed and she fell into his arms into a dead faint. Flaming Arrow drew her from her horse and onto his lap. He raised his hand and ordered his people to stop. Holding Valerie close in his arms, he slid from his saddle and carried her over to the embankment of a creek.

The Blackfoot came and stood around him, silent as they watched him bathe Valerie's pale face with water. Star Dancer, with whom Valerie had made a fast friendship these past several days after land had been reached, came and knelt down beside the couple.

Brian ran over and knelt at Flaming Arrow's other side, his eyes anxious. "What is wrong with my sister?" he cried, reaching out to touch Valerie's lily-white cheek. "Why is she so pale? Why did she faint? Is she ill? Flaming Arrow, please tell me she isn't ill."

"Young brave, do not be afraid," Star Dancer said, covering his hand with hers. "Your sister is not ill. It is something beautiful that has caused your sister to faint."

"How could fainting be beautiful?" Brian cried, yanking his hand away. "Can't you see? Something is terribly wrong with Valerie."

"The cause of her fainting spell is something wonderful for you, Brian, and for you, Flaming Arrow," Star Dancer said, dipping a buckskin cloth in the water, slowly dabbing it across Valerie's brow. "It is even something more wonderful for Valerie, for she will experience the true wonders of a child growing in her womb. *She* will feel its first kick!"

"Child?" Brian and Flaming Arrow said at almost the same moment.

Flaming Arrow gazed in wonder down at Valerie. "She is carrying my child?" he said, stroking his long, lean fingers through Valerie's golden hair.

"All symptoms point to it, for they are the same that I experienced when I became pregnant with my first child," Star Dancer said, smiling at Valerie as Valerie's eyes began to slowly open.

Valerie's eyes widened when she found herself on the ground, her head resting in Flaming Arrow's lap.

She looked quickly around and saw everyone watching her expectantly. Then she gazed up at Flaming Arrow. "What happened?" she asked, slowly rising from the ground.

"You fainted," Flaming Arrow said thickly. He brushed her hair back from her eyes. "How do you feel now? Do you still feel dizzy?"

"No, I don't feel dizzy," she said, but swallowed hard when she felt the bitterness rising again in her throat. She had felt this way since the morning meal. It was almost time to stop for the noon meal and she dreaded it!

How could she explain to everyone why she would rather that someone else prepare the food for her husband and brother? Even *she* didn't understand why she had such a revulsion for food!

Again she looked around her at the people. Her

gaze lingered on Star Dancer, who was kneeling beside her. There was something about the way Star Dancer was gazing at her.

Valerie looked quickly at Brian, who had the same look of wonder in his eyes!

"Brian?" she said, raising an eyebrow.

She glanced back at Star Dancer, and then around her again at how everyone else seemed to be holding some sweet secret inside their hearts as they smiled at her.

She then looked up at Flaming Arrow and saw that he, too, was looking at her as though she were something very special . . . something to be in awe of!

"Why is everyone looking at me like that?" she blurted out. "I . . . I . . . just fainted, that's all."

"Sis, it's more than that," Brian said, beaming.

Valerie quickly sat up. "What do you mean?" she said softly.

She was truly puzzled when Star Dancer quickly rose to her feet and went around the circle of people, whispering. Soon everyone left, except for Flaming Arrow. Even Brian had gone off with the others.

She watched the people busy themselves, rearranging their travel equipment or brushing their horses or washing themselves in the creek quite a distance away from Valerie and Flaming Arrow.

It was obvious to Valerie that she and her husband had been left alone for a purpose.

She gazed almost timidly at her husband. "I

guess I'm the only one who doesn't know what's going on here," she murmured. "Do you want to tell me or leave me guessing?"

"If what Star Dancer says is true about your condition, why you fainted, we, you and I, are to be blessed with a child," Flaming Arrow said, his eyes dancing. "My wife, all of your symptoms are those of a woman who is carrying a child within her womb."

Suddenly it came to Valerie how her mother had behaved during her early pregnancy with Brian!

She'd had the same fainting spells.

She couldn't stand to be in the same room with food that was cooking on the stove!

For the first several weeks of her mother's pregnancy, *she* couldn't stand to eat!

She had lost a lot of weight, and when the morning sickness, as her mother had called it, had passed, *then* she had made up for lost time and had eaten until she had blown up almost like a toad.

"I'm with child," Valerie murmured.

She softly placed her hands over her abdomen. She felt mushy warm inside to think of a child growing in her womb.

Her eyes bright, her smile wide, she gazed up at Flaming Arrow. "Darling, we are going to have a baby!" she cried.

She flung herself into his arms, her excitement greater than at any other moment in her life. To be carrying the child of the man she loved was something so wonderful she could hardly contain herself with the joy she felt over it.

Flaming Arrow held her close. He burrowed his face into her hair to hide the tears that burned at the corners of his eyes, his own joy matching his wife's. "A child," he whispered. "Ours. Yours and mine."

"I will give you a son first and then a daughter," Valerie said. "I know the importance of sons to Blackfoot warriors . . . to their *chiefs*. It will be a son, my darling. I promise you."

Flaming Arrow chuckled. "It is good that you wish so hard for your husband," he said. He framed her face between his hands and gazed lovingly into her eyes. "But, my wife, if the first child is a daughter, this husband would be as elated as were it a son, for a daughter in my wife's image will make this husband's heart sing!"

"Of course you would say that to lessen my disappointment if the child I carry is not a son," Valerie said softly. "Hear me now, my *no-ma*, husband, I *will* give you a son first. I *will*."

"When the child is born, whether it is a boy or a girl, you will be so proud you will forget such promises made today," Flaming Arrow said, chuckling.

"Yes, I know that I will," Valerie said, returning his smile. "It's just that I want so much for you. A son would be a great gift to such a husband as you."

"A daughter would be as great a gift, for I have

held many a friend's newborn daughter and could not get over their tininess and sweetness," he said softly. "When such a daughter is placed in my arms, and I know it is *mine,* it would be a time of magic miracles."

He rose away from her and looked around him.

His eyes widened when he saw that his people had started making camp. A huge fire had already been built beside the creek. Someone had even gone out and killed a deer with his silent arrow. The meat was already dripping its juices over the fire.

Valerie also saw what was happening. "Your people saw that you needed more time with your wife at such a moment as this," Valerie said, taking his hand as he helped her from the ground. "Your people are astute to their chief's needs. If only it could be that way among the white community. So many people are selfish and only look out for themselves and their own needs. Your people work as a unit in all things."

"This is why I wish to have the best for my people," Flaming Arrow said, slipping an arm around Valerie's waist as they both stood and watched the activity around them. "I *must* find the best place for their new home."

Valerie badly wanted to encourage him to go on to Kansas where she had been raised as a child. Perhaps even her family had returned there! But she knew that there were several forts in Kansas that did not take kindly to Indians settling there.

It was best *not* to go there.

"I'm sure you will make the right choice," she

said, then felt the terrible stinging in her throat and knew that this time she could not hold back the urge to retch.

She yanked her hand from Flaming Arrow's and ran quickly away from him, getting only a few yards before it burst forth. She fell to her knees and leaned her face toward the ground as she threw up until nothing was left in her stomach.

A soft hand was suddenly on her brow, followed then by a cool, wet compress.

"Come with me," Star Dancer murmured. "My husband has made a lean-to for you and Flaming Arrow. I encouraged Flaming Arrow to go on there as I tend to you and your discomfort. He is not familiar with these women things, so he did as I asked. He waits for you. Let me help you go to him."

"I wish he hadn't seen me . . . seen me . . ." Valerie said, her knees so weak she could hardly stand as Star Dancer helped her to her feet.

"It will not be the only time he sees you like this," Star Dancer said, laughing softly. "It will be several sunrises before you feel like yourself again. I know. I have gone through this five times with five sons."

"Five sons," Valerie said softly. "How proud your husband must be!"

"As proud as your husband will be when your child is born," Star Dancer said. She helped Valerie to the pile of soft blankets just inside the lean-to, where Flaming Arrow awaited her.

"Until you feel better I will prepare the food for your family," Star Dancer said. She placed her hands at the small of her back as she straightened, revealing her own swollen abdomen, a *daughter* hoped for this time.

"I don't even want to think of food," Valerie said, wincing. "But thank you for helping me in chores that I cannot bear to do right now myself."

"It is always good to do for others," Star Dancer said, then waddled away as her five children, ranging from age two to eight, came and walked with her to their own lean-to.

"There goes a good woman," Flaming Arrow said, then held out his arms for Valerie as she moved into his embrace. He held her close and slowly rocked her back and forth, as though she were a child, he the father. "My *nita-ile-man,* wife, my love and pride of you could never be greater than now," he murmured.

"I wish you hadn't seen me. . . ."

"I will see more than that in the days and weeks to come," Flaming Arrow said, chuckling. "I have seen many pregnant women in my time, you know."

"But this time the pregnant woman is your wife," Valerie said, sighing.

She still could not believe that she was going to have a baby!

It did seem a miracle that she was pregnant, especially now, when she had recently lost her father . . . and perhaps not only him, but also her mother, Aunt Hillary, Aunt Elaine, and Uncle Harold.

It was nice to have something good and wonderful to erase the bad.

27

Here love received immedicable harms,
And was despoiled of his daring arms.
—JOHN DONNE

The sun had just cleared the horizon, and sparkling hoarfrost covered everything. The frost was so fragile that a breath would send it swirling away.

Valerie sat away from the others and sipped on some broth for breakfast while everyone else ate something more substantial. She recalled the autumns of her past when the pumpkins lay ripe on the ground in her mother's garden in Kansas.

She would never forget the first time her mother had shown her how to carve faces into the pumpkins after their seeds and insides were removed. It had delighted her so when her mother had placed a candle inside the hollowed-out pumpkin and lit it, causing the face on the pumpkin to seem to come alive.

At night when they had placed the pumpkin on the porch for everyone else to see, Valerie had enjoyed sitting outside on her swing that her father had hung from a tall limb of a tree and just sit for hours watching the fluttering of the candle in the pumpkin.

And when Brian became old enough to enjoy such things with her, they had delighted in seeing who could carve the funniest face, and then whose candle would burn the longest inside their pumpkins.

Next autumn she would have her own child to introduce to the magic and mystery of pumpkins in the autumn. Although her child would be too small yet to understand it, at least the child could sit and watch the fluttering candle through the face of the jack-o-lantern.

Dressed in his warm buckskins, a blanket wrapped around his shoulders, Flaming Arrow stepped away from the others and sat down beside Valerie, their fire warm and cozy inside their tepee. Although decisions had not yet been made about where they would establish their village, after Flaming Arrow had heard of Valerie's pregnancy he made certain she had a much warmer and more comfortable place to spend the night. He and Fox Eye had erected the tepee in less than fifteen minutes!

"Is the broth adequate enough for you this morning?" Flaming Arrow asked, repositioning the blanket that hung around her shoulders. "Are you warm enough?"

"I get the feeling that while I am pregnant you

are going to spoil me rotten," Valerie said, laughing softly.

"And you do not enjoy being spoiled?" Flaming Arrow asked, his eyes twinkling.

"By you?" Valerie said, setting her empty bowl aside. She snuggled against him and sighed. "Yes, darling. I will enjoy every bit of your pampering."

"Are you warm? Is the broth enough?" he repeated, placing a finger beneath her chin, urging her eyes up to meet the concern in his. "You must not go too much longer without eating that which will not only benefit you, but also the child."

"The morning sickness should soon pass, and then, like my mother when she was pregnant with Brian, I will make up for lost time," Valerie said. Her gaze absorbed his handsomeness. She felt so fortunate that he loved her . . . was her *husband.* "You will then urge me to stop eating, for I imagine I will get as fat as a butterball."

"Butterball?" he said, raising an eyebrow. "What is a butterball?"

"Oh, darling, it is just another way to say things in an effort to be amusing," Valerie said, smiling up at him. "Do you find me amusing this morning, husband?"

"I find you beautiful and radiant," he said, bending to brush a soft kiss across her lips.

He turned away from her and shoved a log into the flames of the fire. "I have made a decision that might please you," he said, giving her a quick glance.

"You have?" Valerie scooted closer to the fire and pulled the blanket more closely around her shoulders. "What sort?"

He shoved another piece of wood on the fire. "As you suggested, we *will* make our home here in Missouri, on this very land where we have stopped for the night," he said thickly.

Flaming Arrow wiped the dirt from his hands on the tail end of a blanket, then sat down before Valerie. He took her hands in his. *"Nito-ile-man,* my wife," he said, "you have told me how you admire this land called Missouri. I have observed myself the beauties of the hills and valleys. I have seen enough wildlife to know there will always be food on our tables and enough hides for our people's clothes. As you said, there is this place called St. Louis where my people can trade. I believe everything we wish a home to be can be found here."

Surprised by his quick decision, Valerie was for a moment at a loss for words. She gazed at him, her lips parted, her eyes wide.

"Why are you truly staying here?" she blurted. "You never hinted earlier about staying. I thought you were going to venture just a bit farther and see what else the land had to offer."

"Things changed when I discovered your pregnancy," Flaming Arrow said, taking her hands, affectionately holding them. "You have been forced to travel far enough on my people's quest to find a home. The child has endured the travel thus far. But who is to say how it would fare if we continued onward? I have seen how tired you have been in the evenings. And since you cannot eat adequately as you should, due to your pregnancy, you are not as strong as you would normally be. Traveling under those conditions is not good for you *or* the child. We will stay here. You will get rest. And soon you can begin eating foods that will give you your strength again and the nourishment that is necessary for the child to be born healthy into this world."

"You care so much for the child," Valerie murmured, near tears. "You care so much for *me*."

She slipped her hands from his and hugged him. "Oh, darling, how I love you," she murmured. "And yes, whatever you think is best for me and the child will make me happy. I believe your people will do well living here. It is a lovely place for us all to make our home."

"I shall bring my people together today for a council and tell them my decision," Flaming Arrow said.

He drew away from her when Fox Eye spoke his name outside of the lodge. Flaming Arrow's jaws tightened, for he heard too much caution in his warrior's voice. He had spoken Flaming Arrow's name quietly and guardedly.

Valerie sensed her husband's sudden tenseness. "What is it?" she said, gazing at the closed entrance flap when Fox Eye once again spoke Flaming Arrow's name.

Flaming Arrow discarded his blanket and secured a sheathed knife at his waist.

"Darling, it's only Fox Eye," she said. "You look as though it might be someone else . . . an *enemy*."

"Fox Eye's voice reveals to me that perhaps an enemy is near," Flaming Arrow said, going to the entrance flap. He turned and gazed at Valerie. "Or someone who might be, in the future. Caution must be used in this new land until we are certain we are welcome."

Valerie was now aware of an approaching horse outside the tepee. She scrambled to her feet, clutched her blanket more snugly around her shoulders, and stepped outside with Flaming Arrow.

She stood stiffly beside him as he and his people silently watched the white man's approach. He was alone. She could see he was a young army lieutenant.

Valerie had to believe that the soldier was from Fort Jefferson Barracks. She knew that most of the soldiers there were friendly with Indians, yet there were always those who thought of all men with red skin as savages.

The soldier wheeled his horse to a stop beside the large outdoor fire and he looked slowly around him, one hand resting on a saber to his right side. No one spoke or welcomed him.

"Who is in charge here?" the young lieutenant asked, his blue eyes still roaming, his uniform neat and clean beneath the soft rays of the early morning sun. "Who is chief? What tribe are you from?

I've never seen you before. Where do you hail from?"

Still no one spoke to him.

Valerie was getting nervous, wondering why Flaming Arrow did not approach the man and introduce himself.

But Flaming Arrow knew this soldier was young for his rank. Those could be the worst kind, feeling a need to prove themselves to their superiors. What better way to prove oneself in uniform than to stand up against a band of Indians?

When the soldier's eyes finally found Valerie, he gaped openly at her in surprise. He was further surprised when he saw Brian, as Brian stepped up beside Valerie and stood square-shouldered beside her, meeting the man's studious gaze with steady eyes.

The lieutenant dismounted and walked over to Valerie. "Ma'am, why are you and this lad with Indians?" he asked, clasping his hands behind him. "What tribe is it? Can they speak English?"

"She is my wife and the young brave is her brother," Flaming Arrow said suddenly. "And as you can see, I can speak English well enough to know what you are saying. I am Blackfoot. I have led my people from Montana Territory to find a new home. I have chosen this place. Everyone will soon be building their lodges. My warriors will soon be hunting on this land and making trade with your people."

This was the first time the Blackfoot had heard

this news, and they gazed at their chief. He understood the silent question in their eyes. He had not had time yet to tell them of his plans.

The soldier looked more closely at Valerie. His gaze raked slowly up and down her body, and then he gazed into her eyes. "You have married an Indian?" he said, his involuntary shiver proving his disgust. "You . . . fornicate . . . with an Indian?"

Insulted, embarrassed, her very soul inflamed by the man's rudeness, Valerie stepped up to slap him in the face. But sensing what she was about to do, Flaming Arrow took Valerie's hand and gently held it to her side.

"You are here for what purpose?" Flaming Arrow said, controlling his own temper. He had not thought to be tested so quickly in this new land. And a man insulting his wife was truly the worst test of all!

Flaming Arrow wanted to fight for his wife's dignity, yet this was not the time. His whole band of Blackfoot would suffer.

"I am here because I saw your fires," the lieutenant said. He again looked slowly around him, at the number of Indians who circled him. "It has been some time since a band of Indians took Missouri land as their own."

"It is theirs to take, is it not?" Valerie said, boldly lifting her chin.

"If it were up to me, I'd tell you and your Indian friends to hightail it outta Missouri," the young lieutenant grumbled. "But it isn't my duty to give those orders."

Valerie sucked in a wild breath when he swung around and mounted his horse. He gave Valerie one last lingering stare, then wheeled his horse and rode away without another word.

This frightened Valerie. She knew that he would report what he had seen to his commander.

She turned to Flaming Arrow. "I'm afraid," she cried. "That young man is going to be nothing but trouble for us."

"We will take it one day, one soldier, one intruder at a time," Flaming Arrow said, pulling her into his gentle embrace. "I did not expect things to be easy. The Blackfoot learned long ago the trials and tribulations of being red-skinned instead of white. We have endured. So shall we still."

"The soldier was so . . . so insulting," Valerie said, gazing up at Flaming Arrow.

"The insult cut like a knife into my heart, yet I could not fight for your honor," Flaming Arrow said, swallowing hard. "My people are in a new land. They are facing new challenges, new hates, new prejudices. It seems you are a target now for the hate. Can you live with that? Insults are something familiar to the Blackfoot—to you they are not. Can you accept them, turn the other cheek, and go on your way as though it was not spoken to you?"

"For you and your people, yes, I can do whatever I must to assure your safety," Valerie murmured.

She watched Brian, who was now scampering with his Blackfoot friends—ah, so quickly having forgotten the soldier. But she couldn't forget him that easily. She knew he would urge his commander at the fort to confront the Blackfoot.

She prayed that the fort's leader would be a decent, caring man, who saw all men as one no matter the color of their skin.

Would the army force them to return to the reservation? That was her worst dread of all, to think that they might be made to take the long journey back to the Montana Territory! Winter was near, and they would meet it head-on during the long weeks it would take to return to the reservation.

She was not sure if even she, or the beloved baby inside her womb, could even survive the journey. Pregnant women were vulnerable to all kinds of sicknesses. She'd heard stories of the many women and unborn children who had died during the long wagon trains that came west.

"Let's leave now for Illinois." She begged Flaming Arrow with her eyes. "I don't feel safe here. Please, Flaming Arrow, let's take down our lodge and leave today!"

"I will not be frightened off this land like a cornered mouse in a cornfield!" Flaming Arrow said thickly. "We *will* stay. It is best for you. It is best for the child!"

"But I'm so afraid," Valerie said, clutching his hands.

Flaming Arrow had never seen this side of his

wife before. Stunned by it, he was not sure what to say in return. She suddenly seemed so vulnerable . . . so tiny. It was up to him to protect her, not only from those who might frighten her, but also her own feelings of fright.

"Be not afraid, for I will protect you," Flaming Arrow assured her. He drew her against him and held her tightly in his embrace. "Do you think that I would ever make decisions that might harm you . . . or our child?"

"You know as well as I that sometimes good intentions are not enough," Valerie said, wanting to take back the words the minute she said them. She could feel her husband stiffen and take a quick breath.

"I'm sorry," she murmured, gazing up at him. "I shouldn't have said that. Forget that I did. And forget what I said about being afraid. I'm not any longer. Truly I'm not. Things will be all right. God is looking down at us from heaven. Your Napi is, also. Did they not guide us safely here? Not one man or woman or child was lost on the long journey. Nor will anything happen to any of us now."

"Let us go now and sit in council with our people," Flaming Arrow said, turning to gaze at everyone who still stood waiting for his leadership.

He raised a hand in the air and looked toward them. "Let us sit around the fire and warm ourselves as we have council," he said. "As your chief, I have much to say to you. You must listen closely. All of our future depends on each of us understanding this new life I have led you to. As you saw by the presence of the white soldier moments ago, life here will still have its times of stress and anger. But we will learn to live with it! We at last are no longer confined to a reservation!"

Valerie gave him a guarded look. She couldn't help but dread the arrival of the commander from Fort Jefferson Barracks. If he hated the presence of the Blackfoot enough on land that was in his jurisdiction, he *could* evict them. He could even order his soldiers to escort them back to the reservation.

Valerie knew that this was just the beginning. She knew now that her life with the Blackfoot would always be one of uncertainty, for that was what they faced every day. Knowing that made her sorely sad—and ashamed—to have been born into a society that made life this way for the red man.

She placed a hand over her abdomen and thought what her child would be born into . . . a time of hate and prejudice against all redskins.

Her child would be a "breed," a word that brought disgust in the eyes of most white men!

Her jaw tightened. She would fight with all her might for the rights of the children born of her love of Flaming Arrow!

She slid her hand into Flaming Arrow's and sat with him on a blanket close to the outdoor fire.

Pride filled her as she watched him stand and talk to his people about his plans. She could tell by how they listened so intently that her husband would always be revered by his people. They saw in him a man of wisdom.

She knew that whatever he told them they would believe. They trusted him implicitly.

She silently prayed that no overbearing army commander would wipe away that trust in one order—the order to return to Montana Territory. She was afraid that, if that happened, her husband might decide to take up arms.

She wasn't sure just how far her husband's patience would run when it was tested to the limit.

28

He that cannot choose but love,
And strives against it still,
Never shall my fancy move,
For he loves 'gainst his will.
—JOHN DONNE

Valerie lifted the entrance flap of her tepee and gazed outside. The sun was just rising. Ascending into the air, thin columns of smoke were creeping from the smoke holes of the tepees that had been erected after the people's council yesterday.

In the distance she heard someone chopping wood for their morning fire. Dogs trotted about, their tails wagging contentedly. Stretching and yawning, children were just beginning to emerge from their lodges.

Valerie sighed. She was glad that, though a full night had passed since the young lieutenant had stopped and questioned the Blackfoot, no other soldiers had come to the campsite. She hoped that meant the commander had not become concerned about the young lieutenant's news of the new arrival.

As Valerie recalled, the young lieutenant had not

even asked for the name of the Blackfoot chief. Nor hers and Brian's. Surely that showed even his disinterest in them all.

"Do you think you can eat the morning meal today?" Flaming Arrow asked. He moved up behind Valerie, slipped his arms around her waist, and drew her around to face him. "The pot of boiled meat that Star Dancer brought to us is warming over the fire."

"I do feel somewhat better this morning," Valerie murmured, smiling up at him. "Yes, I do think I will try my luck at eating."

"The baby will thank you for it," Flaming Arrow said, laughing huskily. He placed a gentle hand over her abdomen. "Soon, when I place my ear to your stomach, I will feel our child's movements. I have watched other expectant fathers do this when their woman is large with child. I have seen their eyes light up with a radiance that is rarely seen in a warrior's eyes. I, too, will show such pleasure at feeling our child."

"Father swore he could hear Brian's heartbeat when mother was pregnant," Valerie said, memories of that moment tearing at her heart, for each day now she seemed to miss her family more than the last. "But, my darling husband, you will have a long time to wait for such discoveries as that. Mother was almost ready to give birth when father said this."

"Sis, can I go ahead and eat?" Brian asked from

behind them, breaking into Valerie and Flaming Arrow's sweet and tranquil moments.

Valerie swung away from Flaming Arrow and sat down beside Brian before the lodge fire, the flames sending their warmth into the hidden shadows of the tepee. "Yes, you can eat now," she said.

She lifted a wooden spoon and ladled the boiled meat into a wooden bowl for Brian, then glanced up at Flaming Arrow. "Darling, I'll dip you some meat, also," she murmured.

He seemed not to hear. In his eyes she saw a sudden wariness. He was cocking an ear toward the entrance flap. A sudden fear swept into Valerie's heart.

Horses! She could hear the approach of many. Their hooves sounded like distant thunder; she could even now feel the pulse of it in the ground beneath her.

"Sis, what's wrong?" Brian asked, looking from Valerie to Flaming Arrow. "Why are you both suddenly so quiet?"

Then he quickly placed his bowl to the floor. "Horses!" he said. "Do you hear the horses approaching the campsite?" His eyes wide, he moved slowly to his feet. "There . . . are . . . so many," he gasped.

"Yes, I hear them, and yes, there are many," Valerie said, rushing to her feet.

She grabbed Brian by the hand and walked outside the lodge with Flaming Arrow.

Flaming Arrow shoved them behind him and

stood tall and straight as he awaited the arrival of the cavalry who were now in sight, the soldier's sabers at their sides glistening in the morning sun. "Stay behind me or go back inside the lodge," he said flatly to Valerie and Brian. "Let me do the talking."

Valerie nodded. Now that she had the baby to protect, she would no longer do anything foolish that might risk its life. But it was hard not to watch the soldiers' approach, fearing the luck of the Blackfoot might have just run out.

Flaming Arrow stood tall and tight in his buckskins. He had left his weapons inside the lodge. He felt that it would best benefit his people if he faced such a number of soldiers without the threat of a weapon to anger them.

It was obvious to Flaming Arrow that the young lieutenant had done his duty well by revealing to his commander the redskins' arrival on Missouri soil. The chief would have expected no less from his own warriors. But now he had to wait and see what the commander's feelings were toward the newcomers.

Would the soldiers choose to make war against the Blackfoot? Or were they arriving with peace on their minds and in their hearts?

When Flaming Arrow saw two faces that he recognized among the horsemen, hope for the future of his people waned. He could not help but believe that he soon would be leading his people back to the reservation, and this time under a military escort.

The commander of Fort Jefferson Barracks was none other than Colonel Randall Thiel. The very man who had imprisoned Flaming Arrow at Fort Harrison! Colonel Thiel's promotion had taken him from the Montana Territory to Missouri.

And the other man whose face was like a sharp thorn in Flaming Arrow's side was Bradley Hart! He was riding beside Colonel Thiel, his face etched with hatred, his hand resting on a holstered pistol at his right side.

Flaming Arrow sucked in a quavering breath to think that this man, who was everything evil, was still alive and had found his way to the very land that Flaming Arrow had chosen for his people!

Fate was like a twisted rope ... as though it were around Flaming Arrow's throat, tightening ... tightening ...

Brian sneaked a peek around Flaming Arrow. He gasped and paled when he recognized Bradley Hart. Trembling, knowing what the presence of that man with the cavalry might mean, he jumped back again behind Flaming Arrow.

Valerie saw Brian's reaction, how he was trembling and how wide his eyes were. "Who did you see?" she whispered. "Brian, you look frightened to death. Who did you see?"

"Sis, I don't think you want to know," Brian said, giving her a wavering look. "Oh, Sis, how could it be that Bradley Hart is here? He's alive and he's riding with the cavalry. He's surely been appointed Indian agent for this area."

Valerie felt a sinking at the pit of her stomach. She recalled seeing Bradley on the grounded riverboat, staring holes through her when he had seen her gazing up at him.

At that moment she had known he could be trouble for her and Flaming Arrow's people, yet she had not expected it to be this soon, or in this capacity.

"He's riding with the cavalry?" she whispered, taking Brian's hand and squeezing it. "That doesn't have to mean he's going to cause harm to the Blackfoot . . . or to us, Brian. Just keep faith in Flaming Arrow's ability to talk to them. I'm sure things will be all right."

A double line of troops remained at the edge of the newly established village, and Colonel Thiel rode on through the campsite. His eyes never left Flaming Arrow. The Blackfoot chief stood at the end of a long line of people who stepped back and made way for the colonel. Bradley Hart rode quietly beside him.

The Blackfoot chief's eyes shifted from Bradley to the colonel and back again. The Indian band hated both men, for their experiences with them had been ugly.

The colonel had imprisoned their chief. The agent was evil through and through and had survived the punishment the Blackfoot had devised for him. Now they both were surely there to reek even worse havoc than before on the Blackfoot.

Colonel Thiel and Bradley Hart drew a tight rein before Flaming Arrow, but Bradley positioned his horse so he could get a direct look at Valerie as she stood behind Flaming Arrow.

As their eyes locked, Valerie defied him with a set stare and lifted chin. Not wanting Bradley to think she was frightened of him, she yanked on Brian's hand and urged him to follow her as she stepped up and stood boldly at Flaming Arrow's side.

She could see Flaming Arrow's quick glance and knew that her action displeased him. Yet she would not let Bradley see her cowering like some frightened ninny!

"Flaming Arrow, we meet again," Colonel Thiel said, his voice tight. He nodded toward Bradley. "And I imagine you remember Bradley Hart? Well, Chief, he's just been hired on at Fort Jefferson Barracks as my Indian agent. Seems the world is small sometimes, isn't it?"

Flaming Arrow's lips were tightly pursed as he glared at the two men.

"Lieutenant Dunn came to me yesterday with the news that you Blackfoot had arrived on Missouri soil," Colonel Thiel said, running a finger around his tightly starched collar, his shirt spanking white against the blue of his uniform. His brown hair had been recently trimmed and lay neatly just above his collar line.

The colonel leaned forward and rested an elbow on one of his knees as he stared at Flaming Arrow.

"You still have nothing to say?" he said, arching an eyebrow. "Or are you afraid to? You know as well as I that you should be back in Montana Territory confined to a reservation. If Fort Harrison hadn't been closed, you'd still be behind bars. You'd best open up now, Chief, and explain yourself."

"You know that reservation life is like a prison for all men with red skin," Flaming Arrow said stiffly. "You know that it is not a fair thing to do to people whose land was wrongly taken from them. The treaties signed by my forefathers were wrong treaties. My people must be free to live as they have lived since the beginning of time. They must be free to hunt where they wish to hunt! They must be free to trade with whom they wish to trade! This land called Missouri offers all of these things to my people."

He paused, then took a step forward. "Would you again deny my people those things?" he asked thickly.

"I never, alone, forced your people on the reservation," Colonel Thiel said, clearing his throat nervously under the close scrutiny of so many Blackfoot. "It was not even I who wrote the orders that put you in the stockade at Fort Harrison. Although I have the impressive title of colonel, there are others above me who give me orders. I follow them."

"Are you saying that someone besides yourself will decide whether or not we Blackfoot will stay where we have placed our lodges now?" Flaming Arrow said, folding his arms across his chest.

"If *I* say you will stay, you will stay," Colonel Thiel said, squaring his shoulders. "In my new position at Fort Jefferson Barracks I have more authority than I had in Montana Territory."

"And what will you say?" Flaming Arrow said, prodding. "Stay? Or go?"

"Make them leave," Bradley Hart bit out. "I told you what they did to me. I'm lucky to be alive."

"I know you well, Bradley," Colonel Thiel said flashing Bradley an irritated look. "I've hired you as an agent here in Missouri only because you are kin. But, Cousin, were you just an ordinary man asking for a job, I'd deny you. I know what little you did for the Blackfoot in Montana Territory. They had just cause to resent you."

"But they sent me away, unclothed, with all intentions of letting me die," Bradley said, his voice a thin whine. "Send them away. I don't want to have to deal with them."

"That can be arranged," Colonel Thiel said, his eyes gleaming. "I know several men who would enjoy having your job. Are you ready to move on? Or shut up?"

His face red from embarrassment, Bradley glared back at the colonel, but clamped his mouth tight and said nothing more.

"That's more like it," Colonel Thiel said, sighing.

He again gazed at Flaming Arrow. "You can stay," he said softly. His gaze shifted to Valerie. "And as for you, I know you are the chief's wife. Stay away from the fort. I don't think my men would take kindly to knowing that you, a white woman, are married to a redskin."

Valerie had always known how white people felt about white women marrying Indians. But never had she felt that they would be this openly prejudicial! Yet the soldiers would surely look to her as someone who had committed the forbidden.

She would hold her head high. *She* knew how wrong the white people were who looked to the Indians as savages. That was enough to make her know that she could live with such malice toward her.

Colonel Thiel shifted his gaze back to Flaming Arrow. "But, Chief, any time some of your pretty young things wish to come to the fort and entertain my *men,* they are more than welcome," he said, his eyes dancing. "My men get lonesome. They don't care whether the woman's skin is white or red, just as long as they get what they want from them. They don't intend to marry those they fornicate with . . . just have fun with them."

It took all of Flaming Arrow's willpower not to grab the colonel from his horse and hit him. But besides those insulting words, thus far, things were amicable enough between himself and the colonel. He must control himself. As it stood now, this new land was the Blackfoot's to use!

"None of my people's daughters will be play the woman for soldiers," Flaming Arrow said sullenly. He gestured with a hand toward where he knew the city of St. Louis stood on the waterfront. "Tell your men to go elsewhere and find white women who are willing to lift their skirts."

The colonel laughed throatily, then became solemn. "You'd best tell your warriors to behave themselves while living close to my fort," he said, his voice filled with a low measured warning. "You make sure the warriors know their limits . . . what's expected of them. Tell them to watch their step. Most white men are not eager to befriend a redskin. But of course you know that, don't you?"

"My warriors, my people, follow my lead, for I am their chief, their *voice*," Flaming Arrow said, lifting his chin proudly. "What I say, they will do."

"Good," Colonel Thiel said. "Chief, come to the fort tomorrow. We will have council. We will share a smoke."

"I will consider the invitation with an open heart and mind," Flaming Arrow said, his eyes locked with the colonel's.

"Do that," the colonel said, his voice measured.

The colonel and Flaming Arrow stared quietly at one another for a moment longer, then Colonel Thiel wheeled his horse and nodded at Bradley Hart. "Come on, Brad," he said. "Let's get home. My wife has a pretty thing she wants you to meet. Cousins must look after cousins, right?"

The colonel's booming laughter could be heard as he rode off with Bradley and joined the others. They all rode away, leaving a strained silence in the Blackfoot village.

"They are really gone?" Brian was first to break

the silence. "They are allowing us to stay?" He tugged on Flaming Arrow's shirtsleeve. "Do you trust them, Flaming Arrow? Do you truly trust them?"

"I believe I can depend on the colonel keeping his word," Flaming Arrow replied "But Bradley Hart? No. I do not trust that man. He has a hunger for revenge written in his eyes. He will find a way to feed it!"

Valerie was stunned that the Blackfoot had gotten through this confrontation with the colonel so easily. They had fled reservation life and were not going to be forced to return!

But the more she thought about it, the more she understood. It was apparent to her now that all that the government had cared about was taking the land from the Blackfoot in Montana Territory, for the gold that had been discovered there and for the riches found in the animals and land. Once *that* was achieved, it didn't seem to matter where the Blackfoot decided to live, after all—whether it was in Missouri or on the moon!

Yet she could not be comfortable with what had happened today. Although Colonel Thiel bragged about being in charge here, was he truly? Valerie could not help but be afraid that things had been just too easy today.

What of tomorrow?

And what of Bradley? she thought, a tremor coursing through her veins. He was not one to let things go this easily.

He would be back.

29

No lover saith, "I love," nor any other
Can judge a perfect lover;
He thinks that else none can, nor will agree
That any loves but he.
                    —JOHN DONNE

Valerie was surprised when Flaming Arrow awakened her early the next morning and told her to get dressed . . . that she was going on an outing with him.

She presumed he was going to the fort for his council with Colonel Thiel. She was stunned that he was including her. Colonel Thiel had made it clear he didn't want her at the fort, *ever*.

But she did not question her husband. She knew that if her husband had chosen to include her, he had thought this decision over carefully. In his heart he surely felt it was right that she should arrive at the fort by his side.

Nevertheless, as she dressed in her finest beaded buckskin dress, she felt anxious about not only the colonel's reaction, but also that of all the soldiers stationed there.

Valerie rode beside Flaming Arrow away from

the village. She worked hard at hiding her uneasiness. She expected to be humiliated by the colonel and his men.

If so, she was afraid that her husband would not stand by and allow it. And if Flaming Arrow defended her honor in the presence of so many soldiers, who was to say what their reaction might be?

They might imprison him and start a full-scale war with the Blackfoot, for she knew that Fox Eye would never stand for his chief to be imprisoned again, not for even one day. And if Fox Eye arrived at the fort painted in war colors?

"Today is a surprise day for my wife," Flaming Arrow said, making a wide right turn through the tall grass.

Valerie's eyes widened. He had taken a turn in the opposite direction of the fort.

"Darling, the fort is to the left, not the right," she said, though she wished to go anywhere today with him but to Fort Jefferson Barracks.

"I am aware of where my travels take us," Flaming Arrow said, smiling mischievously at her. "That is a part of the surprise I mentioned. Where I *am* taking you."

"Where?" Valerie sidled her horse closer to his. "Why be so mysterious about it? All along I thought you were going to the fort."

"I did not mean to cause you anxiousness about the fort," Flaming Arrow said as it dawned on him what she must have thought. "I thought that you knew that I would never take you there, especially after the colonel insulted you and told you to stay away. I thought you surely knew that my surprise today had nothing to do with the fort."

"But you told Colonel Thiel that you would go there today and have council with him," Valerie murmured.

"I made no promises to anyone that I would go to the fort for council," Flaming Arrow grumbled. "I doubt I shall ever go there. If council is held, it can be held in our village where we are surrounded by Blackfoot, not by whites."

"I'm so glad," Valerie said, sighing with relief. "I don't think the colonel has good intentions by asking you to the fort. I don't trust him. Do you?"

"There have only been a few whites in uniform that I have trusted," Flaming Arrow said thickly. "And Colonel Thiel is not one of them."

"I can hardly believe that Bradley Hart is an agent again," Valerie said sullenly. "Heaven forbid he comes to our village trying to use his powers as agent. You know that he will *never* come with good intentions."

Seeing that talking about Bradley made her husband uncomfortable, Valerie smiled and leaned closer to him. "Now tell me more about the surprise," she said, her eyes dancing.

"We are going to the city of St. Louis to acquaint ourselves with it before my people go there to trade," Flaming Arrow said. "Not only is my purpose for going there today for my people, but also for you, my wife. I sense that you miss being among white people."

Valerie tried to look excited over the prospect, for under any other circumstances she would be anxious to go there. But she had begun to realize she would be shunned at St. Louis, traveling with her Indian husband.

She wasn't sure if she could stand much more of this . . . but she wasn't concerned so much for herself. She was frustrated over how people could be so pompous and shortsighted . . . so prejudiced! If they only knew the wonderful man her husband was, no matter the color of his skin, they would understand why she chose to marry him!

"Yes, I will enjoy our outing today," she forced herself to say. "It soon will be too cold to travel far. And with my pregnancy, I soon shall have to refrain from getting on a horse."

"That is so," Flaming Arrow said, dropping his hand down to pat his buckskin travel bag. "And because you may not get to travel with me again to St. Louis until our child is born, I have brought pelts today to trade so that you can experience how it is done. I shall search for a special necklace for you for which to trade my pelts. *Nito-ile-man*, wife, would that please you?"

"Very much," Valerie said.

Then she thought that she heard something in the deep shadows of the forest at her left side. She looked guardedly over at Flaming Arrow. "Did you hear that?" she murmured, then looked past him at the bluff that ran along the Mississippi River not far from where they were traveling. There was a sharp drop-off at the very edge of the bluff. Should they become threatened by a traveler, there would be dangers in being so close to the bluff.

Flaming Arrow didn't have a chance to respond to her question. Bradley Hart was suddenly there blocking their path, a rifle aimed at him. His eyes flashing angrily, Flaming Arrow reached over, took Valerie's reins, and drew her horse to a shimmying halt along with his own.

"Get off your horses," Bradley said, motioning with the barrel of his rifle. "Now! Do as you are told! I've got you dead in your tracks! You don't dare make a wrong move or I'll plug you both!"

Valerie glanced over at Flaming Arrow.

He nodded to her, a silent way of telling her to do as Bradley said. As she slid from her saddle, Flaming Arrow swung out of his.

"Bradley, reconsider what you are doing," Valerie said, glad to have Flaming Arrow's protective arm around her waist. "You know that if any harm comes to us, you won't only have the entire Blackfoot nation to answer to, but also Colonel Thiel. If you kill me and Flaming Arrow—"

"Shut up, you damn Injun lover," Bradley said, his face red from a frustrated anger. "Just do as I say. Flaming Arrow, you step away from Valerie."

"Please don't harm him," Valerie said, then wished she hadn't when her husband's arm tightened around her waist. She knew she should not have pleaded for her husband, a proud Blackfoot warrior and chief. It made him look small in the eyes of the white man.

"My child!" she said, trying to draw attention away from what she had said about Flaming Arrow. "Bradley, I am pregnant. Do nothing to harm my child!"

This enraged Bradley even more. His cheek twitched. His jaw tightened and loosened as his breathing quickened.

"A child?" he said, his voice rising in pitch. "You are carrying this savage's child inside you?"

He dismounted and motioned with the barrel of his rifle toward the bluff. "Over there!" he said in an almost hysterical scream. "Do you hear me? Both of you get over there! Valerie, I'm going to make sure you don't give birth to a savage brat! I'm going to make sure this savage you call your husband will not be around to twist your mind any longer about what is right and wrong in life! Marrying a redskin is cause for eternal damnation in hell! Having his child would cinch it!"

Flaming Arrow took Valerie's hand. "We will not do anything you say," he said tightly.

"Especially not stand close to that cliff," Valerie blurted. "Do you think we're idiots? We know what you plan to do. You will shoot Flaming Arrow and then throw his body over the side of the cliff so that no one would ever find him and blame you for his death."

"I don't need you to be over there for me to

shoot that savage!" Bradley screamed, aiming his rifle, his finger trembling as he slid it toward the trigger.

A rifle shot rang out like a slap of thunder.

Thinking it was Bradley's, and that he had shot Flaming Arrow, Valerie screamed.

But then she saw Bradley suddenly drop his rifle and clutch at his chest, where blood gushed through a hole in his cotton shirt, seeping through his fingers.

Someone else had fired! The target had been Bradley Hart!

Bradley sank to his knees. He looked wildly up at Valerie. "We could have been . . . so . . . good . . . for one another," he gasped, then fell over face first on the ground, dead.

Stunned, Valerie stood over him for a moment, staring. Then a familiar voice broke the silence.

"Valerie!"

She spun around. Her lips parted in a gasp and her eyes widened in wonder when she saw her precious Aunt Hillary rushing out into the open with a smoking pistol held at her right side.

"Aunt Hillary? It was you? You shot him?" Valerie cried, then ran toward her aunt and fell into her arms, sobbing.

Flaming Arrow stood stoically quiet as he watched his wife hugging a woman unfamiliar to him.

But he knew who she was from Valerie's stories of her family. This was Valerie's favorite aunt.

What he could not understand was why she was there, and how a woman could be brave enough to shoot a white man—*any* man!

He gazed at her. This woman was even taller than he! She was stout and her flesh was tanned almost as dark as the skin of a Blackfoot's.

And she wore clothes of a man.

She even seemed brusque like a man.

Her voice, even, was deep like a man's.

She was most certainly nothing like Valerie, who was a true woman in every sense of the word.

Valerie slid out of Hillary's arms. "I don't understand how you could be here," she said.

Valerie, too, was surprised by how mannish her aunt looked in her man's attire. Even her hair was drawn up and hidden beneath the crown of the hat. This was a side of her aunt she had never seen before. If no one knew any better, they would think she *was* a man!

"How did you know we were here?" Valerie asked anxiously. "Do you know that if you didn't arrive when you did, my husband Flaming Arrow would be dead? Bradley would've shot him, then—"

"I know," Hillary said, interrupting Valerie. "Because I came by just in time to see him accost you and say what he had planned for you."

She glanced at Flaming Arrow, then gazed at Valerie. "Val, when Bradley was courting you, I knew then what a despicable man he was and what he might be capable of," she said. "I was so glad when you told him you weren't interested in him and sent him packing. He would have made a miserable husband."

"But how is it that you are anywhere near here?" Valerie persisted. "And, Aunt Hillary, if you are here, is Mother, also?"

"Yes, your mother and I are living here," Aunt Hillary said, sliding her pistol into its holster at her right side. "Also Elaine and Harold. They live just across the meadow from our cabin."

Hillary glared down at Bradley Hart. "He would have soon discovered that we were living here," she said icily. "To assure our silence, I would hate to say what I think he might have done to us."

Hillary slid her gaze back to Valerie. "For you see, Val," she said, her voice drawn, "we—your mother and I—know a lot about Bradley that no one else knows."

"What do you know?" Valerie asked, glancing down at the dead man, shivering at the sight of him.

"Bradley is responsible for your father's death," Hillary said in a low hiss as she again glared at the man. "Bradley had stolen clothes and a horse from a man making camp at night. He had come upon your father while Royal was out feeding the livestock. I saw your father and Bradley arguing. Bradley drew his pistol. They began wrestling. A shot rang out. Bradley killed your father."

"No," Valerie said, placing a hand to her mouth.

"Before I could get to your father, he was dead and Bradley had ridden away," Hillary said, swallowing hard. "I didn't bother looking for him. Your mother was my main concern. I had to tell her what had happened to her husband. She had just come out of being seriously ill. I was afraid she was too weak to take knowing that her husband was dead."

"But you told her and she came through it all right?" Valerie asked softly.

"Yes, well . . . *some*what, and after your father's burial, your mother said she wanted to go back to Kansas," Hillary continued. "But we didn't have enough money to get that far. We stayed in Missouri instead when we reached that far and the money ran out. We are homesteading a small piece of ground. I am trapping to make enough money for us to live on." She laughed. "I must say my trapping has done us quite well. Our home is now filled with trinkets that we could not afford otherwise."

Hillary's gaze slid over to Flaming Arrow. A slow smile shaped her lips. "And so this is your husband, eh?" Her eyes showed her approval, for although she was manly and gruff, she appreciated a handsome man, and this man was more handsome than any she had seen before.

She even admired the color of his skin. She especially liked his eyes and the way he was looking at her. She knew that he saw her difference and somehow enjoyed it.

Valerie saw her aunt and her husband assessing one another. She stepped over to Flaming Arrow, took him by the arm, and led him back over where her aunt stood.

"Aunt Hillary, this is my husband Flaming Arrow," she said softly. "Flaming Arrow, this is my most favorite aunt in the world, my Aunt Hillary, whom I've told you so much about."

"And so she has discussed me with you, has she?" Aunt Hillary said, lumbering closer to Flaming Arrow, extending a gloved hand toward him. "Let's shake on knowin' one another and on your being smart enough to marry my niece."

When Hillary placed her hand in Flaming Arrow's and shook it, he was impressed with her grip. It was much tighter than most men's.

More and more he saw her as a unique and very likable woman.

"You don't seem at all surprised to know that I'm married, and to a Blackfoot chief," Valerie said. "Why is that, Aunt Hillary?"

"Word has spread in St. Louis and among the settlers about the Blackfoot's arrival," Aunt Hillary said, again smiling at Flaming Arrow. "When one of the women talked about a chief with a white wife, of course I didn't know then that it was you. But when I came upon you with the chief here in the forest, I had to know then that it was you who had married an Indian."

Her smile faded into a frown. "But what I don't understand, Valerie, is why after you met and married this chief you didn't return home and tell us that you did it," Hillary said. "And what about Brian? Why didn't you bring him home?"

"It's all a long story," Valerie said, sighing. She glanced down at Bradley and shivered again. "I'd rather tell you after we get this behind us."

She looked quickly up at her aunt. "But know that Brian is all right," she said. "He's been living with me and Flaming Arrow. He's healthy and happy. And he will be so glad to see you and Mother again. When we came by the cabin and found everyone gone, it took a while for Brian to get over worrying about you all."

"Well, we'll have to do something about that," Hillary said. "And *soon*. I can hardly wait to see the scalawag."

Flaming Arrow took a step closer. "Today what you did to save my life was the most honorable act a man can perform," he said thickly. "To show that he is brave, to prove by some daring deed his physical courage, his lack of fear, is something all braves wish to brag of. In my eyes, although you are not a man, you have proven yourself worthy of being called a great warrior. I thank you for your courage and daring."

Hillary laughed and tipped her hat back with one of her forefingers. "I might not be a man who can take on the title of warrior, but I appreciate the thought anyhow," she said. "It was indeed a pleasure saving your life today, Chief."

She leaned toward him. "It was quite a pleasure, indeed," she whispered. "Are there any more like you in your village? If so, I'd like to meet them. I'd not mind having a husband like you slide between my blankets with me each night."

Trying not to be too shocked at this woman's boldness, and certainly seeing more and more about her that was different than his delicately sweet and demure wife, Flaming Arrow's eyes danced. "I might have just the man," he said, thinking of his best friend Fox Eye and how Fox Eye would be attracted to such a woman as this. "Yes, I might have just the man for you."

"Let's get this thing with Bradley Hart behind us and then I'd like to go and see Brian . . . and that particular hunk of man," Hillary said, laughing softly.

She grew solemn as she stared down at Bradley.

Valerie gazed down at him, also. "What *are* we to do with him?" she asked.

"There is only one thing that is right to do," Flaming Arrow said, his voice drawn. "We must have the courage to take this man's body to the fort and hope that Colonel Thiel will listen to reason."

"I'll tell him what happened," Hillary said, resting her hands on her holstered pistols. "I know the colonel. We're old friends. He'd have no reason not to believe me when I tell him why I shot and killed Bradley. If I had known that Bradley was in these parts earlier, I'd have gone to the fort and pointed an accusing finger at him and told the colonel that he shot Royal Ross in cold blood, as well as the man he killed to have his horse, clothes, money, and weapon. I'd have made sure he was thrown in the hoosegow! If given the chance to, I'd have placed the hangman's noose over the bastard's head."

"But still there is the chance he won't believe a word you say," Valerie said. "Especially when he sees you with me and Flaming Arrow. I have a sinking feeling that the colonel will grab this opportunity to order Flaming Arrow from Missouri!"

"He doesn't have the authority to do that," Hillary said flatly.

"He has more authority than one can imagine," Valerie said solemnly.

"No matter what the chances are, we must take this man to the fort," Flaming Arrow said. He bent down and swept Bradley Hart into his arms. He carried him over and slung him across Bradley's horse and tied him to it.

Valerie stood back watching, her pulse racing as fear rose inside her over meeting face-to-face with the colonel so soon, especially under these circumstances.

And she so baldly wished, instead, to go and see her mother! It had been so long!

"Come and let us get this behind us," Flaming Arrow said, reaching a hand out for Valerie.

She hesitated, then took his hand.

30

So, so, break off this last lamenting kiss,
Which sucks two souls, and vapors both away;
Turn thou, ghost, that way, and let me turn this,
And let ourselves benight our happiest days.
—JOHN DONNE

As Fort Jefferson Barracks came into view, looming like a vast, stone-walled castle on the embankment of the Mississippi River, Valerie could not
help but be afraid of the chore they were forced
to do today.

Not only was she arriving at the fort against the
colonel's cold orders for her never to come there,
she was also transporting the colonel's dead cousin.
Although Valerie could tell there was no love lost
between the two, she could not help but be afraid
of telling the colonel that Bradley was dead

And what of the rest of the soldiers? When they
saw a dead white man brought to the fort's gates
by a Blackfoot Indian and two women, would they
arrest them first and ask questions later?

"You are so quiet," Flaming Arrow said, guiding
his horse alongside Valerie's.

"I don't think bringing Bradley to the fort like

this is a very good idea," Valerie blurted, glancing over at her Aunt Hillary.

"I'll take care of things," Hillary said, reaching a reassuring hand to Valerie's arm. "I'll explain to the colonel."

"I will be the one to speak for us," Flaming Arrow said. "It would look less dignified for a chief of my stature to sit back and let a woman speak on his behalf. I know the colonel. He will listen to what I say and be fair about his decision."

Hillary shrugged her shoulders. "Whatever you say," she said, then dropped back and followed Valerie and Flaming Arrow.

"You didn't have to be so short and gruff with my aunt," Valerie whispered to her husband.

"If I did not correct her now, it would have been done in the presence of others," Flaming Arrow said, his spine stiffening. "That would have been embarrassing for her."

"Don't you like my aunt?" Valerie murmured.

"I have mixed feelings about her," Flaming Arrow said. "She is quite bold in her behavior, would you not say?"

"Yes, which surprises even me," Valerie said, looking over her shoulder at her aunt. "She seems to have changed since I last saw her in Montana Territory. All the years that I have known her, as a child in Kansas, and as an adult in Montana Territory, I never once saw her dressed in such a manner, nor was she this brash. I wonder what changed her."

"Perhaps she has not changed at all," Flaming Arrow said, drawing Valerie's eyes back to him. "Perhaps she has always been this way and she kept it hidden from you."

He gave Hillary a quick glance over his shoulder. His eyes swept over the woman again, at how she was dressed, and how she held herself so tall in the saddle like a man.

Then he smiled over at Valerie. "Yes, she *is* different," he said. "I cannot help but admire her." He chuckled. "As I am sure will Fox Eye."

"You truly think that she and Fox Eye will enjoy each other's company?" Valerie asked, eyes wide.

"I believe Fox Eye will enjoy the challenge of the woman, as well he will enjoy looking at her," Flaming Arrow said. "She is quite a beautiful woman, do you not think?"

"I have always thought my aunt was beautiful," Valerie said, feeling a surge of jealousy to hear her husband speak so fondly of another lady. "So you think she . . . is more beautiful than your very own wife?" Valerie said, blushing when she realized she'd revealed her jealousy.

Flaming Arrow reached over and placed a gentle hand on Valerie's cheek. "My wife," he said softly. "No one in the entire world is as beautiful as you." His lips formed a soft smile. "Jealousy most times makes a person ugly," he said. "On you . . . it is pretty."

"Pretty?" Valerie said, arching an eyebrow.

She then laughed softly and covered his hand

with hers. "I believe you would think me pretty even if I had mud splashed all over my face," she said.

Soon they arrived beneath the shadow of the high fort wall, upon which they saw armed sentries staring down at them.

Valerie expected the soldiers to shout down at them to stop, especially after they saw Bradley Hart's lifeless body across the back of his horse. She looked straight ahead as they rode past the sentries without being stopped. At the opened gate, more sentries stood poised on either side. Valerie gazed guardedly from one to the other.

She started as though she had been shot when a soldier stepped from the shadows and shouted at them, a rifle clutched in his right hand. "Halt!"

Valerie and Flaming Arrow both quickly recognized him as the young lieutenant who had first come upon the Blackfoot campsite. The husband and wife exchanged quick glances.

They watched the young lieutenant go to Bradley's horse and inspect his body. Hillary sat silently watching, her horse only inches away from Bradley's.

The young lieutenant suddenly whipped his rifle up and aimed it at Hillary. "Ma'am, step down from your horse," he ordered. His gaze swept over her and her attire. He chuckled amusedly. "Or should I call you *sir*?"

Disgruntled over his taunt, Hillary slid from her saddle.

The lieutenant nervously leveled his rifle at Hillary, then slid it around and aimed it at Flaming Arrow. "You, too," he flatly ordered. "Also the woman."

The other sentry came quickly and grabbed Flaming Arrow's weapon from his holster, and the rifle from his gunboot.

"Are you actually arresting us?" Hillary asked, edging over closer to Valerie. "Without asking for the truth, you have the nerve to arrest us?"

Flaming Arrow cast her a dark frown for having spoken up when he had made it clear he was to be the one to speak on their behalf.

He opened his mouth to correct the situation, but instead gazed at Colonel Thiel as he suddenly came from the fort and looked quickly from one to the other, and then at Bradley's dead body. When he saw the mortal wound on Bradley's chest, he turned and quietly questioned Flaming Arrow with his eyes.

"As my wife and I were traveling toward St. Louis, this man, your cousin, accosted us," Flaming Arrow said levelly. "If not for this woman, who is my wife's aunt, this man would have shot me."

"Bradley was going to kill Flaming Arrow and throw him over a cliff," Valerie quickly interjected, then regretted having spoken up when Flaming Arrow gave her a hurtful glance.

Colonel Thiel stood for a moment staring at Bradley's body, then walked slowly toward Valerie and Flaming Arrow, his eyes sweeping suddenly over to Aunt Hillary, then lighting up in recognition.

He hurried up to her, placed his fists on his hips, and smiled. "Why, if it isn't Hillary Ross," he said, chuckling. "I see you still prefer men's clothes over women's."

He placed a hand on her shoulder. "It's been a long time," he said throatily. "Goddamn it, where've you been keepin' yourself? Damn it, Hillary, what've you been doing?"

Valerie was stunned to see the colonel's behavior. Obviously they had known each other in the past.

"Damn it, Randall, you ol' cuss, it *has* been a long time," Hillary said. Her manner seemed to be flirting! "When I left the pony express, well, I just went on home to Kansas and became . . . a lady."

"Like hell you did," the colonel said, slapping her on the back as though she were a man. "Anyone who could down shots of whiskey like you could, could never settle down to the serene life of a lady. I've never seen a woman who could out-drink and outshoot men like you did."

Valerie paled to hear how her aunt had truly lived in her past. She did recall her aunt telling her more than once that she had had a colorful past. But she had never told her exactly *how* colorful. She could hardly wait to sit down and hear it all from her aunt!

"Now tell me, Hillary, did you truly shoot my

cousin the way the Indian said it happened?" Colonel Thiel said, leaning his face near Hillary's.

"If I hadn't shot him, I'd say by tonight you'd have a Blackfoot Indian uprising on your hands," Hillary said, her jaw tightening. "Bradley Hart was ready to shoot Flaming Arrow. I got off a shot first and downed Bradley. It's as plain as the nose on my face, Randall. Goddamn it all to hell, *yes,* I shot the sonofabitch."

Valerie gasped and placed a hand to her mouth. Until today, she had never heard her aunt utter one curse word! Yet it seemed strangely natural for her aunt to behave in such a manner. It looked right on her, as though she were born this way!

But Valerie felt uneasy for Flaming Arrow. His gaze was locked angrily on Hillary.

Valerie could tell her husband was not amused by her aunt's behavior. Nor did she think that he now wished for his best friend Fox Eye to become acquainted with the woman, after all. It was obvious he no longer admired her. Instead he seemed to silently be despising her.

"Well, Hillary, I think you've said enough to clear everyone of the crime committed today," Colonel Thiel said.

Then he went to Flaming Arrow, his hands clasped between him. "Chief, you are to be commended for being brave enough to bring a white man's body to the fort, knowing that it might endanger not only yourself, but your people," he said thickly. "I like such courage in a man. I also ap-

preciate the fact that you felt you could expect to
be treated fairly by me. That shows trust."

Then the colonel kneaded his chin thoughtfully.
"But one thing puzzles me." He slid his gaze over
at Valerie, then looked again at Flaming Arrow.
"You said you and your wife were on your way to
St. Louis. Didn't you and I have plans today that
did not include your wife? Weren't you supposed
to have council with me today at the fort?"

"*You* made plans for such a council," Flaming
Arrow said flatly. "When my wife was excluded, it
was I who chose not to have council at the fort
without her. Instead, we were headed for St. Louis
to acquaint ourselves with the city."

Again the colonel gazed at Valerie.

Then he looked over his shoulder at Hillary.
"Hillary, this lady is your niece, eh?" he asked.

Hillary came and stood beside Valerie. She slid
an arm around her waist. "My very own," she said,
smiling proudly at the colonel. "And if she can't
come to the fort, nor shall I." She winked at the
colonel. "And I think you'd miss my visits now that
you know I am in the area, wouldn't you? Don't
you think it'd be nice once in a while to sit and talk
while we smoke cigars and chug-a-lug an occasional
glass of whiskey?"

Valerie's lips parted in a gasp as she stared at
her aunt. "Cigars?" she said, her voice drawn.
"You even actually smoke cigars?"

"Yep, I've been known to enjoy one or two in
my lifetime," Hillary said, her eyes twinkling. "You

might want to try it sometime, Valerie." She glanced down at Valerie's stomach and frowned. "But not while you're pregnant."

"Pregnant?" the colonel said, his face flooding with color. "You are pregnant? With an Indian's child?"

"Yes, I am pregnant, and yes, with Flaming Arrow's child," Valerie said, boldly lifting her chin.

She saw the colonel's eyes take on a coldness that seemed to reach inside her heart. She turned to Flaming Arrow. "If we're going to get to St. Louis today and have time to enjoy it, don't you think we'd best leave now?"

"Valerie," Hillary said, grabbing her hands. "Surely you want to go and see your mother first."

Valerie gazed sullenly at her aunt. "I thought you might be too busy with the colonel," she said, realizing she was speaking far too coldly to her aunt.

"Honey, you come first, always," Hillary said, grabbing Valerie into her arms, hugging her. "I'm sorry if I've embarrassed you today. I promise not to do it again."

"You didn't embarrass me," Valerie said softly. "You *shocked* me."

"I'll not shock you again," Hillary said, looking past Valerie's shoulder at Flaming Arrow. "Nor you, Flaming Arrow. From here on out, I'll behave."

Flaming Arrow wanted to believe that she was speaking from the heart. He wanted to like her again. But he saw too much in her behavior that made him wary.

Colonel Thiel clasped a hand on Flaming Arrow's shoulder. "Do come again and let us have that smoke," he said softly. He glanced over at Valerie, then again at Flaming Arrow. "And bring your wife anytime."

Flaming Arrow was touched deeply by the colonel's change of heart. He smiled and clasped his hand on the colonel's shoulder. "We will talk soon," he said thickly.

Then he swung away from the colonel and took Valerie's hand. He led her to her horse and helped her into the saddle.

Hillary mounted her horse and rode up next to Valerie. "Ready?" she asked. She yanked her hat from her head and tossed it away, then shook her hair down to hang long and wavy down to her waist. "As soon as we arrive home I'll discard these clothes. I'll turn myself into a lady as fast as you can snap your fingers."

Seeing that her aunt was going to try to behave properly made relief flood Valerie's senses. She laughed softly. "I'll be more than glad to help you choose a dress," she said. "I think it should be all lacy and pretty, don't you?"

Hillary's eyebrows rose. Then she laughed throatily. "Yes, all lacy and pretty," she murmured, then sank her booted heels into the flanks of her horse and rode off with Valerie and Flaming Arrow.

Valerie saw out of the corner of her eye that her aunt looked over her shoulder and gave the colonel a wink. By that, she knew her aunt would not cast all her bad habits to the wind.

She could just see her aunt sitting in the colonel's office with her boots propped on the corner of his desk, a cigar hanging limply from the corner of her lips while the colonel poured her another glass of whiskey!

"Valerie, what are you thinking about?" Flaming Arrow asked as he edged his horse closer to hers. "Your eyes are dancing."

"Oh, I guess I was just thinking about things I would have never imagined before in a million years," Valerie said, laughing softly.

She gave her aunt a quick glance and saw she was deep in thoughts of her own. "I was thinking about my aunt and . . . and . . . cigars and whiskey."

Her eyes widened when Flaming Arrow broke into a fit of laughter. "What's so funny?" she asked, watching his laughter fade into a lingering smile.

"Since my first moments with your aunt I have had mixed feelings about her," Flaming Arrow said. "But now? I can accept her any way she wishes to be."

"Did someone say something about me?" Hillary asked, looking quickly over at Valerie and then at Flaming Arrow.

"Aunt Hillary, I think you will be a topic of conversation between me and my husband for many years to come," Valerie said, giggling. "Lord, how you have surprised this niece today."

Hillary's eyes twinkled. She then rode on ahead of Flaming Arrow and Valerie, but only to give them privacy to say what they wished in her absence.

"Aunt Hillary, come on back here," Valerie shouted. "We're not going to tease you anymore. Honest!"

Hillary gave them a slow stare, then wheeled her horse around and came back to ride with them.

"Aunt Hillary, I can hardly wait to see Mother," Valerie said softly. "And now that I know of your acquaintance with the colonel, you two being such good friends and all, I believe he will be there always to look out for you and mother."

"And with Bradley Hart finally dead, everyone can feel much safer," Hillary said, sighing.

Flaming Arrow smiled, himself feeling uplifted and hopeful for the future of his people.

With a friendship now forming between himself and the colonel, his people would be able to live a peaceful coexistence with the whites in the community!

Yes, for the first time in many moons he had true cause to hope!

Missouri *would* be their home!

His people *would* prosper there!

No longer would the word *reservation* be spoken among them, for they were now free again.

They were as free as wild mustangs!

31

As the moon's soft splendor
O'er the faint cold starlight of Heaven is thrown—
So your voice most tender
To the strings without soul had then given—
Its own.
—PERCY BYSSHE SHELLEY

Valerie could hardly believe she would be seeing her mother in a matter of minutes. Up ahead, through a clearing in the trees, sat a cabin, so serene and lovely beneath the colorful foliage of the autumn leaves.

"Nancy won't be able to believe her eyes when she opens the door and sees you standing there," Hillary said, smiling at Valerie as they rode closer to the cabin. "It's been hard on your mother . . . her husband being murdered in cold blood, and you and Brian disappearing. She thought you were dead."

Valerie had been so caught up in her eagerness to see her mother she had absolutely forgotten about Brian! He should be here, she thought desperately. Oh, Lord, he should be here!

She turned quickly to Flaming Arrow. "Flaming Arrow, after you have met my mother, would you go to the village and get Brian? Darling, mother will be so anxious to see him. I only wish he were with us now. Mother will want to see him so badly."

"I will go for him," Flaming Arrow said. "But do not fret over your mother. When she knows your brother is alive and well, that will be enough to sustain her until she sees him."

He looked away from her for a moment, his eyes wavering. He felt guilty now for not allowing Valerie and Brian to return to their home in Montana Territory to reassure their parents that they were all right.

He had been too immersed in his own problems to think of the wrong he had done his wife and her brother . . . and especially their parents. He turned quickly again, to apologize to his wife for his neglect, for allowing his own problems to create those for others. Especially for the woman he loved!

But suddenly Valerie broke away and rode at a hard gallop toward her mother's home.

Flaming Arrow and Hillary stayed back, to allow Valerie some privacy for the first few moments with her mother.

"Now Nancy will have a reason to live again," Hillary said thickly as she cast Flaming Arrow a sorrowful glance. "I didn't tell Valerie the condition her mother is in, that she rarely smiles anymore. She doesn't even carry on a lengthy conversation with anyone. Not even with *me*. She's withdrawn. She has been living in her memories.

Only they have sustained her. Otherwise, I believe she would have been totally lost in her despair."

"Today, except for her husband, she gains it all back," Flaming Arrow said.

"She gets more than a daughter and son today," Hillary said, smiling over at Flaming Arrow. "She gains a son-in-law."

"She might not be too happy to see who the son-in-law is," Flaming Arrow said tightly. "She may not want to accept a man with copper skin into her family."

"If this man is the one her daughter loves, Nancy will love him also," Hillary said, reaching over to place a reassuring hand on Flaming Arrow's arm. "She is a woman with a big heart. There isn't a prejudiced bone in her body."

When a loud shriek of glee reached them, they rode onward in silence, watching the reunion of mother and daughter.

Tears filled Flaming Arrow's eyes. The wondrous scene before him touched him to his very core. Ah, but he would be as jubilant if he could only be reunited with *his* mother! She had been so good! So soft-spoken! So sweet!

"Everything Valerie is, my mother was," he whispered, drawing Hillary's eyes quickly to him.

"Did you say something?" she asked, wiping tears from her eyes.

"I was thinking out loud," Flaming Arrow said. "Only thinking out loud."

He drew his horse to a halt and gave his wife a

little more time with her mother. Hillary drew a tight rein beside him.

Valerie clung to her mother and inhaled the familiar, wondrous scent of her mother's skin, which she always bathed in rose water every morning to keep it soft. It was so wonderful to have her mother's arms around her again . . . to hear her soft voice and be able to look into her blue eyes!

"Mother, oh, Mother, I'm so sorry I worried you so much," Valerie murmured. "And yes, Brian is all right! You'll see him soon! Oh, Mother, Brian will be so glad to see you! At first, when we discovered you were gone, and that . . . that father was dead, Brian became so withdrawn and quiet. In time he became all right. But never has he forgotten you! He'll be so happy! Oh, Lord, so happy!"

Tears streamed from Nancy's eyes. "Daughter, daughter," she cried. "My life has been so empty! It has not been worth living! Oh, now it will be so different! I have you! And Brian! Oh, how I have missed my little boy!"

They eased from one another's arms and gazed at one another.

"I can hardly believe you are here," Nancy said, wiping fresh streams of tears from her cheeks.

"Nor can I believe *you* are here," Valerie said, brushing away her own tears. "It's like a miracle that you are."

"I want to hear all about where you have been and why you didn't return home," Nancy said, clutching Valerie's hands. "Daughter, life has been so empty!"

"I'm sorry," Valerie said, swallowing hard. "And yes. I'll tell you everything."

Valerie looked over her shoulder and saw Flaming Arrow and Hillary waiting in the shadows of the forest. She then looked back at her mother. "Mother, there is *so* much to tell you," she murmured. "First let me say that I am happy. So is Brian. Then let me say that your daughter is no longer single."

She watched her mother's eyes brighten. She was warmed through and through by her mother's smile.

"And, Mother, that isn't all," she murmured. She placed one of her mother's hands over her stomach. "Mother, feel it? Inside lies your first grandchild."

"You are with child?" Nancy said, a tremor in her voice. Her eyes were brilliant with happiness.

Valerie hoped that knowing about the child might help her mother accept just who her daughter's husband was—a man whose skin was not white like her own! Although she knew her mother was not a prejudiced woman, how might she truly react when she was told that the man who had entered her daughter's life was an Indian?

Valerie's heart thudded as she searched for the courage to tell her mother, to prepare her for Flaming Arrow's arrival.

And once her mother knew the full truth about why Valerie and Brian had not returned home to let their parents know that they were alive, would she then hate Flaming Arrow for being the one responsible?

Yes, there was much for her mother to accept. And she must, or again lose her daughter and son. Valerie knew that Brian would never live anywhere else now but with the Blackfoot! He had adapted well to their environment and wanted nothing else but to be a part of their lives, as one with them, as though he had Blackfoot blood flowing through his veins.

"A child," Nancy said, looking adoringly at Valerie's stomach. She gently rubbed a hand over it. "I am so very, very happy for you. And for *myself*. A grandchild! Oh, what a joy a grandchild will be. And, Valerie, when will I meet your husband?"

Valerie heard horses approaching behind her. She knew Flaming Arrow was now out in the open, riding beside Hillary toward the cabin, for suddenly Valerie's mother had become quiet, her eyes wide, her lips parted, as she watched Flaming Arrow's approach.

"My word," Nancy gasped, placing a hand to her throat. "An *Indian*. What on earth is an Indian doing with Hillary?" She laughed softly. "Your aunt has changed, of late. She's become as wild and woolly as she was when she was a teenager. Lord knows who she'll bring to supper. Tonight it seems it's a stray Indian."

"That 'stray Indian' is my husband," Valerie

said. She caught her mother's elbow when she saw her face drain of color.

"No, not your husband," Nancy said, her eyes imploring Valerie. "You didn't marry an Indian." She looked, petrified, at Valerie's stomach. She gasped and took a shaky step away from her. She grabbed at the doorknob and steadied herself. "The child. My grandchild! It might be Indian?"

Valerie's heart sank. She was at a loss for words. Never would she have expected this kind of reaction from her mother!

The woman who taught Sunday School classes back in Kansas City, who taught the children that all people were alike, no matter the color of their skin? The woman who always felt pity for Indians because they had been mistreated?

"Mother, *please,*" Valerie said, reaching out for her. "Please don't react this way. Mother, Flaming Arrow is the kindest, gentlest man I've ever known. He has a heart of gold! Oh, Mother, if you treat him unjustly, I won't be able to stand it!"

Valerie gasped when her mother rushed into the house and closed the door. She felt weak in the knees when she heard her mother bolt-lock the door to keep her and Flaming Arrow out.

Hillary drew up, jumped from her horse, and hurried to Valerie's side. "I saw what your mother did," she said, sliding a reassuring arm around Valerie's waist. "I should've told you that your mother hasn't been herself. Since your father's death, it seems as though her brain has snapped. You know that she wouldn't have reacted this way earlier, when she was her normal self."

"That doesn't change how her reaction is going to hurt my husband," Valerie cried, sobbing as Flaming Arrow strode up and took one of her hands.

She turned to him and moved into his arms. "Mother isn't herself," she cried. "Oh, Lord, Flaming Arrow, don't let what she did cause you hurt. She isn't behaving normally. If she was, she wouldn't do anything to hurt your feelings." She gulped hard. "Or *mine*."

"We will go home, then come back later," Flaming Arrow said thickly. "We do not want to cause your mother any more unnecessary pain and hurt."

Valerie drew away and gazed up at him, grateful for his understanding. "You aren't hurt by her behavior?" she murmured. "You are, instead, ready to forgive her and do what you think is best for her?"

"She is your mother," Flaming Arrow replied, placing a gentle hand on Valerie's cheek. "How can I not have feelings for her? In her, there is much of you, and in time I know that she will realize that what she has done today is wrong. She will embrace you again. She will, I hope, embrace the idea of who you have married."

"She was so happy to know about our child," Valerie said, swallowing back a sob. "I so badly wanted her to be happy about you."

Valerie turned with a start when the door sud-

denly opened a crack. She scarcely breathed when
she saw her mother peering out of the small space
at the door, her eyes searching Flaming Arrow up
and down in a studious fashion.

Valerie started to say something to her mother,
but Hillary placed a hand on her arm.

"Wait," she whispered. "Say nothing. Do nothing."

Valerie sighed and acquiesced. Yet she couldn't
help but feel her mother was acting as though she
were a trapped animal.

It saddened Valerie deeply to see this . . . to
think this. But it was true! Her mother was behaving so irrationally, Valerie wondered if she could
truly ever be the same mother she knew as a child.

"Valerie?" her mother whispered. "Come close.
Hear what I say."

Valerie's eyes widened. She gave Flaming Arrow
a questioning look.

He nodded.

She slipped over to the door. "What is it, Mother?"
She found it hard to contain her grief over her
mother's actions.

"You said that Indian is your husband," her
mother whispered, her eyes wild as she stared past
Valerie at Flaming Arrow. "Has he ever taken
scalps?"

Valerie's heart sank again as all hopes of her
mother accepting Flaming Arrow flew away in the
wind. "No," she said, gulping back the urge to cry
again. "He has never taken scalps. But, Mother, he
has stolen my *heart.* I love him, Mother. He loves

me. And he will be such a good father to our child. Please open the door. Let me introduce him to you. Give him a chance, Mother. I love him with all my heart."

"Brian isn't alive, is he?" her mother whispered back. "The Injun killed him, didn't he?"

"Heavens, no!" Valerie cried, paling. "Mother! Stop this foolishness! Open the door! I want to bring my husband into your house! I want you to see what a kind man he is!"

Valerie hoped that this harder line with her mother might work better than being so soft and careful with her.

"Mother, I said open the door," she said flatly, yet feeling guilty for talking in such a disrespectful way.

Suddenly the door began sliding open more widely.

Then Valerie's mother stood at the fully opened door.

What she did then totally surprised and confused Valerie, but it made her so happy she could hardly contain the joy she felt at that moment.

"Come and give me a hug," her mother said, holding her arms out for Flaming Arrow. "Any husband of my precious daughter is welcomed in the arms of her mother."

Stunned speechless, taken aback by the lady's change in mood, Flaming Arrow wasn't sure what he should do. He wasn't sure whether to trust the woman's sudden change. He had seen white people pretend friendship one minute and slam a knife into the backs of the Blackfoot the next!

"Go on," Hillary whispered, giving Flaming Arrow a gentle shove. "Hug her."

Valerie clasped a hand over her mouth and fought back tears as she watched her beloved husband sweep his arms around her beloved mother and draw her slight form into his embrace.

When her mother wrapped her arms around Flaming Arrow, Valerie could not hold back the tears of joy any longer. They streamed from her eyes. She sobbed, wiping at the tears with the backs of her hands.

"I'm sorry about those things that I said earlier," Nancy said, patting Flaming Arrow on the back as he continued to hold her in his arms. "I have forgotten how to trust. Ever since my Royal was gunned down, everything inside me seems cold and filled with hate."

"I have felt the same emotions when I have lost loved ones," Flaming Arrow said thickly. "But I learned early on that bitterness eats away at one's heart. It is something that one must fight hard to combat."

"My daughter has returned, and soon I will also see my son again," Nancy said. "I will soon forget my bitter feelings. My children will fill the lonely spaces in my heart once more."

She eased from his arms and gazed up at him. "You are welcome there, also," she said, wiping tears from her eyes. "If my daughter loves you so much, how could I not love you as well?"

Valerie went to her mother and hugged her. "Thank you, Mother," she said, choking back a sob. "Oh, Mother, you had me so worried."

"Things will be all right," Nancy said, gently patting Valerie on the back. "I . . . I . . . sometimes get lost to reality. Please help me get all of the way back, Daughter? Please?"

"Yes, I'll help you," Valerie murmured. She smiled at Flaming Arrow over her mother's shoulder. "Flaming Arrow is leaving now to go and get Brian. Soon you will have both your son and daughter to hold and to love."

"Also a grandchild," Nancy said, gently placing a hand on her stomach. "A child. I can hardly believe my little girl has a child growing inside her body."

"It's hard for me to believe, as well," Valerie said, laughing.

"I'm going with Flaming Arrow," Hillary said, grabbing her horse's reins, swinging herself into her saddle. "I'm anxious to make the acquaintance of the Blackfoot. I've always wanted to see what it's like to be in an Indian village, especially a tepee."

"Hurry back," Valerie said, sliding an arm around her mother's waist, drawing her close to her side.

Flaming Arrow gave Valerie a smile, then rode off with Hillary at his side.

Valerie smiled at something she felt was best left

unspoken for the moment . . . that just perhaps there might be another Indian warrior who could become a part of the Ross family. If Valerie knew her aunt very well, the Indian warrior didn't have a chance.

Valerie could remember the men back in Kansas City who crowded the family doorstep as they came to woo Hillary. Only those her aunt wanted to court her stayed and were welcomed in the house. Valerie remembered her aunt had ways with men that got her any her heart desired!

Valerie laughed to herself as she thought of the way her aunt was dressed today. Even that would not keep a man from seeing just how special Hillary was! Hadn't Flaming Arrow seen past it?

"Let's go inside and get some food cooking on the stove," Nancy said, taking Valerie by an arm, leading her inside the small cabin.

Once inside, Valerie looked slowly around her. She was stunned to see how simply her mother lived. It was even more humble than the small cabin her father had built in Montana Territory! This was only a three-room cabin with a small loft bedroom overhead. Everything was crowded.

But the furniture was pretty and plushly upholstered. And she recalled Hillary's words about buying trinkets for the cabin. Valerie noticed a lovely clock on the fireplace mantel, a hutch standing against a far wall with sparkling crystal and beautiful china behind the glass, and lacy doilies across the backs of each chair.

Yes, even though it was small, it had taken on the feeling of home as Valerie remembered it in Kansas.

Valerie's mother caught her staring at everything around her. "Yes, I know it isn't very much," she said. "But it's enough for me and Hillary. It's home."

"Yes, it's home," Valerie said, going to the fireplace and picking up something familiar to her. A pipe, which her father was smoking the last time she had seen him. Oh, how she did miss him.

She put the pipe back on the mantel and joined her mother in the kitchen.

Every once in a while Valerie glanced over at her mother, hearing her speak softly to herself as though carrying on a conversation with some invisible person.

It gave Valerie a cold feeling inside her heart to know that her mother had a long way to go to be normal again. It did seem that she was struggling to emerge from a world that had belonged only to her and her imagination.

Valerie only hoped that in her strange world, her mother would continue to accept Flaming Arrow in her life.

"Now tell me about yourself," her mother suddenly said. "I want to hear it all. Do you have a pretty cabin? Or do you live in a wretched Indian tepee?"

"I live in a tepee, but it's anything but

wretched," Valerie said, laughing softly. "It's my home, Mother. I love it."

"How could anyone love living in a tepee?" her mother said, shuddering. "And that Indian! How could you let him put his hands on you? He's surely scalped plenty of people in his time." Her mother stared up at Valerie. "Has he shown you his scalps? Has he?"

Valerie could hardly hold back her tears to see the troubled side of her mother surface again. She now doubted that her mother would or could ever be the same again!

But Valerie would not love her mother less! She would give her much love and understanding.

Beyond that, Valerie doubted that she could do much else to bring her mother back to her as she had always known her.

"He is ever so handsome, though," her mother suddenly said. "The Indian. Your *husband*." She laughed throatily. "Why, he's handsome as sin."

"Yes, he's handsome," Valerie said, setting a coffeepot on the stove. "And he's good to me."

"That's all that matters, sweetie," her mother said, patting her on the arm. "That he's good to you."

"Yes, that's all that matters," Valerie said, turning to her mother and suddenly drawing her into her arms. The two women desperately hugged each other.

32

Her beamy bending eyes, her parted lips
Outstretched, and pale, and quivering eagerly.
He reared his shuddering limbs and quelled
His gasping breath and spread his
Shuddering arms to meet . . .
Her panting bosom.
— Percy Bysshe Shelley

Several years had passed and life was good at the Blackfoot village, especially for Valerie. In her womb again lay the seed of her great Blackfoot warrior! A son had been born to them first. They now wished for a daughter.

It was spring. The heavy rains had triggered growth throughout the land. Oaks were draped with their conelike flowers, giving their limbs a golden glow. The hickories' buds were swollen, while buckeyes were already wearing their leafy cloaks of summer.

It was the time of year for the wildflowers to perform their orchestra of color. While the blue-eyed marys formed a carpet of white and pale blue petals with their flowers, the larkspurs grew taller cones of purple blooms, like tiny horns playing a symphony for the bees.

Sweet white violets, with their dark heart-shaped

leaves, grew everywhere. Phlox added their own spice to the mix as they circled the spindly stems with their blossoms of pale violet.

Valerie and Flaming Arrow were sitting outside during the Blackfoot's celebration of spring. A huge fire burned in the center of the village. The feasting had begun early in the morning and would continue through the night. The choicest foods had been prepared.

But before all of this began, Flaming Arrow had drawn all of the warriors together and cut up some tobacco to share with them, carefully mixing it with *l'herbe.*

After filling the bowl of his pipe with this mixture of tobacco and first smoking it himself, he had then passed it from one to the other, beginning with the first man on his left.

When the last man had smoked, the pipe was passed back around the circle this time to the right of Flaming Arrow.

It was then that the spring celebration truly began, the feast enjoyed, and now the dancing.

Games would soon follow. One main game to be played today involved gambling.

Valerie felt apprehensive about her husband gambling. It had been the downfall of her father.

For now, she enjoyed these wonderful moments beneath the beautiful blue spring sky with her family and the Blackfoot people.

She and Flaming Arrow laughed softly together and held hands while they watched their four-year-old son dancing among the others around the great outdoor fire. Bright Arrow was the exact image of his father, with his copper skin, long and flowing black hair, and eyes the color of midnight.

Brian, now fifteen, was also enjoying the fun along with all of his friends. His skin was bronzed almost the same color of the Blackfoot's. But the sun had bleached his hair almost white, always there as a contrast to his friends' coal-black hair.

Today Brian wore only a breechcloth and moccasins as he danced and sang around the outdoor fire with his friends.

Valerie gazed warmly and with much pride at her mother. She had slowly emerged from her cocoon of insanity and was laughing and clapping her hands today in time with the music played on the drums and the large rattles ornamented with beaver claws and bright feathers.

Valerie spent as much time with her mother as possible, helping to keep the void from creeping again into her mother's heart. It had been fun last spring planting her mother's favorite flower in her flower garden. Snapdragons!

This year there would be many more in her mother's garden. Valerie had made sure of that. She had gone even while the frost still lay across the ground and planted the snapdragon seeds in the garden, *and* in her mother's new flower boxes that Brian had made for his mother and hung beneath each of her windows.

Valerie's gaze shifted, this time to her Aunt Hillary, who was also there, but not with the husband Valerie or Flaming Arrow had expected. Hillary had married Colonel Thiel, with whom she was endlessly happy!

Valerie smiled when she saw Fox Eye with a lovely Shawnee maiden whom he had met on the waterfront at St. Louis. She was now his wife and *very* pregnant!

Valerie ran a hand over her own abdomen as she glanced down at it. She felt aglow inside and out to see that she was now showing her pregnancy.

She wore a garment of antelope skin to keep her warm. Her leggings of deerskin, heavily beaded and nicely fringed, warmed her legs on this early spring day.

Her hair was drawn back in two braids, tied with strips of fur from a rabbit pelt.

Her deerskin moccasins matched her husband's, with parfleche soles and worked with porcupine quills.

She glanced over at Flaming Arrow, whose own fringed deerskin clothes fit him more snugly than when she had first married him. Marriage seemed to have agreed with him, for he had put on some weight. During the long winter months, especially, when activity was lessened among the Blackfoot people, she could often find her husband lying back on his couch, moving his turkey-wing fan as he contentedly watched the fire burning in the fire pit.

But now was different. Soon her husband would lose at least some of his winter paunch. The earnest hunts had begun. The Blackfoot warriors' hunt was eager this year. Prime skins were selling from four to five dollars each along the waterfront at St. Louis.

She looked over at Flaming Arrow and watched how his eyes never left their four-year-old son as Bright Arrow continued to dance with the other children and adults.

Flaming Arrow's lips curled proudly when their son spinned majestically without falling, then lifted his feet and stamped them in time with the music, as his head bobbed and his long braids danced along his back.

Valerie leaned closer to her husband. "Isn't Bright Arrow so very precious?" she said. "And isn't he so mature for his age? Just look how well he knows the steps to that particular dance. Look at how well he keeps time with his feet!"

"Yes, he is special, so very, very special," Flaming Arrow said proudly, squeezing her hand affectionately. He gazed over at her. "As will our daughter be special." He laughed softly. "But she will be much prettier. She will look just like her mother."

"You think I'm still pretty, even though I am no longer as tiny?" she murmured.

"Nothing will ever take away your loveliness," Flaming Arrow said, placing a gentle hand on her fleshy cheek. Valerie had gained much more weight this time in her pregnancy. "And do you not know that when you are with child you are even prettier?

My wife, your eyes shine. Your skin is pink and, ah, so soft."

Thinking this might be the right time to question him about gambling, Valerie's smile waned. "Darling, do you truly have to play the gambling game today?" she asked guardedly. "Do you truly?"

"Your concern is understood," Flaming Arrow said, dropping his hand away from her face. He slid it around her waist and drew her around to face him. "My wife, I know about your father and how his downfall came from gambling. But it is not the same sort of gambling that will be done here today among my people. You have seen it before. Surely you saw it was always done in fun. No one is the true loser."

"But you gamble for *some*thing," Valerie said softly. "That constitutes a winner, doesn't it?"

"Yes, there is always a winner," Flaming Arrow said. "But do you not see? *Every*one is a winner at this game. The winner will receive the first pelt caught this spring while our men were on the hunt. Do you not know that all of our warriors brought home pelts? Do you not see that means no one is without because of the gambling game?"

"The one who caught the pelt that is gambled for is a *loser*," Valerie said, trying to make sense out of her husband's point of view. "If he has to give away his pelt, then isn't he a loser?"

"You do not know, then, how the first animal is downed?" Flaming Arrow said, arching an eyebrow. "Have I forgotten to explain that part of the game to you?"

"No, you didn't tell me anything about that," Valerie said, then smiled at him. "I do remember several times when you started to tell me, then were interrupted by this or that. *Now* tell me, husband, for I am all ears. There is no one to interrupt—"

Bright Arrow came suddenly to them, yanking on first Valerie's arm and then Flaming Arrow's, another interruption that would delay Flaming Arrow's tale of the pelt.

"Mother, Father," Bright Arrow said, still yanking on their arms. "Can I go and play with my friend Fire Wolf? Then can I stay the night with him and his family? They are going to pop corn and tell stories after the celebration is over tonight."

Her child asking such a grown-up question as that, and wanting to do such a grown-up thing, tugged at Valerie's heart. He did seem so much older than four. She could tell that his intelligence matched that of a ten-year-old child. In the white community he would eventually be labeled a genius. He even knew the ghost of chimney mountain story by heart. She had listened with much pride the first time she had heard him telling the story to his spellbound friends!

She turned questioning eyes over to Flaming Arrow. "What do you think, darling?" she asked softly.

"It is good that our son has such good friends,"

Flaming Arrow said, nodding. "Yes, I think staying the night would be all right."

Valerie saw dancing shadows in the depths of her husband's midnight-dark eyes and knew that his quick approval of their child staying the night with a friend had a double meaning. Brian was going to take his and Valerie's mother home and was planning to stay the night with her. That meant Valerie and Flaming Arrow would have the whole tepee alone the full night! That was rare. It was something they would take advantage of.

She lifted Bright Arrow onto her lap and hugged him. "Yes, you can stay the night with Fire Wolf," she murmured. "And be good. Don't eat so much popcorn that it gives you a bellyache. And go to bed when you are told."

Bright Arrow wrapped his tiny arms around Valerie's neck. "I will, Mother," he said as he gave her a big hug. "I will be good. And I will not eat too much popcorn. I do not like having a bellyache."

He jumped from her lap, hugged Flaming Arrow, then scampered away and joined many other children as they ran toward Fire Wolf's tepee.

The music stopped playing.

The warriors walked away from the fire and clustered together where the gambling game was going to be played.

Flaming Arrow rose slowly and majestically and offered Valerie his hand.

"Come and stand near me during the game," he

said. "See how the gambling is done this time. Always before, you sat back and only watched from afar. See the fun in the gambling. You might even then see why your father enjoyed it so much. You might even find a way to forgive him inside your heart."

"I have forgiven him," Valerie said, taking his hand, rising to her feet. "Long ago. But I shall never forget what gambling did to our family. It has never been the same since he lost everything to bankruptcy.

She swallowed hard. "Father would be alive today had we not been forced to leave our home in Kansas City and move elsewhere," she murmured. "He would not be lying in a grave alone in Montana Territory except that he gambled his life's savings away in Kansas."

"Try to place it from your mind as you stand with me during the game that is fun for my people," Flaming Arrow said gently. "This game will not lose us our home, or our dignity. Come. Watch. I believe you will also enjoy it if you will allow yourself."

"Just being with you is all I need to make it enjoyable," Valerie said, holding his hand as they walked toward the cluster of men who were going to participate in the gambling.

Earlier in the day the men had drawn sticks to see who would play the game this time. Only a few participated each time. Today their chief had drawn the longest of the sticks. He would be the first to play the game.

The Blackfoot people who would just be observing the game stood aside to make room for Valerie and Flaming Arrow. She could see Brian standing with their mother on the far side of the crowd. She smiled and waved, and then stopped and stood beside Flaming Arrow as preparations were made to start the game.

She looked slowly around her. A level, smooth piece of ground had been selected, a log placed at each end. The men would be gambling with a small wheel called *it-se-wah*. The wheel was about four inches in diameter and had five spokes, on which were strung different-colored beads made of bone.

The game was to begin with two men at a time who gambled against each other as the crowd surrounded them, betting on the sides.

But there was only one main prize. The team who first reached a certain number of points would win the special pelt.

The pelt was hung from a low limb in a tree for everyone to see, and Valerie was stunned to see how it was riddled with holes, which to her made it useless. No one could sew anything from such a hole-riddled pelt.

"And so you see the pelt that is to be gambled for," Flaming Arrow said, lifting his bow and drawing a brightly painted arrow from the quiver he had just slipped onto his back. "You can see the many holes in the pelt. That is from arrows of each of my warriors so that no one is an actual loser. Although one man shot and killed the deer, each of my warriors took part in the kill by then sending arrows through the downed animal. The animal then belonged to everyone. Not only one man. The one who gambles best today will be the true victor of a pelt that is useless to everyone. It is the sport of the game that makes it worthwhile for those who not only play the game, but enjoy watching it played."

His eyes gleamed as he smiled at her. "And the one who downed the first deer, who then gave it up for the game today?" he said. "He did not go home with empty arms. His chief, your husband, downed a second deer that day for that warrior."

"But what is the true sense of the gambling if . . . if—"

"Like I said. It is just the sport of the game that counts, not the winner or that which is won."

Valerie's eyes were wide as she tried to sort through his explanation to make sense of it. She laughed softly instead, and said, "I see."

That was all that she had time to say. She stepped back from her husband as he positioned his arrow in his bow, drew back on it, then, along with the other warriors who were participating, sent his arrow flying toward the wheel as a warrior sent the wheel rolling along the course.

Before the wheel reached a log at the opposite end of the track, points were already being counted as each man's arrow passed between the spokes, the position and nearness of the different beads to the arrows representing a certain number of points.

The game continued thusly until each arrow from each warrior had been fired.

Laughing, their bows and arrows left alongside the playing field, the warriors mingled and finally declared a winner.

Fox Eye was lifted on the shoulders of several of the warriors and was pranced around for everyone to see and praise.

And when he left the field with the riddled hide, everyone began to scatter, to once again return to the fire and resume their dancing, talking, and feasting.

Valerie saw Brian and her mother walking toward her. She broke away from Flaming Arrow and went to them.

"What a strange way to gamble," Nancy said, laughing throatily. "For certain if Royal had been here, he'd have been one of the most eager gamblers. Even if the winner only won a strange sort of pelt filled with holes."

"Had father had such innocent gambling advantages, you'd still be living in your mansion in Kansas City, Mother," Valerie said, hugging her mother.

"Daughter, I'm happy enough," Nancy said, returning her hug. "How could I not be? I have so much to be thankful for."

Flaming Arrow came to them and received a

generous hug from Nancy. Then he and Valerie walked Nancy and Brian to the wagon.

Brian helped his mother up in the wagon, then settled in on the other side and lifted the reins. "See you all tomorrow," he said, snapping the reins.

Valerie's mother blew her a kiss, then chatted with Brian as they rode away.

It made Valerie proud to see how her mother had accepted the Blackfoot into her life, especially after her mother's first reaction to them. It gave her shivers to think back to the day when her mother had closed the door between herself and Valerie and her Blackfoot husband.

She felt blessed that things had changed so much and that her mother was her old sweet self and enjoyed life and family once again.

She was drawn out of her thoughts when Hillary and Colonel Thiel walked up to Flaming Arrow and Valerie.

"We must leave now," Hillary said, hugging Valerie. "We don't like to travel as far as the fort after dark."

Valerie returned the hug, then watched as Hillary went and cuddled close to Colonel Thiel, her smile radiant.

"Thank you for asking us to be a part of your spring celebration," Colonel Thiel said, offering Flaming Arrow a handshake. "It is interesting to learn your people's customs. I truly enjoy it. And the new agent? Is he working out for you and your people?"

"He is a kind man who works for the best interest of my people," Flaming Arrow said, clasping his hand around the colonel's and shaking it. "Yes, he is a good man, who is welcomed each time he comes to have a smoke or council. He cares. My people care for him."

"That is good," Colonel Thiel said, then gazed into his wife's eyes. "Ready, hon?"

"Yes, darling, I'm ready," Hillary murmured. The look she gave her husband was one of utter adoration.

Valerie was amazed at how marriage had brought her aunt back to her softer side. Hillary even appeared to be a bit too fragile for her own good sometimes. But Valerie sensed that it was all pretense on her aunt's part, to look feminine and sweet in the eyes of her husband.

Valerie smiled as she watched her aunt allow the colonel to help her up into the fancy buggy.

Valerie giggled when her aunt waved a lacy handkerchief as the colonel climbed on the other side of the buggy and soon had the horse carrying them through the village.

"Come again soon!" Valerie said, waving back at her aunt.

"They are a happy couple," Flaming Arrow said, smiling down at Valerie. "It is a good thing to see."

Suddenly, overhead, an eagle soared low and studious, then its wings banked away upon the wind and it was gone again.

"Did you see that?" Valerie asked, gasping at the sight.

"It is rare that one sees that happen," Flaming Arrow said, drawing Valerie into his arms, gazing into her eyes. "Do you not know the meaning?"

"No, I don't," she murmured, searching his eyes.

"My woman, that is a good omen," he said thickly.

He brushed a soft kiss across his wife's lips, then placed an arm around her waist and led her toward their home. "We do not have to wait for night to be alone in our lodge," he said huskily. "While the eagle and its silent message of good faith is fresh in our minds and hearts, let us go and make love."

Valerie sighed and snuggled against him. "Yes, let's," she murmured, feeling so at peace with herself and with life. "It is such a perfect time for us to be alone together. It has been such a perfect day."

"They are all perfect for this Blackfoot chief, for he has them to spend with his sweet, beautiful wife," Flaming Arrow said, loving the way Valerie laughed so softly when he paid her such heartfelt compliments.

It was a perfect life with a perfect wife!

Dear Reader,

I hope you enjoyed reading *Flaming Arrow*. Exclusively for Signet, I am writing a Dreamcatcher series. This series began with *Running Fox* and *Shadow Bear*. The next book in the series is *Falcon Moon*, which is filled with much excitement, romance, and adventure. *Falcon Moon* will be in the stores in January 2008.

Many of you say that your are collecting my Indian romances. For my entire backlist of books, or for information about my fan club, you can send for my latest newsletter and autographed bookmark. For a personal response from me, please send a stamped, self-addressed, legal-sized envelope to:

Cassie Edwards
6709 North Country Club Road
Mattoon, IL 61938

Thank you for your support of my new Dreamcatcher series!

Always,

Cassie Edwards

cassieedwards@consolidated.net

Also from
New York Times bestselling author
CASSIE EDWARDS

SHADOW BEAR

South Dakota 1850. Before he died from the
Indian arrow that pierced his body while he was
hunting gold outside Fort Chance, Shiona Bramlett's
father, the colonel, revealed a shocking secret. Now,
armed only with her father's map and her courage,
she's determined to honor him—and to fulfill her
own destiny.

After a fierce prairie fire, Shadow Bear, Chief of the
Grey Owl Band of the Lakota tribe, is desperately
looking for his missing brother Silent Arrow. His
search leads him to a beautiful woman in
desperate need of help. Shadow Bear loathes the
white man—but he cannot help but protect her. With
a passion that is undeniable, they must learn to put
their mistrust aside and share their secrets before
all is lost.

Also from

New York Times bestselling author

CASSIE EDWARDS

RUNNING FOX

Nancy Partrain's life in pioneer Michigan has
become a nightmare since her mother married
her stepfather, who has involved her in his
underhanded whiskey trading scheme.
Then Nancy meets handsome Running Fox,
chieftain of the Fox band of the Lakota tribe,
who wants to put an end to her stepfather's
corruption of his people. In each other they stir
feelings of hope, freedom...and longing. Stolen
away to eerie Ghost Island by Running Fox,
Nancy finds herself falling for her abductor.
But can she allow his tender passion to finally
heal her wounded heart?

Also from
New York Times bestselling author
CASSIE EDWARDS

FALCON MOON

After trekking across the country, Wylena is
happy to arrive in Arizona Territory to reunite
with her brothers, but less happy to learn of
their troubles. Her brother, Jeb, is wrongly
accused of scalp hunting. He's also been
courting a lovely Apache woman who is sister
to Chief Falcon Moon. And the anger of the
ruthless Mexican general on Jeb's trail is nothing
compared to the ire of a protective sibling...

Then Wylena is kidnapped by Mexican troops—
and the handsome chief comes to her aid.
Now she must not only clear her brother's
name, but fight her burning desire for her
valiant rescuer.

*Available wherever books are sold or
at penguin.com*